MIDNIGHT,
Water City

MIDNIGHT,
Water City

○ ○ ○

CHRIS McKINNEY

Published by
Soho Press, Inc.
227 W 17th Street
New York, NY 10011

Library of Congress Cataloging-in-Publication Data

McKinney, Chris, 1973– author.
Midnight, water city / Chris McKinney.
Series: The Water City trilogy; 1

ISBN 978-1-64129-240-5
eISBN 978-1-64129-241-2

1. Science fiction. I. Title
LCC PS3613.C5623 M53 2021 | DDC 813'.6—dc23
LC record available at https://lccn.loc.gov/2020055355

Interior design by Janine Agro

Printed in the United States of America

10 9 8 7 6 5 4 3 2 1

MIDNIGHT,
Water City

1

Forty years ago, in the year 2102, the asteroid Sessho-seki hurled toward Earth at nineteen miles per second. Only one person could spot it: Akira Kimura. Scientist, savior, hero of the goddamn human race. She did so with the largest telescope ever built, atop the tallest mountain on Earth, to map its trajectory and engineer a weapon to counter it: Ascalon, the cosmic ray that saved the world. It fired with so much energy that its path remains visible, a permanent slash across the sky. People call it Ascalon's Scar.

One in every four girls born in the last decade is named Ascalon, including my youngest daughter, who's nearing eighteen months. Irritating, but my wife insisted. At least the name's popularity is down from one in two, which it was after those world-saving events. I'd guess that by now, only half of the population can recall the name Sessho-seki—The Killing Rock—but everybody remembers Ascalon. Probably doesn't help that Akira gave the asteroid a Japanese name. But being Japanese is coming to mean less and less anyway. Being white, Black, Latino, too.

177 atmospheres below sea level in Volcano Vista, the

world's largest seascraper, is where I'm heading. That used to be the crush depth of a super-sub, but we beat crush depth like we beat global warming, Sessho-seki, and sixty being old. I'm eighty now, finally the right age to collect Social Security, but I'll need to grind away another five to ten years. I'm on my fourth marriage and quite a few kids, but Ascalon is the most like me—can't sit still, never sleeps, loves to walk backward. It's probably deluded and egomaniacal to *like* that she takes after me. I'm basically old enough to be her ancestor.

The older I get, the more I care about numbers. I think about them too damn much, which is funny because I'm getting worse at running calculations in my head. At least my iE can do that for me.

The elevator opens, and a boy, maybe sixteen and completely tat-dyed blue, steps out. He's got the indifferent swagger of a teenager and androgynous pink hair draped over the right half of his face. He's trying hard to look like a cartoon. Maybe that's all we ever wanted from the beginning, to look like cartoons. Well, we're certainly succeeding. We all wear the same snug, temp-controlled foam fits spun from synthetic yarn coated with conductive metal. It's like an old-school wetsuit, except it's got a scaly metallic sheen to it that can change pattern and color. Some people, like my wife, like to wear a thin overcoat over theirs. Kids nowadays, they like to retract the sleeves and midriffs, while us older folk constrict it to take advantage of its girdling abilities. Either way, adjust the temp with your iE, and you're good to go for rain, shine, or a frolic in the ocean. This boy, he's wearing one, too, of course. He scratches his mechanical blue tail with an unusually long pinky finger as he walks past me, diving into his uncanny valley, a synthetic form of natural reality that looks plain creepy. Maybe fake tails, like the slang "hemo" and "semi," are in with the kids now? Who knows or even wants to. A weary-looking couple steps into the elevator with me, the woman fighting to re-convert her umbrella-style skirt back into a stiff, conical one. The skirt's clearly winning, and I get it. As the door closes, I look in its mirrored surface at my own reflection. I'm fighting age so hard, I look like a ventriloquist's doll.

This couple has the look of twelve-volt-intellect renters who could never really afford this place. Working their hardest the last decade but not breaking even. They get off at atmosphere five, and I'm alone in the gorilla-glass tube as I continue down. I look out onto a Volcano Vista feed observation platform. A cloud of plankton, freshly released. A school of fish swoops in, mouths wide open, constantly moving, constantly feeding. Then marlin and sharks come for the small fish to keep the food chain spectacle going. Down deeper still, darkness. The sprinkle of marine snow. Biolumi-nescent jellyfish and creatures that drip instead of swim. I find myself half-wishing the glass would web and shatter, killing this old man by drowning or water pressure imploding my skull. I feel like I'm drowning anyway, and everyone around me is trying to throw me anchors.

This building I'm descending is in essence a buoy, and the life drawn to it gets weirder and weirder-looking as I go. At atmosphere ninety-nine, a vampire squid with glowing blue eyes swims by slowly. Always slowly—the absence of heat and light from the sun forces them to conserve energy. This species is older than dinosaurs. The creature turns itself inside out. Something must be coming for it. Ah, no, it's just spooked by the giant cubes of trash being parachuted up by massive, billowing mechanical jellyfish. Now we're getting close to where The Money lives. The deeper you go, the more primo the real estate.

At 177 atmospheres, the bottom of the ocean, the elevator slows to a stop. Outside are black volcanic chimneys, one source of our geothermal energy. Zombie worms also live out there, grinding whale bones to dust. I spot the hull of a passenger jet from that day, decades ago, that the Great Sun Storm knocked all the planes out of the sky. Oh, and a cannonball from an old pirate ship—there's no way that's the same one I dropped from above the surface all those years ago?

The elevator beeps, and I pivot back toward my reflection. Behind this door is the woman who's supposed to help me. My oldest and perhaps dearest friend. Years ago, before she became a deity among us, she used to tell me I was her best friend, too. People have told me this often. It used to make me feel good, until I realized I was surrounded by people without friends. There was a reason no one else could stand these motherfuckers. And for Akira Kimura, that reason was probably that it's tough to put up with the smartest person on Earth.

Akira has called me to moonlight as personal security for her, just like in the old days. She says she's been getting the weird sense that she's in danger. A vision. A halo. And once again, a woman who says she trusts only me. But she's always been a little paranoid. She's offered to pay me well, more than enough to get myself out from under. That's the funny thing about The Money. They'll gift each other artifact and libation equal to most people's annual income. But anyone who ain't them's gotta work for it. *I'll give you this, but you've gotta do something for me.* Because they know a gift to the Less Than is truly a gift, not a trade. And rich or poor, no one wants to give away a thing for free.

I look into the elevator's facial recognition scan. I have clearance, just like she said. Right before the door slides open, my wife pings me on my iE. It zooms to a halt in front of my face to emphasize the importance of the message. Sabrina's got this psychic power for pinging me at the worst times. But if I'm being honest with myself, it's not that hard for her to figure out. I'm not in love anymore, so they're all the worst times. I pluck my iE out of the air and tuck it into my shoulder pocket before stepping into the penthouse.

The place is half furnished. This is a woman who lives at work, at her telescope, so the lack of armchairs isn't surprising. I'm way too early. Around thirty minutes, so I poke around. Doesn't look like she's home. Odd—she's more pathological about punctuality than me. I peep through her ocean telescope and look up through the atmospheres. All this modern underwater architecture, lit up with bioluminescence. Condos, aqua resorts, plazas, lighted vac tubes connecting them all. Like a twenty-first century skyline flipped upside down and dropped into the ocean. Refuse drones designed to look like yeti crabs claw out of septic cubes and scurry to the surface, flexing their mechanical limbs. Everything is hydro-powered, motion-powered, geo-powered. Sewage, heated and pressurized into biodiesel. Holographic ads circle their gilded prey, telling people they can somehow live forever while looking like a million bucks. The underwater city is always on, data-scavenging all our habits and using the info to create a more efficient place. An underwater panoramic, lubricated by the grease of America.

And that's when I see green. A small wisp of it, weaving

its way under Akira's bedroom door, its scent an ambergris perfume.

I step inside and look around closely. Nothing out of the ordinary. The only pieces inside are a dresser, a Japanese tea table with two black cushions, and a bullet-shaped AMP hibernation chamber, a grade people would kill to own. I sense death. I can hear it like an off-key strum. But I don't see blood. Even though I'm colorblind, I know what it looks like, and there isn't any.

But the perfume is overpowering in here. The wafts start coming at me. Other people can't sense them. You can't recreate them through canvas or theater. I've tried to paint them hundreds of times myself and never gotten it right. Murder has a smell like pure ambergris, and I'm the only one who knows it. Death is red, murder green.

I finally see them more distinctly. The faintest red circling the AMP chamber, its seal lined in green. The way that thing is constructed, nothing can seep out. So I know murder's been locked in there.

I step over to open it. It won't budge. An old-school padlock is holding the machine's opening handles tightly together. I take out my knife and crank the heat up on its blade, then cut through the clunky shank. The lock clanks on the floor as I open the hatch. Mist puffs out of the chamber. I swat the freezing cold puffs away. A solid, cloudy chunk glows from within the chamber. There's a frozen body in all that nitrogen, but except for a pair of hands flexed, pressing upward, it's tough to make out a face. I pull out my knife and start chipping away at the solid nitro. It's harder than ice. I turn the heat up even higher on my blade and stab at it again and again. A chunk breaks off. My iE alerts me that my blood pressure is rising quickly, that my pulse is racing. I silence it and turn my blade to where the head is.

I'm desperate now. I need to see if it's her. I thrust the blade into the block with everything I've got. Again and again. The smell gets stronger and stronger the closer I get to the face. The green wafts are making me tear up, but I've gotta know. It could be Akira in there. I cut and twist. A small chunk flies out of the chamber and skids across the room. I look down. An eye. Open. Always open, always seeing. The pupil is cloudy. Barely perceptible green curls up from them. Akira Kimura, one of the greatest minds to ever exist, has been reduced to breathless ice.

I stand up. Close my eyes. The smell is giving me a ferocious headache. The lock means she was trapped in there. And the green . . . This was murder, not suicide. I think for a moment, but it's tough to hang onto the flotsam of each detail in this mental flood. *Procedure*, I tell myself. *You're a detective. Stuff the personal. Procedure.* But I look at the broken lock and melting chunks of nitro on the floor and know I've already crossed that line.

I ping the chief and call it in. At first, he thinks I'm messing with him. He's never liked me, and the feeling is mutual. "The most brilliant scientist in the world, dead? Really," he says.

"You think this is a fucking prank call?" I say.

"No jokes, please," he says.

It's tough to convince someone of the death of a demigod, especially the kind of guy who goes through life like he's playing an efficiency simulator. Gods don't die, no matter how many sims you run through the quantum. My voice is shaking as I tell him about the lock, the chamber, the arms locked in an outward push. The clouded eyes. And when he realizes I'm not joking, he finally asks real questions. "Chamber malfunction?"

"I told you, the lock. Besides, someone flooded this thing with nitro instead of AMP. And the chamber's got controls on the inside."

"Assisted suicide?"

"No way," I say. "What's the point of sleeping in an AMP chamber every night if you aren't trying to live forever?" I don't tell him about the green. I never tell anyone about it. And I certainly don't tell him that if Akira Kimura were to ask anyone to help her kill herself, it would probably be me.

He gasps, then asks the obvious question. "Why would anyone want to kill her?"

I have no answer. The chief wants me to sit tight until he gets here. We have to secure the area and confirm it's her; we have to avoid a media shitstorm. Procedure. Then he asks what the hell I was doing there. I tell him the truth. She's an old friend who feared for her safety and offered me a job. *Her iE?* he asks. She never had one. Not even when she was busy saving the world. *Can she be saved?* the chief asks. Unlike every other member of The Money, Akira never kept a stockpile of farmed organs. She was old-fashioned through and through. He tells me again to sit tight. But I can't stay here anymore. My headache is now a full-blown migraine, the smell choking me. I need to leave. But I can't. I'm missing something.

I step to the chamber and press the heat button, which I would've done in the first place if I'd been thinking clearly. I tell myself to stop. Think. Wait. Procedure.

As the nitro melts, the chamber vents seep up the liquid. First, it's the hands, then the arms. The ones that were pushing up slide off at the shoulders and drop beside her. I take a step back. Next are the feet. Then the legs. They separate in half at the knees. I see her eyes, even after death, aimed upward as usual. Looking, always looking, just like I'm looking at her now. Then her head slides off, spins face down, and bobs in the remaining liquid nitro.

Someone locked the chamber and cranked up the AMP. Maybe Akira was startled and put her hands up. But it was too late. So much AMP flooded her liver that it put her into instant hibernation. Then whoever it was cut her to pieces. With such precision that the body didn't fall apart, and Akira slept through the whole thing.

Then that someone cranked up the nitro to put her on ice. Why put the lock back on after all this? I know the answer to that one: this was Akira Kimura. Whoever did this probably thought there was a chance she could somehow reassemble herself and get out. These are the thoughts that go through someone's head when they try to kill a living god.

I close my eyes and take a breath before looking again. The cuts are surgical. Her torso cracks in half, diagonal, from clavicle to hip bone. I turn away. Kick the cut lock across the room, put my hands on my face, and squat in frustration.

For some reason, I find myself telling the chief that at least she lived well. That she succeeded, then had a good, long life. An inappropriate sentiment made by a man needing to get out of the room. The chief tells me again to stay put, but the green wafts have now formed a narrow stream that juts outside the bedroom. I see them floating to the elevator. I cannot bear to look at Akira like this. And I cannot let the trail go cold.

I get into the elevator and am finally able to take a breath. I try to rev down. The chief tells me to relax. He tells me,

Calm down, old man, you're gonna have a heart attack. And I don't know why, but I say again: *At least she succeeded. At least she lived well.* The chief says, *Stop saying that,* then pauses. He says the grass is always greener. I wouldn't know. Murder is the only time I can see green.

2

As a kid, I was diagnosed with two conditions: colorblindness and synesthesia. Colorblindness is easy enough to explain. Like most of the afflicted, I can't see red or green as others see them. I'm in my blended-wing-body SEAL now, gliding above the island toward Akira's Telescope, and the lava below looks brownish-yellow. The rainforests, like the ash plumes that block the sunlight, appear in varying shades of beige. I fly higher. The brown-yellows and beiges become vague, blending together.

Synesthesia, on the other hand, is a diagnosis with plenty of possible combinations. Most simply put, it is a condition in which a person senses something in two different ways. Some synesthetes not only hear music but see it in colorful swirls. Others feel certain sounds, like burning skin when a baby cries, and yet others might touch the rough surface of old concrete, the stuff we used to make buildings out of, and taste fish waffles. Some may listen to dripping water and smell sulfur. Most simply see something more in words and numbers. For example, a small number, like two, may appear to be closer to the reader than the number two hundred. Or some read the word "big" and see the word itself as bigger on the page.

And all this is theoretical. A number of scientists think it's simple hallucination. I don't talk about mine because it sounds crazy, like feral hallucinations that have escaped the confines of reality. At least most cases of synesthesia correspond to the basic and objective five human senses in a logical way, with something everyone can perceive with two of the following: sight, sound, taste, smell, touch. The synesthetes everyone knows exist, the ones we depend on to feel comforted that we all perceive reality pretty much the same way.

And maybe my synesthesia has roots in this. It is, after all, a sight and a smell. But their triggers are things I shouldn't be able to sense. Music that really hits me somewhere deep comes floating in red notes. Murder—before and after— wisps before me in strands of green. Death, heavier than music, is always a cloud of red. I perceive these violent delights in colors I'm not otherwise able to see. And only when murder is inevitable, like back in the war, do these colors coil and mesh together.

People don't like to hear this kind of bullshit. They would never believe it, and I don't blame them. It's often been said that the human mind is a prediction machine, so maybe it's just some kind of overpredicting on my part. A heavy psychodynamic pour of my unconscious into my conscious. A splash of Charles Bonnet syndrome, since I'm visually impaired and recognize that what I'm seeing isn't real. A twist of delirium and astronomer's gambit. As much research as we've done, the human brain remains a puzzle. Not even Akira figured it out. But people born mute sometimes hear voices in their heads. We can see the auditory parts of their brains kick in when they do. The chances of someone having all four of my disorders at the same time is billions to one. And the way I figure, all four need to be firing when this happens, or the whole thing will break. Just because what I see ain't real, doesn't mean it ain't accurate. I have a murder-solve rate that's unprecedented in the history of the police force. Colorblindness has been curable for years now, but I never had any interest in curing mine. And I've prevented crime in the past that no one else saw coming. So I may not be a legend like Akira, but I protected her so she could do a hero's work.

The chief won't stop pinging, and I'm getting irritated. He doesn't get what I do. He doesn't have a clearance rate anywhere near mine. He didn't have a hand in saving jack shit. So why won't he just let me do my thing? I can't block the chief's pings—chain of command is programmed into my iE—so I look down from my SEAL to distract myself.

A color that I see as vividly as anyone is blue. And as the SEAL steers higher and higher, the ocean blue surrounding the island brings back memories. My father, a hydronaut, worked in aqua construction back when engineers and architects were trying to build the first seascrapers from the seafloor up. Humanity was on a roll back then, and scientists were coming up with a bunch of crazy ideas, shook from the Great Sun Storm that almost knocked us a century or two back. They built seascrapers that protected us from solar flares with deep-water habitation. We made rail guns, giant ones that could fire plasma to outer space. We came up with pills that could change skin color. Organ farms. AMP therapy that could slow down the aging process or turn the work day from twelve hours to twenty-two. After an hour in that thing, a person feels like they've gotten a full eight hours of sleep.

Then there was the iE, which blew cell phones and every other piece of smart tech out of the water.

One day, my dad came home from work with a chunk of ambergris the size of a soccer ball and showed it to me and my mother. Plunked it right there on the kitchen table. And when he told us what it was, the indigestible stuff sitting in a sperm whale's belly until the whale itself dies and rots on the ocean floor, my mom told him to throw it away. He laughed and said it was what the most expensive perfume was made of, worth a fortune. The smell hit me first. That headache of a smell. Then the color. Faint, like the smoke rising off a snubbed wick, but growing stronger and stronger, forming into a ghost being called by a séance. That was when I saw green for the first time in my life. And I was awestruck. The green wafted over to my father.

"The whale didn't rot on its own," I said. "Did someone kill it?"

He frowned at me. "How'd you know that?" he asked.

I shrugged. He nodded. "We set off a charge in the vista, and the whale got caught in it," my father said. "I felt horrible about it, killing the thing, but I found this after. Lucky, huh?"

It was one of the last times I saw my father happy. Over the next year, as the world population hit twelve billion and we raced harder to make something new and bigger, he dove deeper and deeper into the ocean to build underwater scrapers that would be insulated from power outages in sun storms. He eventually got the bends one too many times. He spent the last year of his life crippled, pissing into a catheter until he became a ghost himself. I responded with hate. I hated his work. I hated the company he worked for. A part of me might even have hated him.

That was when I started getting into trouble. Started leaning into life, fists first. As a child, I thought my color-blindness would be the only way I'd be able to see my father again, because I was sure his death wasn't his fault. He broke depth records. He was invincible in the water. When he died, I waited for his green ghost to confirm that it was someone else's fault, but it never showed up.

The chief pings again. I relent and answer, voice only.

"Where are you going?" he asks.

"To her telescope."

"Come back for the autopsy."

"Autopsy? Have you seen her yet? Somebody killed her with an autopsy."

"I did see," the chief says. "You shouldn't have touched a thing. You should've reported it immediately. I need to supervise this one. I need you to inform me about the moves you're making before you make them. Drum-tight procedure on this one. The governor's already aware. The president. The *president*! This is national security. You need to get clearance every step of the way on this. And under no conditions are you to talk to the press. If we show the public what happened to this woman, there will be chaos."

My head is pounding. "Okay, Chief."

"The president is already sending his people here. The president!"

"Got it, Chief."

"Stop calling me that. I'm your captain."

"Aye-aye."

I click out. He didn't explicitly tell me to stop my mission to Akira's Telescope, which I'm nearing now. Sitting above the clouds, on the tallest mountain on Earth, this telescope isn't just a telescope, it's an entire complex that barely fits on the peak. I look up at Ascalon's Scar, then down at the island below, which I can see since it's a clear day. Only someone my age would recognize those buildings as normal looking. The rest of it nowadays—the seascrapers, the cloudscrapers, the theme parks—it's all architecture that celebrates our newfound admiration of the natural world while we've crammed it with nearly thirteen billion souls, forcing us to build into the depths of the ocean or so high that we scrape the top of the troposphere. Glass behemoths that look like monster tulips, clouds, or bamboo shoots. No right angles. Spit shined in parrotfish blue and trevally yellow. Nothing like a near-miss extinction to create a world that looks like a giant tossed salad. But this building I'm hovering over to, it's not a building trying to look artful by imitating nature. It is a building whose nature is clear: to look further into the unknown than anything man has ever made. To look inside the swirls of galaxies drybrushed in wisteria.

What I see are the slight green fumes wafting from its god-like eye. And for some reason, I think back to my father, and the fact that the dead are the only extinguished lights we can never really see again.

3

Crazy as it sounds, I first met Akira Kimura on a dating app fifty years ago. I had just jettisoned marriage number two, and she'd worked so hard her whole damned life that she'd somehow missed the whole pairing off and Noah's Ark pro-creating we were all supposed to do. Signing up for the app was her version of a midlife crisis.

We met at an old-fashioned Korean-Irish soju pub called Maru Bollix. I'd chosen this cop bar because back then I was still going for my cynical, noir detective vibe on dates, trying to be one of those "sensitive tough guys" we only remembered in black and white. But when Akira stepped in and I saw her reflection in the saloon-style mirror behind the bar, I didn't need any synesthesia to see plain fact. We were immediately disgusted by each other—and ourselves.

But she sat down and ordered a drink, and we went through the motions. She had two PhDs, one in astronomy and one in astrophysics, and was pursuing a third in mechanical engineering while working to improve cloaking tech, which she described as a cheap second-rate hat trick. I told her I was working on solving the murder of a woman who had starved her twins to death and, for sympathy, claimed a terminal illness had taken them. She paused, then said the list of suspects must be long. I said yeah, cracking this one's probably as tough as a PhD in mechanical engineering.

We relaxed a bit after that. She was different from my most recent ex, who, adding together makeup, plucking, gym, makeup removal, moisturizing, and exfoliating, spent about four hours a day in front of the mirror. According to my math the one time I clocked her, that was how she spent about seventeen percent of her existence—twenty-five percent of her waking hours. It was tough to judge her, though. I spent about the same amount of time solving the murders of those who probably deserved to die.

Akira, though, spent one hundred percent of her time trying to figure out anything and everything except herself. I once told her I was an art history major in college. She seemed surprised the subject still existed. I told her it didn't anymore, but had surprisingly lasted longer than philosophy, photography, journalism, and religious studies. I told her education was probably the next to go. She said, no, as long as people needed babysitting, the field of education would be intact. She called babysitting the world's second-oldest profession. I laughed and agreed. She added that despite all the advances in neuroscience, psychology wasn't going anywhere either. I nodded. It would be around for as long as there are people who wanted to babble about their problems. So, forever.

She told me she didn't know much about art, but that I reminded her of the man in the suit sitting alone in Edward Hopper's *Nighthawks*. I told her my favorite painting was *The Great Wave off Kanagawa*. That was a wooden block print, she corrected, not a painting. Then she asked what I thought about Matisse's *Music*. I told her I didn't care for it much. We went on and on. All the masterpieces. And the only thing we really agreed on is that some of the best art is a cry for help.

"Did you know . . ." she said.

I was beginning to notice that, like most overeducated people, she habitually started sentences with that question. "Did you know that the female giant octopus starves itself to death for six months while it takes care of its eggs?"

"Sounds admirable," I said.

"That's because you're a man," she said.

I laughed. Then we somehow ended up on the piano. Maybe because we'd discussed Renoir and how he liked to paint young women playing the instrument, and this Irish cop pub had an old dusty out-of-tune one sitting there. I decided to sit in front of it and show off some—Akira was impressed, and I told her my mother had wanted me to be a concert pianist. That I'd always had a knack for it. I didn't tell her why, that I heard and saw red when good, really good music played. That musical notes blared in front of me in crimson letters and numbers. Songs, or at least the ones I liked, read to me as stories. My concert pianist dreams were dashed once parents started genetically engineering their kids to have six fingers. Back then, genetic enhancement, with the exception of freak athletics and evil genius IQ, was legal. A six-year-old, six-fingered kid once played at a concert and took my breath away. I knew I'd never be as good as him. And after that, I no longer wanted to play. But I didn't want to lay all that history on Akira, so instead of talking about it, I finished my song and told her once they created the PhD program in useless skills and knowledge, I'd be the first to receive an honorary diploma.

She smiled and looked at the piano, teary-eyed. She said her mom had forced her to take piano too. She said that she was terrible at it from the beginning, so she rigged the piano to be self-playing and would sit there in front of her mom and pretend she was making progress. The ruse lasted about six months, until her mom surprised her by entering her in a competition. She went and made a fool of herself. Worse, she made a fool out of her mother. Wistful, I told her about my first wife and child, how I'd enlisted in the army to make enough to take care of them. Then Desert Storm 15 erupted. After three years of rail gun sniper and MP work, I walked out a master sergeant with two farmed organs on reserve for future use. Part of Federal benes. In the meantime, the wife had walked out on me. She'd hooked up with a G therapy nurse during my deployment and taken the kid to live in Portugal with him. I know what it is to make a fool of yourself, I said.

By the end of the night, me and the yet-to-be world-renowned genius and terrible piano player Akira Kimura had agreed on a few things. First was that the last thing I needed right after a divorce was to be near any romantic entanglement, period. Second, that she admitted that the whole dating thing was a meltdown for her, an attempt to satisfy the craving to be normal. She was, in fact, not normal, not actually interested in being normal, but like that piano-playing version of herself who wanted to satisfy her mother, she sometimes felt guilty for just being who she was. In the end, I got married two more times, and she never went on another date. Even with the heft of her fame and reputation, people didn't fully realize how powerful this woman was. Squashed a personal crisis with a single date. That's why it never surprised me, given three years and change, that she also squashed the fuck out of globe-killer Sessho-seki.

When I exit the SEAL and climb the steps to Akira's Telescope, the adrenaline I've been running on the past hour begins fading fast. It's cold up here, and the bad knee starts clicking, the teeth start aching, and the heartburn percolates. My fingers, once thick and strong, feel crooked and hollow. I'm feeling old again. My iE pings. The wife. I don't respond.

It's been ages since I've been to this place. In the years I ran security for Akira, I practically lived here. Some people would say that using the word "security" for what I did for Akira is a stretch. But it's what I did. I kept her safe by any means necessary. That instinct hasn't faded. I wish I'd been there for her back at the penthouse. No matter how old I might be, I would never have let anyone cut her to pieces like that. Back in the days of Ascalon, people on all levels tried to take her down. And I silenced them all. Aching joints now, perhaps the loss of a step, but when I'm in mode, I know I've got a power bomb or two left in me.

But it's been ages since I had to be in mode. Decades. I get to the telescope door and let its scanner flash over my face. Even after all these years, it recognizes me and opens, and for some reason, I'm surprised. Not that I still have clearance, but that the machine even recognizes me. Because the older I get, the less recognizable I am to myself.

4

The guts of the most powerful telescope in the world resemble a cathedral of twentieth-century office antiquity. I almost leave my iE floating outside in sleep mode out of habit, her strict rule. Then I remember that she's dead and enter. Upon stepping in, I stand on a cylindrical pedestal of the full-body scanner and laugh to myself remembering how much Akira hated this thing. She'd step on it, this little platform, and her eyes would narrow as the neon rings of blue light lit up and gyrated around her. Today, no neon blue rings alight around me. The inside-out body scan is probably decommissioned now, just like me. I step off the pedestal and into the middle of the grand chamber. The chair in front of the eyepiece, a steel folding chair, looks impossible to sit on comfortably. Lining the wall are file cabinets filled with binders—binders filled with actual paper from back when people could chop down trees with impunity. Now, the unauthorized chopping down of a tree that's a hundred years or older gets a wannabe lumberjack charged with murder, the same if he or she gunned down a grandma in the street. "Streets" being a metaphorical term nowadays.

Only people around my age and older remember rubber tires. Meanwhile, our own tires are running on worn treads down to the tartan of steel, fiberglass, and rayon barely holding us together.

I look across the room and spot her desk under the *No iEs Allowed* sign. It's the same desk from back in the day, sitting in the exact same place. A wooden desk with actual handled drawers. A flat screen, or what laughably passed for flat a hundred years ago, hangs above it. It's hooked up to a literal handheld remote control. On the desk, a telephone with buttons. The childhood photo of her at a playground—the only real evidence I ever saw that she had a childhood—is gone. Next to the desk, a platoon of med bots. Off to the right, a chalkboard filled with the powdery ghosts of calculations I couldn't even begin to fathom. Shelved underneath, erasers caked with the remnants. Akira was always afraid of someone stealing her work. Trying to do what only she was capable of doing correctly. Afraid her work would be used as a weapon. Maybe that was part of the reason she trusted me so much back then. She knew I didn't understand a damn thing she was scribbling on that board.

But the strangest thing isn't this antiquated office and its chalkboard. It's the grand piano cordoned off with velvet rope. That wasn't here the last time I visited. I ignore it for now, step over to the desk, and grab a drawer handle. I pause. For the first time in years, I'm shy about invading someone's space. It's like touching the property of a saint. I open the drawer and it's empty. I look around. No green wafts. Not that I expected to see any. It's not that easy. I still need to use my brain and figure my way through the gaps, through what Akira would call the dark matter, which takes up more space than the trail, just like in the heavens, those devoid gaps between swirling galaxies.

Even though we go way back, once Ascalon did its work, I was never invited here again. I suppose some places are so sacred to us that we don't share them with anyone else unless we absolutely need to. And this place is personal. For her, personal meant work. There are zero signs of the public Akira Kimura here, no holos of her thousands of awards, no vid doc of the conversations she had with practically every head of state in the last forty years. So the piano, which cannot be work related, is very strange. I want to laugh at the thought that the largest thing in the room is a reminder of her biggest and perhaps only life failure. I wonder why she had this thing lugged in.

I let my iE out of my shoulder pocket to record all this, which feels like a violation because no iEs were ever allowed in here. The floating orb hovers and scans and reminds me that I forgot to take my pain and memory pills. The last thing I need is a memory pill. I'm feeling for the first time in a long time. And it don't feel good. I'm usually tired by this time of day, but right now, I'm wired. It's depressing that maybe my old friend's death excites me. On top of this mountain with some native name that escapes me, her death balloons life into me.

I can't take my eyes off the piano. I step up to the brass stanchion and detach the velvet rope. A vacuum revs and nearly makes me jump. It hovers over the rubber flooring, a machine with one job on its mech mind. Watching it reminds me what Akira said to all the nay and doomsayers when she unveiled Ascalon. Some people were terrified of an object that powerful calculating trajectory on its own. No one, not even Akira, was going to pull the trigger. Ascalon would do that on its own. People freaked out. And Akira responded by saying that no one should fear AI. We've all known for centuries that a piece of hardware can do any one thing a man can do, sometimes infinitely better. But no single AI can come close to doing what a single human mind can do across the board. Don't fear Ascalon, she said. Be thankful that she may be able to accomplish the one thing we could only dream of doing with perfect accuracy.

I sit at the piano and the vacuum stops. I think about what Akira must've felt like, playing in front of all those people and letting her mom down. It's always been hard to imagine Akira as a child. The same image always pops up, and it's not the one in the picture that adorned her desk. Instead, I imagine a girl in a lab coat, sprung from her father's forehead. I laugh to myself and sigh as I strike a few keys. Then I stare down at the keyboard, trying to remember the song I played fifty years ago in that bar with Akira.

All of a sudden, I see them. The curls of smoke rising from between the keys—faint, almost imperceptible. I strike a single key, and the smoke kicks up like dust. I begin to play the same song I did the first time we met. An old jazz standard, loaded with improvised sorrow. I close my eyes. I feel the tears and know there ain't no color to them, just clear.

Then I notice. The piano has begun to play on its own.

I stand and step away. It's playing what I'm playing, but the song slowly transitions into another one. One I've never heard before. The music turns red. A rush of words and numbers, coming at me fast. Too fast, keys undulating quicker than any one person could tap them. I try hard to listen, to memorize this barrage of red letters and numbers. But I can't.

Now I wish I'd taken my memory pills. My iE can't record those letters because no one, not even my robotic substitute brain, can see them but me. Procedure. I try to calm down and remember that this is music. Even if my iE can't record the letters and numbers, it can record the song. I calm. The chorus repeats. Some of it is soaking in. It's an insanely complex piece of music. Way too complex for Akira to have written. Then who wrote this for her, and why? Is this her *jisei*, her death poem? It would be too complex for anyone else to understand, just like her work.

Then the telescope begins to groan. I tell my iE to keep its focus on the music and walk to the eyepiece. I almost trip over the velvet rope on the way there. I chastise myself. I saw the green emanating from the lens from outside. The first thing I should've done was look through the damn telescope when I got in. But I got emotional. I forgot procedure, just like an hour ago back at the penthouse when I was trying to chip away solid nitro with a knife. Besides, even back in the day, just about no one was allowed to look through the telescope besides Akira. I don't remember doing that even a single time.

When I arrive, the telescope stops its groan. I put my right eye to the eyepiece.

It's aimed down at Earth, at above-ground lava rocks not fifty miles from here. A single marble tombstone scribbled with katakana is the only thing standing on the vast basalt field. Fresh flowers sit in front of the tombstone, and at first, they look brownish yellow. But as the song gets to the chorus, the flowers begin to turn red.

Before I can start to think about what it means, the piano stops. Voices outside. The telescope groans back into its original position.

The chief and two corporals walk in. The chief is the kind of man who uses his facial hair to make some kind of masculine statement, his very large beard perfectly trimmed as usual. It's a beard worthy of old missionary schoolmasters, jutting out to create the illusion of an elongated chin so prominent that it hides his tightly buttoned blue coat collar.

"I told you not to go in," he says.

I want to grab that ridiculous beard and yank it off his face. "I was gonna get here eventually."

"Now you'll be heading back out with us."

A PD drone floats behind me. I immediately get it. I'm a suspect. I drop my hands and make cuffing easy for it. Magnetic coils wrap around my wrists and lock them together. "If you think I did it, you're crazy, Chief."

The chief shrugs. "Orders from way up. All persons of interest detained immediately. This is just a formality. You're a person of interest. Covering all bases. Honestly, if you weren't one of mine and I didn't know how dangerous you were, I wouldn't even bother cuffing you."

I don't complain. Persons of interest. The roundup. I used to do this sort of work back in the days of Ascalon. For her. One of the corporals takes my knife from me.

"Analyze it," the chief says.

The PD drone keeps its camera eye on me. "There's no way whoever cut her up like that was using a knife," I say. "And I haven't been dangerous in years."

The chief waves off the drone and grabs me by the cuffs. He whispers, "We both know you killed for her."

"That would make me the last person who'd kill her. You ever kill anyone, Chief?"

"I'll ping your wife and tell her you'll be late," he says.

The chief walks away and signals for the corporal to take over the arrest. "Your DNA was all over that place, for God's sake."

"I had to confirm it was her."

"You didn't follow protocol. Instead, you polluted the entire crime scene, and you know it."

"I don't leave my friends like that."

The chief ignores the comment, his mind drifting elsewhere. "My God, did you see her AMP chamber? iE compatible and crush-proof with nitro bath? My entire lifetime salary wouldn't cover the cost of one of those."

AMP. Everyone's dream. The mitochondria. Krebs cycle. Hibernation. We all run on electricity. And AMP chambers help to preserve our battery lives. Most have to pay a serious bundle just to go to a clinic to get the occasional treatment. Akira's crush-proof chamber of youth is probably worth more than her crush-proof penthouse. And she has two of them, one at the penthouse and one in her bedroom at this lab. The fact that the chief is fantasizing about affording one right now pisses me off. "Crush-proof like your stupidity," I mutter.

"And yet, I outrank you."

"Yes, you do, Chief. Yes, you do."

"She didn't look a day over forty," the chief says. "Not a single day."

This asshole actually picked up the head of a god, and the first thing he thought was how young she looked. This piece of mediocrity who couldn't solve a fucking ten-piece jigsaw puzzle. I feel my wrists battle with the cuffs, skin chafing. My body wants to go fists-first, like it did sixty years ago. The magnetic cuffs sense the struggle and tighten, so I take a breath and force myself to calm down. "Go ahead and run tests on all the knives in the world," I say. "Those cuts were laser."

"Still, we've got to make sure. Procedure."

I'm led outside. The vog at this altitude makes it hard to breathe, so thick that it dulls the sun to the point that I can look straight at it. I'm walked toward the chief's SEAL, thinking about Akira. About my wife and baby at home. About all my wives and babies, my mistakes and fears. I picture the piano inside Akira's Telescope. I wonder if she thought about her own mistakes and fears every time she set eyes on that damn thing.

As I look back, there are no green wafts, no red letters and numbers. The song replays in my mind, gasping to get something out. The memory crystallizes into one thought. A word. *Ascalon.*

Great, another Ascalon. Just what the world needs. Wasn't the first one enough? Maybe Sessho-seki really should have reduced all of us to tinted gas like the one enveloping us, smearing the sun.

I inhale sulfur and think about Akira. I try to picture her reaction the moment she saved the world, but I can't. I was there, wasn't I? Why can't I remember? I just imagine her in her usual calm. She told me once that she was disgusted by all animals with their involuntary twitching and gnawing nature. Maybe that was why she never did anything involuntarily.

Or maybe when you have the sheer force of will to keep doing something over and over again until you get it right, winning feels more like relief than anything else.

5

Interrogation rooms are no longer what they were for centuries of criminal investigation. This one is warm and inviting, with cushioned chairs, soft light, and music, like the suspect is in for a full-body massage instead of relentless questioning. We finally came to understand that when people feel threatened, they're more prone to lie. I sit in the recliner and put my feet up. The concrete ceiling is a butterflyfish yellow that does a piss-poor job at hiding its impenetrability. I met my wife, Sabrina, in this exact room. She was a young cop with talent. I'm impressed with that, like anyone else. Weak to it. She was the type people seemed to want to tell the truth to, with a breathless ability to articulate empathy. So much potential. But what I forgot is, talent often peaks when you're young. And empathy isn't that hard to pull off if you've got no personal stake in a thing.

I know what she saw in me. The brilliant mentor. Formerly Akira Kimura's personal sentinel. The one senior cop with the seemingly inexhaustible ability to tell her things she didn't already know. But now she sees a broken old man in debt who does practically nothing around the house with the excuse of a time-consuming job that doesn't pay much. Pay, like talent, typically caps out when you're young. And now that we can get so old, everything under the cap eventually wastes away. So whenever I'm home nowadays, I feel like one of the criminals she used to question for a living. But her questions aren't the paranoid, "Where have you been?" type. More like, "How the hell did I end up with you?" And she's not really asking me, she's asking herself. Either way, I haven't got a good answer.

The chief steps in, a company man through and through, with just enough self-knowledge early on to know he had no talent. Armed with that, he did the sensible thing and chased rank fast and hard and climbed the ladder. He's more than thirty years my junior, and his salary doubles mine. He's the kind of mindless go-getter a corporation would make up executive positions for. A man singularly bent on being on the top of a heap of a stinking pile of average.

He sits down and puts my knife on the desk. I wanna grab him by his obnoxious beard and slam my fist through his face. Instead, I say, "Lawyer's been pinged. I'm going to take a nap till she gets here."

The chief starts going on about how I'm a member of a team, a brotherhood, that he's trying to protect me, blah blah blah. He knows it's bullshit, but the cameras are on, and the show he's putting on is what's expected of him. My iE hovers above me, recording the same thing. Privacy rights and all. The warrant to confiscate a person's iE is the toughest one to get. Everyone knows that's because The Money has always made most of the rules, and they're not The Money because they're dumb. Just like anyone else, if they're in a legal bind, the last thing they want turned over to cops is the device that contains their entire history, personal and otherwise. The only time law enforcement can gain immediate access to an iE is to observe the last hour of a victim's life if foul play is suspected. Either way, I belatedly hand it to Akira. Showcasing one more aspect of her genius by refusing to ever have one.

The chief drones on. The background saxophone jazz and chiming of crystals sound more to me like shattering glass. It makes me furious. I imagine Akira frozen, hacked to pieces in that capsule. The futile noise of my knife chipping away at that solid nitro block. The sound of things breaking. I find myself wanting to do even more of it. So I decide to break from the script the chief probably figures we'll play out.

I sit up and look at him. He's startled by it. I'm not supposed to do that. "Procedure," he says. "I know you didn't kill her, but why didn't you just follow procedure?"

The word "procedure" pisses me off, maybe because he's said it a hundred times now, maybe because he's right. I crushed procedure into a fine powder under my foot on this one. Maybe because whenever it comes to Akira I go into sentinel mode, and thought I could hunt unleashed. Even though it's been decades since protecting her has been my duty, that I let her die is my failure.

I stand. The chief frowns. I'm not supposed to do that either; I'm supposed to sit back silently until my lawyer gets me out. Now he's scared. Like most idiots, he loves repetition and hates improvisation. Me, I just want to destroy everything. "No elevator security vid, I take it," I say.

The chief starts to say something, then pauses. Then he says, "You know The Money. They like their privacy."

"List of people who had access to her penthouse?"

"You."

"And?"

"A person of interest. A person named Ascalon Lee."

I laugh. "There are probably more living Ascalon Lees than dead John Smiths."

"Yes, a fake name, I would guess," the chief says. "But we're looking into it."

Ascalon. I hear the song in my head again.

The chief tries to get us back on script. "You need to help us on this. And help yourself. Let's get you cleared so we can work together to find out who did this."

My iE pings and the music pauses. We both look up. Sabrina calling again. I don't answer, even if I'm technically allowed to. It'll be just like this interrogation, the same script I've heard hundreds of times. I tell my iE to ignore the call.

"Life's just gotta be more than this," I say to the chief. "This same dialogue with every person who sits in this fucking chair. We're like programmed androids on some shit vid cast. Not even one of the main ones."

"You need to calm down, detective," the chief says. "Don't worry. This is not an arrest. I just need you to answer some questions. Procedure."

"Yeah, pretty sure you said that already," I say. "What kind of imbecile parrots himself every sentence?"

"Mmm, uh."

I'm as surprised at my behavior as he is—he's still my superior—but at this point, I'm just rolling with it. Fuck careers, hierarchies, pay caps, loans, responsibilities. Fuck pushing the boulder up the hill over and over again. I'm too old. I don't got the back for it nowadays. Plus, I haven't been able to piss in the last several hours, which at my age must be some kind of record.

"I quit," I say.

"You can't!" he sputters. "These, uh, these things take time to process."

"Well, let me help you out with that, Chief."

"It's Captain."

"I'll send over this recording of my resignation to HR by iE the minute I leave this room." I pick my knife up off the desk and step toward the door. "Let me out of here."

He puts his hands up. "You know this makes you look suspicious."

He's really grasping now, as if saying that will somehow make me recant and sit back in that damned plush leather chair. At this point, I'd even go for the electric kind instead. I point my knife at the interrogation room entrance. "Out," I say.

The door slides open. As I head for it, he asks, "Why do you always insist on calling me chief instead of captain? That rank hasn't existed in decades."

I turn to him. "You don't know why?"

He shakes his head. "No. Before my time."

I point the knife at him. "That's the thing. For anyone to solve a problem today, they should be looking backward first. And, like just about everyone else, you refuse to. The title 'chief' was taken off the books because when Sessho-seki was coming and Ascalon was being built, the president's chief of staff almost mucked up the entire thing by trying day and night to convince the president that Ascalon wouldn't work and should be aborted. That Sessho-seki didn't even exist."

"And?"

"Thankfully, the president didn't listen. The chief lost his fucking mind. And after Ascalon saved us, the word 'chief' stopped meaning what it did and started to mean 'fucking moron.' So every organization took the title off the books. Do you know what Akira Kimura did to figure out the asteroid was coming for us?"

"What?"

"She had to see where it had been to predict where it was going."

The chief thinks for a moment. He glares at me, and for a second I'm tempted to slice that stupid wannabe goatfish beard from his face. Instead, I walk out for good with just one question running through my head: who would have wanted to kill Akira Kimura forty years after she saved the world?

6

For the most part, the only people allowed to live on the south and east sides of the island are subsidized preservation workers who spend their days planting and caring for indigenous species or eradicating invasive ones. They're all neo-hippies required to live in primitive huts and tree houses designed to not ruin the natural aesthetic of the island. They live under rules kind of like town associations back in the day. They also run the theme park millions of tourists flock to while they're here on their pilgrimage to pay reverence from the side of the mountain to Akira's Telescope, nicknamed The Savior's Eye by fanatics. Its construction was a deal brokered by Akira. Maybe she'd chosen that spot for its clarity in viewing the stars, or maybe she'd chosen a spot that high up so she could limit access to her telescope, to her. I was never sure.

Most of us, The Less Thans, don't live on the island or on the low floors of new seascrapers and the high floors of old skyscrapers. We live in the float burbs, clusters of domed townhouses that bob on the ocean surface and descend two stories underwater. From above, they look like sinking flowers. The townhouses are magnetically moored far enough from the shore that they aren't an eyesore. Mostly government workers, plastic skimmers, trade people, coral gardeners, small business owners, and resort and theme park middle management, we live on means just enough to enable us to do nothing after we put in our forty hours. Maybe we can afford a once-a-month trip to the AMP clinic. Maybe we save and purchase a week-long family tour of Epcot or Lucky Cat City once a year. Maybe we collect enough social security to experience a mundane retirement after eighty. Octogenarian Boredom on a Budget, or OBB, as we call it. It's not great, but it's better than living on the continent. Three hundred million surrounding the quad state Great Leachate, the biggest landfill in the history of man. Penicillin rivers running like veins from Missouri to the Nashville Dam. We pretty much gave up on trying to clean that up. Figured it was easier to just come out here and start a vertical expansion.

I'm hovering home through the satin gunmetal sky. I've just quit my job. I'm still reeling. I realize I forgot to take my insomnia and anxiety inhibitors. I have access to the kind a person is only supposed to take for space flight. I've been double-dosing every day before I get home. The second dose curbs my anxiety about taking too many anxiety pills.

A trip would be nice right about now. Not a one-week quickie family package, but maybe a long solo tour of something far from the ocean, like pitching in a hand to replant Yosemite National Desert. I sigh. I haven't volunteered for anything my entire life except war. Besides, I couldn't keep a fern alive in a rainforest. It's too late for me now, anyway. I dock my SEAL and step onto the wharf.

I walk toward my unit across planks that light up as I go.

The sun is setting and a man, about a hundred years old, a retired cryptocurrency assistant to some VP, is fishing in front of his slip. Fishing in water too deep to bring up anything with that pathetic spool of line. "Any luck, Fred?" I ask as I walk by.

"Not yet," he says, legs dangling over the edge, his short-legged plaid foam fit humming cool air onto his skin while sweat drips down his face.

Not ever. Poor guy. I pass him and hear the blaring of a neighbor's iE projection, probably a classic movie. From outside, it sounds like the kind of entertainment geared toward an old man, the main character of the program an elderly badass with no romantic entanglements, just a retired guy on a mission, using his skills to help other people. Said skills usually involve a remarkable proficiency to bloody his hands. It's the kind of show for a man whose capacity to dream is the only thing lower than his T levels. I pass the unit and begrudgingly head toward mine.

Two units down, a group of teens on the same color tat pill, probably red because except for their outlines, I can't see them well. The fact that they're half naked and masked up like it's Halloween doesn't help. It's how the kids do nowadays, trying to collectively express their individuality. Hair smart-gelled itself into fins, flower petals, and snakes. They ignore me as I approach—ignore everything outside of themselves, really, whispering empty secrets and doing everything else teens have always done. Like talking about how dumb the world is even though they haven't really had to look at it yet. If anyone undoes the work of Akira, it will be this generation. Too young to remember Ascalon, to appreciate being alive. I pass them, practically a ghost in their eyes, and stand before my front door. The plank light under me is on the fritz again. I regret not taking my astronaut-grade anti-anxiety and insomnia pills. For all I know, the chief might've pinged Sabrina and told her I quit.

The door scans me, then retracts, and I step in and down the three steps to the living room. And just like every other day when I get home, I wince at the furniture I can't afford packed into the apartment I can't afford. Part pleaser, part superficial, I have weaknesses that have always destined me for a lifelong game of catch-up, the goal as unachievable as leprechaun gold. After Sessho-seki, people bought into the idea that money didn't matter, or, you never know, so spend what you've got. I don't have that excuse. I always spent too much, most of the time before I even made the money. I'm not sure where the impulse comes from.

Two steps in, a beaming Ascalon waddles full blast at me, calling out, "Dada." I beam back and scoop her up, and after she gets her split second of affection, she's ready to move on, so I set her back down. She runs off looking for something dangerous to sit or stand on.

Sabrina walks in. Sabrina. Back in college, she was a nationally ranked pulse racket player, permanently injured a year before going pro. The first time she told me about it, I thought, how does a kid bounce back from something like that? A future of fame and fortune shattered in an instant, just like her knee. She went to the best docs to reconstruct it, graphed cloned ligaments, then rehabbed it, but in the end, even though she was still good, that loss of a step, that loss of a .05 on her shuttle time to the pulse, dropped her from world class to pretty damn good. From then on was a life of disappointment. She had to get an ordinary job. She became a cop. One on paid leave now, since she's married to an old man and taking care of a baby in the float burbs instead of winning global racket pulse championships. Saddled with a toddler and probably asking herself every day how time can move so slowly.

I see the disappointment now as she drags a changing table out of the elevator. She shoots me an angry glance because I ignored her calls earlier and I'm not jumping in to help her move the table as some form of apology. She sighs and turns her concentration back to the changing table, seemingly remembering that I'm an old man who might be too weak to move furniture. Who might one day need a changing table himself. At least it doesn't look like the chief told her I quit.

I turn to Ascalon. She's sitting on a remote-control ball, the latest gimmick that's supposed to prep toddlers for iE control when they hit early childhood. Her animated program blasts nursery rhymes. It's a 3D spectacle starring a pig with cracked-out eyes that pilots an impossibly tricked-out SEAL in an animated retro-world—currently the size of our living room—filled with fins and fenders. Ignoring her show despite the fact that it's all around us, Ascalon picks up her simplified baby remote control and mashes buttons. The ball squirts out from under her and bounces from wall to ceiling, back and forth, zigzagging through her program. Ascalon falls hard on her butt, crying. I switch off the pig and go to pick her up. But all she wants is her mama. I don't resent it. I'm almost relieved.

But Sabrina pays no attention to us as she drags the changing table into the living room, scraping the faux marble floors I can't afford. I think about how many times this very scene must have played out in the history of humanity. I might as well be walking into a cave to an angry, disappointed mate who could've done better, an out-of-control child, and me, a burnt-out troglodyte who predictably didn't bring home enough bacon again. I step to the changing table. Sabrina looks ready to resentfully accept help. I think about what Akira once said to me about how the numbers to the right of a decimal point matter more than the ones before it. How most people only see things as big or small and think big is more important. And how stupid that is. Without the numbers to the right of pi, pi just becomes three, she said. As I think about Akira, I put the baby down. That someone just cut Akira up like that. I hope she was doped up enough when the laser burned through all that bone and sinew. The thought that maybe she wasn't puts my fists into tight balls. Instead of helping Sabrina, I punch a hole through the changing table and leave. And the bones in my fingers no longer feel hollow. Maybe I haven't lost a step, and my violence was just in hibernation, hungry again now.

After I exit into the chewing heat, I head to my SEAL. I pass the teenagers toiling in gray cloud humidity and boredom. I pass the neighbor's, the one blaring his iE, but I don't hear his program anymore. Even Fred the Fisherman isn't fishing anymore. Instead, he's standing at the edge of the wharf, looking up. His eyes are welling.

Others step out of their units, mostly youngish and middle-aged couples dressed in self-adjusting trouser shorts and sleeveless air-conditioned crops. They step out of their units and look up. At this point, I look up, too, but I see nothing but dark clouds and Ascalon's Scar. A couple sobs behind me. Then it hits me. I turn and the float burb crowd gathers, teary-eyed. The news has broken. Everyone knows Akira Kimura is dead.

At first, I find it odd that they are all looking up. But then I get it. They're looking at the scar. To me, Akira was a friend. To them, some of whom aren't even old enough to remember Sessho-seki, Akira Kimura was a deity. Deities have always lived in the sky, beyond what we can see, but this one, unlike the others, was kind enough to leave her mark up there, granting people a secure feeling of divinity. She has given us a glimpse of what none of us can truly reach. She reminds us every day that we are lucky to be alive.

I head to my SEAL, and before I lift off, I catch the crowd growing out of the corner of my eye. Their necks are craned in unison up toward Ascalon's Scar. The quantum clocks have stopped. Everyone is weeping except for the teenagers who, masks pulled down, are frowning at the grievers with a pure lack of understanding.

7

I'm flying at top speed above the ocean. Looking down at the pleats of breaking water, I am amazed at how well-organized something as chaotic as the sea can look from afar. I break to the west side of the island and dip down to the well-lit coast. Seascraper cabana beach caps to the right, the giant aquatic theme park connected to the beach, shaped like a giant oyster with a pearl-like dome in the middle. Golf courses. A couple of shabby ones for the OBB, the rest exclusively for The Money. This side of the island is where a few of The Money live, the older ones who prefer land under their feet, who own prime acreage cut from lava rock fronting vast manmade white sandy beaches. I'm gliding over the estate of Idris Eshana, inventor of the iE. He died a few years back at 121. His château is being converted to a museum, soon to be another stop on The Savior's Eye pilgrimage. It's next to the shuttlefield where people transport to the continents and other faraway water cities. The whole scene probably looks like any point in the history of civilization, really, the past smeared with the present.

I remember that when Sabrina and I first started dating,

she was in awe of the people I knew. Of course, there was Akira, but when this island became the center of the world, I also knew top brass like NASA Director Parker and tech moguls like Idris Eshana, who came to help plan the construction of Ascalon. This is when a lot of The Money showed up to try to pitch in, or if their help was turned away, to witness. After Ascalon did her thing, a lot of The Money ended up staying. The island is conveniently located between the Mainland US and Asia, the world's two financial, recycling, and tech giants. I stayed friends with some of these people. I may have even saved a couple of them back in the day, when zealots came and tried to blow up the entire mission. The crazies who believed that the apocalypse was meant to be. Sabrina heard old Idris tell the story of me pulling out my rail gun and seemingly firing at random into a crowd of protesters. My own security team thought I had gone crazy and almost gunned me down. The truth is, I fired once. And it wasn't random. I saw green. And the kid I shot was packing a dirty bomb in his backpack. But to hear Idris tell it, I performed like an action hero, and Sabrina was smitten. Idris winked at me after she walked away. Nothing like having the richest man in the world wingman you.

It's easy to drift into nostalgia up here in a SEAL. Not many fly them, so there's never really traffic. SEAL licenses are only granted to first responder, military, and science personnel, and even then, you need to be of a certain rank. I own mine, but I put it up for collateral to buy the float burb unit, so who knows for how much longer. Kind of like me, it's becoming obsolete anyway. There aren't really serviceable roads on the island anymore, and vac tube trains, hovers, and heli-taxis get everybody where they need to go. The Money still have their SEALS and employ ex-cops and ex-military like me to chauffeur them around, dangling supplemental pension and all, but even they hardly use military-grade flying vehicles anymore. We just don't gotta go that high.

Maybe I'm feeling weepy about the past because of the death of my best friend. Maybe it's the mess I just made back home. But most likely it's because I've called in a couple of favors from The (old) Money pals, and it's always been painful for me to ask anybody for anything. Another of my personal flaws that eighty years of supposed learning never stomped out. I'm hovering over a prepubescent sweep of native trees now, a forest once wiped out and then replanted. They take three hundred years to hit full, majestic maturity, so these are just twenty-foot saplings that are about my age.

Right now, I'm heading to see Jerry Caldwell, a retired attorney from Mile High who's also one of the heirs to the biggest corn syrup company in the world. Like Big Tobacco before it, the industry took a giant hit in the US when there was outcry that these companies were knowingly poisoning the children of the nation with GMO junk food. And like Big Tobacco, her family's company simply concentrated production and sales abroad and continued to thrive by poisoning foreign children in countries who supposedly weren't as free as in the US, but let their people poison themselves all they wanted. Jerry came here with her parents when the rest of The Money did, offering to throw their fortune into the Ascalon Project. But they were among the rejected who ended up just staying in their brand-new deep-sea lofts to watch. Akira was downright mean about it to Jerry's father—the thought makes me laugh to this day. What she said to one of the richest men in the world was, "What are you proposing we do? Bribe a carbonaceous chondrite meteorite with a carbonated beverage and ask it to smile and go away?" The old man never got over the insult. But like everyone else, he stayed for the show.

Jerry and I go way back. I actually met her through Akira. They'd gone to grad school together on the East Coast. Princeton-Columbia U. After Akira finished her undergrad degree in Japan, she split and went on to do her PhD in astrophysics. Jerry was a freshman at the time, double majoring in physics and economics. There are thousands of books on Akira's life, but most concentrate on the crazy days of Sessho-seki, while others attempt to recreate her experiences as a childhood genius. Her piano story has been written hundreds of times, on the same level as Newton and his apple at this point. But none of the biographies delve into Akira's college days, when she was actually learning. People aren't into that sort of thing. They want to know what was going on when someone was *doing*, not learning. Besides, Akira has always been a private person. Jerry, too. So any recounting of this time in Akira's life is speculation. And despite the fact that Akira and Jerry were best friends in college, Jerry taking this tween under her wing, hardly any of these books mention Jerry at all.

When the world was ending, Akira hired her old PCU friend as one of her attorneys. Insult to injury for Jerry's old man. But a couple years later, they had a falling out over what Jerry called Akira's "psychopathic ego." She added that if it weren't for the fact that Akira had to live on this planet, she'd have had zero interest in saving it. I found this hilarious. There was probably some truth to it, but Jerry was bruised over the whole thing. Akira, on the other hand, seemed completely indifferent, which was consistent with how Jerry saw her. It's weird having two close friends who hate each other, but neither ever seemed to mind that I hung out with the other, unless you counted silent judgment.

Jerry's the one I called to get me released from interrogation. But I'm not heading to her place now to discuss the case or Akira and the bad old days. I just need a couch to crash on, which through forty years and two wives, Jerry has always provided. She lives on the next island over, the one packed with skyscrapers built by all the rejected Money years back, years after the Great Sun Storm, when storms in general were the least of our concern. The entire place is lit up and reaches into the sky, cloud-breaking bouquets of tech mounted with telescopes that each resident can patch into from the comfort of their high-altitude homes. Besides Akira's Telescope, this place offered the best bird's-eye view to an extinction-level event. When Ascalon's Scar first lit up the sky, some thought it was Sessho-seki coming and jumped. Human feet, broken at the ankles from impact, washed up onshore for weeks after the world was saved. A page-three story to anyone but a cop who had the task of matching feet with names while the rest of the world celebrated. It sucked, too, because we stopped keeping toeprint records by then.

My iF goes off. A reminder to take my blood pressure and anti-plaque pills. I think about my 3D-printed fake teeth, fake hips, fake hair. Neck and jowls nipped and tucked. Already on my second heart and liver, benes used up from military service. The entire thing propped up by titanium in my spine and left leg. Unlike my pain, memory, space-travel grade anti-anxiety and anti-insomnia pills, these BP and anti-plaque pills I take. This is what getting old is, expecting our second or even third livers to hold up the messes we call bodies as we weigh them down a pill at a time. I pop my pharma and descend to the ocean-generated bioluminescence that lights up the scrapers. I head toward the biggest one, the tint of the whale tail–shaped tower breaching two layers of clouds moving in opposite directions.

8

Jerry Caldwell is a sensitive creative trapped in an ancestral line of Money that won resources through ceaseless drive, common sense, frugality, heightened aggression, and a lack of imagination. It's not that they didn't respect imagination. In fact, they recognized it as a key element of success, but one that could be hired. You didn't put imagination at the controls. So even though Jerry did everything right—went to the best schools, got the right degrees, and took the right positions in the company—the scepter was never going to be passed to her. She liked to paint and had an interest in quantum physics. Though her father deeply loved and admired her, he figured you didn't put a daydreaming dauber, a person who thinks this world might not be the only real one, in charge of a multibillion-dollar corporation. When Akira hired Jerry away from her father while rejecting his offer to help save the world, the old man took it badly. He finally understood imagination was helpful when it came to seeing a double left hook heading your way.

I step into Jerry's. Drapes, fixtures, sofas, and counters. Her colors of the week are black and rose gold. Pictures and paintings hang on the walls. Most are priceless, and some may be personal, but it's impossible to determine which are which, because the personal are hidden among a patch of obscure masterpieces. There's one that I have always suspected is personal, one in an alcove of a group of little girls playing next to a giant tree. They all look like they're having fun except one in a yellowish-beige sweater who has her back turned. Of course, the sweater is really red. I just can't see it. As I walk past the painting now, I wonder why I've always been convinced it's personal. Maybe because I know a bit about art and would have recognized it otherwise. Or because there's no signature on the piece. My first reaction to it has always been to wonder what the girl in the red sweater's face looks like, what she's thinking while all the other kids are having fun. I asked Jerry about it once, and she told me that if I can't tell the difference between a random painting and a masterpiece, maybe the random painting is a masterpiece waiting to be recognized. I wonder if that little girl in the red sweater is waiting for the same thing.

In the center of the room, I see that Jerry's still working on the same art project, the one that ponders what it is that makes someone or something iconic. She's been at this thing for at least seven years now. Nobody really likes art that stays still anymore, so it's a digital sculpture that morphs from one three-dimensional icon to another, Marilyn Monroe to Super Mario to Benjamin Franklin flying a kite to the Trojan horse. It's art that asks why so few are remembered and so many are forgotten. Finally, the sculpture morphs from Pearl of Lao Tzu to the original Ascalon, its mighty point soaring near light speed toward Sessho-seki, the asteroid the weapon's strange attractor.

Jerry steps in the room, looking stunningly iconic herself. A hater of foam fit, of any clothing, really, that's practical or doesn't stand out, Jerry dresses every night like she's going to her 150-atmosphere-deep digi opera box seats. Right now, just like her furniture, she's in black and rose gold. She's got the kind of beauty that stirs not lust, but awe. She's holding two lowballs and hands me one. She stands next to me and we watch her sculpture. Now it's Houdini wrapped in chains, then King Tut's tomb. "You know King Tut was only nine when he died?" Jerry says. "He didn't do anything of real significance. It's the look that makes him iconic."

I nod. King Arthur is pulling Excalibur out of the stone. This is a new one I haven't seen yet. Part of the reason this is taking her so long to complete is that it's endless—she's constantly adding and taking away iconic images. Two years ago, there was music. Now, there's none. Ying and yang appear, one of the only mainstays I've seen since the beginning of the project.

"I told Sabrina you were here," Jerry says. "You're an awful husband."

"I know," I say. "No Akira in your sculpture?"

"I don't think they'll remember her," Jerry says. "Just Ascalon."

We clink glasses without looking at each other. "They remember Einstein," I say. We both sip.

"But not Planck. They remember Einstein because of the crazy white hair. Besides, what's your daughter's name again?"

Good point. "You always hated her."

"Not always," she says.

"For the most part."

"She was such a bitch."

I turn to Jerry.

"What?" she says. "We *should* talk ill of people after they're dead. That's when it doesn't matter."

I sip. "I know better than to get into an argument with a lawyer."

She eyes me, toe to hair. "You look awful. Did you stop going to the clinic?"

I think about Akira and her AMP chamber. The sight of her parts sliding onto the floor. It'll be a while before I can go to the clinic and lie in a chamber again. "At a certain point, there are too many appointments just to look good, feel okay, and stay alive."

Jerry laughs. "What else is there?"

"Nothing, I guess."

"You sound like a depressed teenager going through existential crisis," she says.

"That's hitting below the belt," I say. "I saw one earlier. A teen. Blue with a tail."

She's about to say something but stops herself. She takes my glass and heads to the bar. "Thanks for letting me stay here," I say.

"As long as you like. On the condition that you ping Sabrina tomorrow."

"Deal."

"Her, I always liked," Jerry says as she fills the glasses. "I know what it is to want something your entire youth, to kill yourself for it, then have it taken from you. It's excruciating. I know what it feels like not to be wanted. You know what your problem is?"

Jerry often starts conversations with that question. I've

learned to not take it personally. It's actually her trying to be nice. "Which one?" I say.

Jerry smiles and steps to me with the refills. "Never in your life have you failed spectacularly. So you keep doing the same shit over and over again."

I take my glass. I've certainly failed spectacularly. Past wives and children count. And I failed Akira today. But I don't mention that, and we cheers. "I'll drink to that," I say.

We both drain our lowballs. "Whiskey and war," Jerry says, "will never go out of style."

"There hasn't been a war since Sessho-seki," I say.

"There's always war. Sometimes it's just invisible."

Jerry takes my glass and motions toward the guest bedroom. My eyes scan the room before I exit: walls, flooring, furniture, just about everything printed from recycled plastic skimmed from the ocean. Polymers that can change color for the right price. Jerry makes good use of that, redoing the scheme of the place every week. Sometimes, she just throws it all out and starts again. What she throws out will be made into something new for someone else. Is that our new loop? Or the reworking of an existing one?

We stop at the door. It's been a gazillion years since we slept in the same room together. Just a tryst or two between marriages. Maybe the only two good things about getting older is the waning of want and no fear of loneliness. Regardless, we never speak of it. "You didn't see how she went," I say.

"They aren't reporting it," Jerry says. "It must've been gruesome."

She doesn't ask for details, and I don't wanna talk about it anyway, so I just thank Jerry and tell her I'll make this up to her. She tells me I should let it go. That she doesn't get what I'm doing, going so far off the book, quitting my job, leaving my wife and kid for the night, and ending up here with plans to look further into a case I was going to get pushed off anyway. Not even the chief will be able to keep his paws on this one. It'll become Federal. International, if it isn't already. The death of Akira Kimura is a global incident. And with that collective manpower, that brainpower, they'll solve it. Certainly faster than one old man who can't look at the situation objectively anyway.

"Why even do this? It doesn't make sense. If you're hell-bent on leaving your job and a domestic life, then fine. Collect your early retirement, become an expat somewhere, and eat and drink and whore yourself to death like your standard repugnant Less Than. If you think there's no meaning, just a lifetime of wasted effort, then go and do that. Because if you think that and you keep doing what you do, you're dragging down two other people with you, and I have no respect for that. It's weak."

Quite a speech from Jerry. Some of the finer points I've already forgotten, but it's done its job, because two hours later, I'm still wide awake in bed.

I'm mulling over Jerry's words while the song from the piano at Akira's Telescope plays on repeat on my iE. I'm sweating bullets, probably withdrawal from all the pills I didn't take over the course of the day. The song is what I imagine extraterrestrial music sounds like—too fast. There are patterns, but I can't parse them.

Jerry's right. Pack it in. The island is probably already crawling with every super-sleuth in the world. I make a deal with myself: after I check out just one more thing, I'll stop.

While literally the entire police world sifts through Ascalon Lees, every smudge of forensic evidence on anything Akira has ever touched, I'm going to dig up only a single grave tomorrow, marked by a gravestone etched with katakana in the middle of the obsidian cobalt fields on the eastern tip of the island. And if nothing comes of it, I'll start carving out the tombstone of my fourth marriage and move so far away from here that it will be impossible to be tortured by any greens or reds.

As I toss and turn, soiling Jerry's high-thread-count silk sheets with sweat to the tune of Akira's song over and over in my head, I'm thinking that this is so hard, this thing I have to do tomorrow. But that's a lie. The hard thing to do would be to walk away from Akira's death. To patch things up with my wife, with the chief, and go back to normal. What I'm doing right now, including my adrenaline-fueled late-night planning, is the easy thing, practically a compulsion. Which means it's probably not the right thing. All my life, all I've ever done was the easy thing. And maybe, as crazy as it sounds considering her vast accomplishments, that's what Akira always did, too. Is that why Jerry hates her? But there's no way you can go through life, especially taking the easy route, without pissing some people off.

I tell myself for the hundredth time that I should take my pills. I turn down the music and grab the bottle. I imagine little Ascalon smiling and walking backward to her potty. It's adorable. It's one of her great joys, navigating by memory through what may trip her up from behind. I miss my daughter.

Then I stop.

Backward.

I put down the bottle of pills. *Backward*. What did I tell the chief when I quit? Akira had to see first where Sessho-seki had been before she knew where it was going. Backward. I call up the song again. I tell my iE to play it from end to beginning, slowly this time.

And that's when I hear them. Notes I can understand. Red strands that flutter above me, morphing into letters. Lyrics, sung in red:

> *Ascalon is not only the name of the savior*
> *It's the name of the daughter*
> *The one I gave up*
> *Find her for me and tell her that I'm sorry*

I am overwhelmed. It's so clear now, a red so bright I've never seen it before. Laces of notes and words dance together above me. I want a piano so I can play it. So I can feel it etched into my bones. I want to be a part of it. But I resist the feelings it stirs in me and concentrate on the story it's trying to tell me. And it's simple.

Akira had a daughter I didn't know about. That the world never knew about.

No, this has got to be bullshit. Pure hallucination driven by paranoia. But the greens and reds have never done me wrong. Is it guilt, emitting a hormonal scent that I perceive with sight? Does struggle before death emit a chemical in wafts of green? I'm not supposed to be able to see these colors, but no matter what, they are right.

So I start to speculate. She must've had the baby during college, in the years no one knows about, a girl that perhaps instead of aborting, she gave up for adoption. And maybe when she became the most powerful person in the world, she had records of this child expunged. This little girl might not have known she was the child of Akira Kimura. Or maybe she did. Maybe, out of guilt, Akira told her. This child, who would no longer be a child now, could have killed Akira out of resentment. Rage at being denied rightful hereditary fame and fortune and a savior's name. It takes the highest level of rage to cut someone into pieces in that particular fashion— with methodical laser precision, beyond the laws of biology and sanity. If I'd been this baby, would I want to cut Akira to pieces, too? She was known to be heartless, and who knew what a spurned daughter with half her genes could accomplish. Would Akira have granted her access to her penthouse at the bottom of the ocean? Her name really could be Ascalon Lee.

Or maybe that child was an innocent, out there now in need of help. She might be the only living trace Akira left behind. Or maybe I'm losing it, and she doesn't even exist. There are so many possible narratives. I think of Jerry's notions of infinite realities, and I wonder if one day we'll discover that storytellers are actually mystics with the ability to glimpse the alternate realities around us. And when I think of all the variations on this story, the story of Ascalon, I cannot imagine a single one that ends happily. Because I see in red and hear death in the song. This child was killed.

I surprise myself by starting to cry, burying my face in the smooth sheets so Jerry doesn't hear me from the next room over. I cry for my father, bent to the point that he couldn't be straightened out. For the first wife and child, who left me. For the dead ones, buried deep beneath the sea. I cry myself atmospheres deep, until I can drown out the terrible song. I cry for Akira, for her daughter, the first Ascalon. I cry until

I'm all cried out, until I finally reduce my sorrow to a sheet stain that will fade and vanish. I need to get it all out now, because I'll need to listen to the song again and again without this cloud of tears in order to grasp the clues I'm sure exist in it. I will honor Akira's last wish. I will find her daughter, if she has one, and tell her that her mother is sorry.

I catch my breath, slip into my foam fit, and change it from blue to black. I strap on my holsters and pockets and slip into my steel-toed tabis. The smart pleather constricts my ankles. I head to Jerry's bedroom to shout a quick thank-you before I leave. I want to explain the song, but like everything else, it sounds too crazy. They'd have me committed, maybe even reevaluate every case I've worked in my career. And not for a second will they believe me.

That's when I see green wisps, like breath, pulsing at the base of Jerry's closed door. I stop in my tracks, my heartbeat quickening. Is Jerry okay? I pull out my knife.

I burst through the door and step in. Jerry sits up. "What the hell?" Her eyes are locked on the knife in my hand.

I look back at the door. The green tendrils curl and vape past me toward Jerry, who's looking at me like I've lost my mind. "Put that away," she says.

"You've known her for years," I say. "You went to school with her. What do you know?"

"What the hell are you talking about? Have you lost your mind? Put the knife away!"

I step to her bedside. I find my hand curled around her throat. My hand—or her neck—glows green. I can't tell which. I don't squeeze. "Don't lie to me."

"Akira's death has driven you off the deep end," Jerry says. "You need to stop."

"You know something," I say. "Tell me."

"I've never been anything but a friend to you," she says. "An honest one. Look in the other direction for the person who lied to you." She rips my hand from her throat and stands up. She slaps me. Hard. "She told me once she would get you to kill me."

I shake my head. "She would never ask that. And I would never *do* that."

"And yet, here you are, one hand on a knife and the other on my throat. This wouldn't be the first time you killed for her, would it?" Jerry asks.

"I was doing my job. I was protecting her."

"Was it protection?" she whispers.

"Yes. Every single time. Now tell me about her daughter."

She pauses, stunned. Then she turns and grabs a black shawl on her nightstand, draping it around her shoulders. "I don't know what you're talking about," she says. "Now get out."

I glance at her iE, staring down at me.

"I haven't sent that footage yet, but I will," Jerry says.

I head to the door. "You idiot," she says. "All those years, she was just using you like she used everybody else. She isn't who you think."

I turn back around. "She saved me. I wanted the fucking world to end, and she picked me up and saved me."

Jerry smirks. "You'll never see it, will you? She didn't save anyone. She just made you feel alive again."

I want to turn back, walk over, and bury my fist in her esophagus, but the green is gone, and I know the intent is no longer there. I storm out. There's just the red song now leading me through the hallway and to the front door.

The one I gave up. Find her and tell her I'm sorry.

With every step, I know how crazy I might be. The idea that I, and I alone, am the only person who can hear, smell, see a thing. A psychic. An astrologer. A ghost hunter. What people probably don't get or wouldn't buy is that I want to be wrong. I always want to be wrong. I don't want all my senses tied up with death and murder. We all just want to see enough so we don't stumble. People who see more than that end up unhappy. I don't believe in ectoplasm, Santa Claus, reincarnation, or chi. But I see what I see. And I believe one thing: so far, the only thing we have proven absolutely correct is that only the unknown lasts forever. This means that no one, including me, has it all figured out, but also that my ability, even though it's unexplainable, is possible.

I feel guilty leaving Jerry angry and scared back there. She's right. She's always been a friend. And maybe she's right on another account, that Akira didn't save me—she just made me feel alive again.

I step to the front door and am about to yank it open theatrically. I don't even know why. But before I can wrap my hand around the antique knob, I hear the song behind me. I turn. It's faint. And it's coming from Jerry's sculpture, which is stuck on the rendering of Ascalon's ray piercing the heart of Sessho-seki. A burst of red feedback hurts my ears, and then the song is gone. The stuck image vibrates, then morphs. It's now a girl in a red sweater, the one from the painting. Her back is turned. "She killed me," she mumbles. "But I am still here." Then the sculpture reverts back to normal, and the girl is transformed into Houdini.

I want to march back into Jerry's room and pry the truth from her. But for all I know, she's already pinged the police.

Or she's waiting for me with the hand cannon I know she keeps in her nightstand drawer.

I get in my SEAL and take off. I try to ping Jerry. To apologize, I tell myself. But maybe I still want to grill her. No response. She's probably already blocked me, and I don't blame her. The sun hasn't risen yet. I'll try again in the morning.

I point my SEAL down and head to lower altitude. And that's when I see them. A huge crowd is gathered on the beach. Hundreds of people, a thousand maybe, lined up down the coast. A patient crowd. A somber one. The opposite of a mob. They're taking turns stepping into the water like they're about to be baptized. But they aren't there for purification. They're floating lit holo lanterns in honor of Akira Kimura. Hundreds of specks of light drifting on the ocean surface. Not a single one strong enough to reveal what lurks beneath, but enough light to comfort babies trying to sleep in the dark.

I raise my altitude. I cannot believe how much the red song has shaken me. I cannot believe Akira Kimura might have had a child and hidden her from the world. I cannot believe that I pulled a knife on one of my closest friends. Or that for a split second there, I was ready to use it.

I tell my iE to replay Jerry's sculpture morphing from Ascalon to the girl in the red sweater. There is no music. No image. No girl in a red sweater. There's just a crazy old man with his back to a door, holding his ears.

She killed me. But I am still here.

I know I heard it. The voice made my stomach churn because it reminded me of stale beer. But my iE didn't pick up any of it. *Just move forward*, I tell myself. *Forget it and just move on, or your jaw will tingle, your hands and chest will rattle, and you'll suffocate.*

She killed me. This is the voice of a victim heard by a man who, no matter how hard he tries to forget, knows what killing is.

9

When the sun finally rises, I'm standing, sleep deprived, near Fissure 8 of the volcano that has been spewing lava continuously for thousands of years. Over 150 years ago, there was a town here. Before that, a village, probably. One populated by actual natives during a time before the culture died out and the population was completely assimilated. I kick at the black rock with the toe of my boot. It's solid. Some islanders have resurrected the gods of the natives and believe that their fire goddess was preparing to make new life, new land, because she knew the end was coming soon and wanted to get a head start on recreating the world. Others of them believe she continued to spew after the asteroid because she was upset we beat it. The stories of the native gods are very old now, older than electric opera, older than digi-rapture blues. Even older than the hip-hop I caught the tail end of. Music, like the gods, is having a tough time hanging in what Jerry would call "The Pantheon of the Iconic." Not everything survived that damn asteroid, even though it didn't hit.

Speaking of pantheons, my iE feed is running a talking-head program about where Akira sits in the Greatest Scientists

of All Time Hall of Fame. It's mindless dribble that's prefer-
able to the sound of the hydro-drill tearing through lava rock
in front of the single katakana grave. When I told Akeem
Buhari what I needed help with last night on my way to
Jerry's, he was at the world-famous Friday Night Prawn Bake
at the island's theme park. Neo-hippies, all tat-dyed black,
drag a wild boar to the stream and leave it there while they
prep their sweet potato and buried protein. After the other
food is prepped, the prawn catchers return to the boar and
tourists follow with their iEs set to record. The catchers
pull a now swollen boar from the stream, its distended belly
undulating, ripples that stretch the skin to its limits. They
toss the boar on a smoldering fire. The ripples beneath its
crackling skin become violent. The belly bulges more, and
whatever is under the skin appears to be hitting full boil.
Little pincers puncture the skin, and little holes whistle out
gas. Finally, the carcass bursts open, and hundreds of frenzied
prawns swarm from the boar's belly, angry from the heat, and
frantically crawl over each other to avoid falling in the fire.
Minutes later, what's left of the chaotic free-for-all is a heap
of dead prawns, tails tucked under their carapaces, stewing in
bubbling pork fat. I've been to the Friday Night Prawn Bake
with Akeem a number of times. Like most of my other friends
who have at one time or another called me their best friend
or only friend, Akeem is one of The Money. He spends his
on exotic foods, like chicken eggs, a protein source replaced
years ago by farmed, unstressed aquaculture and algae after
disease decimated chickens all over the world. Akeem stops
the drill. "How did I let you talk me into this?"

"What do you mean?" I ask.

"I've never exhumed a grave before. Feels creepy."

"I don't think it's a grave. Just a marker for something."

"Well, how deep then?" he asks.

"Deep enough to hit jackpot."

Akeem shrugs and starts up the drill. "I can cook the perfect egg," he yells while drilling through the grave.

"Oh, yeah? How?"

"Are you kidding? You ask me to dig up a grave or whatever, and now you want my perfect egg recipe? Where you even gonna get one?"

The drill, a machine that used to have to be the size of a small building but can now fold up and be transported like a tent, chops through lava rock. He's only half joking. The funny thing about The Money is that most of them are very paranoid. Always weary of meeting people. Always wondering what someone wants from them. Always waiting for the question that starts with the word "can" and ends with "me." It's tough to blame them. It's paranoia based on personal experience. The Money and I have a silent mutual understanding. I almost never ask for anything, and if I do, it's for their expertise. In turn, they act like I'm not a Less Than.

Akeem, who is now The Money, made his fortune mapping and mining the bottom of the ocean for geothermal energy, which helped make the migration of resources from the continent to underwater cities possible. Now, the food is here. The desalinated water, pure from the deep, is here. The jobs—plastic skimming, construction, recycling—they are here. And like a lot of self-made men and women who've spent their life relentlessly angling and eventually catching their monster fish in this channel of great migration, Akeem's bored out of his mind. Getting him to help me dig was easy. He wasn't really doing shit anyway.

"I'll give you a hint," Akeem says. "Water's involved."

The drill grinds past the six-foot mark. No coffin. "An egg ring and a pan on low heat," I say, safety glasses on, still gazing into the hole. "A teaspoon of water and cover."

"Fucking detective know-it-all," Akeem says.

I shrug. "I was around when all the chickens died. Still a kid, but my dad loved eggs."

The drill breaks through. Akeem tells his iE to pull the bit up. We both look over the edge of the hole. "Interesting," Akeem says. He cracks a bio flare and drops it in. It clunks on the bottom. "How deep?" I ask.

"At least a hundred feet."

"Spelunking?" I ask.

Akeem looks around. He's a big guy, hulkish, but softened by age and money. Most guys built like him age sadly, limbs wilted by atrophy, bellies a solid jelly. But he's got the kind of body that seems to resent the ease of technology. "This makes me nervous," he says. "The islanders don't like people digging around here. They might think we're fucking with their juju. Can't even see them coming, them all tat-dyed black. For all we know, they could be crawling toward us on all this lava rock."

"Natives," I scoff.

"Fine, hippies," Akeem says.

"You're not curious?"

"You got a weapon on you?" Akeem asks.

"I got you. You must be pushing 260 by now."

He laughs. "I'm being serious."

"I have a rail gun packed in the SEAL."

"I thought those were illegal?"

I shrug. "I was issued one back when things were crazy.

Sessho-seki days. Honestly, I don't even know if it works anymore. Almost forgot I still had it."

Akeem smiles. "Screw it. I'll get the rope and remote winch us down."

He steps to the auto drill rig and sets up the winch. "I ever tell you about Panit, the Thai stuntman I used to hang with?"

"Yeah," I say, still staring down into the hole, squinting, searching for wafts. "He wanted you to finance his big budget epic with him as the star."

"Wanted me to? I ended up doing it."

I look up. "Really?"

Akeem drops the rope down the hole and hands me grip gloves. "Oh yeah. It was the worst piece of entertainment ever made. Panit, the poor guy, couldn't even talk in front of the camera, so he'd just stop saying his lines and start elbowing and kneeing stuff around him."

I laugh. "Never saw it."

"No one did."

"What happened to Panit?"

Akeem shakes his head and smiles. "Beats me. That's the funny part. I gave him the money to make his epic, and guess what?"

"What?"

Akeem grabs the rope. "He never forgave me."

I nod. Akeem smirks at me. "I do this for you, you aren't going to do the same thing, right?"

"Hold a grudge against you forever?"

Akeem nods. "We're going down a hole. When people do that, they tend not to like what they find there."

"I'm an expert at finding what I don't like. You don't have to worry about me."

"Okay then," Akeem says. "Let's go."

The winch lowers Akeem into the hole. I grab the rope and follow. It's funny. Akeem didn't ask me whose name was on the headstone. Didn't react to there not being a coffin or any remains buried there. And hasn't mentioned Akira once. I envy him.

But I knew it the moment I saw it. The moment I stood in front of it and stepped on the now-dead flowers.

The one I gave up. She killed me.

The name on the tombstone was Ascalon Lee.

10

When Akeem and I hit the bottom of the hole, he lights up a couple more bio flares and tosses them to our left and right. We immediately see that we're not in a hole, but in a huge cavern, its walls lined with old buildings. We're standing on what appears to be the beginning of a cobblestone path. I take off my grip gloves. Each building is a relic. Some in the style of twenty-first century tropical tourist traps. Others even older. Japanese village architecture. A multicultural ghost town. "These flares are powerful," I say.

Akeem takes off his grip gloves. "I used to use these on ocean floor surveys, on the bottom of the midnight zone. The sun can't even go that deep. You're damn right they're powerful." Akeem looks around. "But I've never dug anything up like this before."

And he's right. This is strange. An excavation of sorts. But this isn't the town that got rolled over with lava a century-and-a-half back. Nothing looks old—it's all in good condition. The architecture is just nostalgic, like the classic seaplanes people like to fly for fun, some painted patina with rocket engines.

"What do you think?" I ask. "This isn't some village that was naturally protected from years of lava rolling over it, right?"

Akeem shakes his head. He rubs his hand against the cavern wall. "That's impossible. This is all pretty newly dug." He looks at the buildings. "Freshly built. A few years old at the most. Expensive as hell and almost impossible to do in secret. Who?"

"Who else?"

Akeem nods. "Akira Kimura."

Akira was originally from Japan. She finished her BS at the University of Tokyo when she was eleven years old. After she got her first PhD in astrophysics a couple years later, she ended up here to get her second PhD in astronomy and help improve what even back then were the most powerful telescopes in the world. She told me once that, like most people who move to an island, she hated it at first. Island fever, she said. Plus, she was a fourteen-year-old kid who'd been sent alone to a strange place. But after a while, she realized it didn't matter. She never got out much anyway.

Akeem and I begin walking down the cobbled path. To the left, a small shop with trinkets like pineapple magnets and fake flower necklaces in its window. To the right, a Zen temple fronted by a garden, perfect circles etched in sand. A big rock sits in the garden, and I wonder if it's Sessho-seki. The Killing Rock in Japanese myth. As the story goes, the rock was the corpse of Tamamo-no-Mae, the nine-tailed fox. The one that killed anyone who came near her. That was what Akira named the asteroid after. As a fourteen-year-old coming to a strange new place, I wonder if she held on to folklore tighter than most of us with the same family roots.

If the stories were like old friends that gave her comfort. She didn't talk to me much about those first years in America. And I met her much later. And like most people, she didn't care for talking about the hard times.

"My dad used to tell me stories," Akeem says. "When Akira started building Ascalon, racist crackpots accused her of being a Japanese sleeper agent looking for revenge for World War II. They thought she was gonna make a robot Godzilla monster that would stomp all over America."

"Yeah, some used to joke that The Savior's Eye should be slanted."

Akeem shakes his head. "Wow. Well, we've come a long way."

I think about that as we pass a small kiosk for diving tours to the left. I've only seen it once but recognize it immediately. A re-creation of the tiny flotilla way out in the cut. I remember the guide. Leathered, lean, muscular, a deep diver. Built like a true explorer of the unknown deep, like my dad, a true hydronaut. The storefront window houses old-school scuba gear—masks without gills. Fins without mini-propellers. I remember the day the tour guide put them on and we went, together, down to the bottom. I can smell his impending doom, and see the graceful, efficient flutter of his fins sink into darkness. I shut it all out. Like Akira, I try not to think about the hard times.

I focus on what that time meant, the slaying of The Killing Rock, and to me and just about everyone else, we *had* come a long way. For the first time in our history, we all had a common enemy. We all hated the same thing and fought it and prayed against it together. After Ascalon saved the world, violent crime plummeted. I stopped carrying a gun decades ago.

And I'll admit, for years, I was bored out of my mind. There wasn't much for me to solve. But after a generation passed, the rates started slowly climbing again. And I started thinking that hate must always exist. It worried me what would fill the hate void that Ascalon left. Nothing had emerged as the frontrunner yet. Most old folks like me would say the world now is still a better place than it was before Ascalon, the opposite of what generation after generation of old men have said about the state of the world for most of human existence. *Kids nowadays. The degradation of morality and hard work. Hell in a handbasket.* Even some ancient Roman once said, "a progeny yet more corrupt." I figured the old men were always wrong, because if they were right, we would've destroyed ourselves long before Sessho-seki headed our way and almost did it for us. But we've still got time to make it worse. Like Jerry's sculpture, worse is a work in progress that's perhaps being created in our underwater scrapers and Earth-core fueled towers. Or maybe it's percolating in the patches of humanity abandoned on the continent, where they wait for The Great Leachate to stop dripping its poison into the Wheatbelt or for the new seacrapers and float burbs to be built in California Nevada Fingers.

Akeem and I pass a replica of the front of some East Coast-style science building. Probably the one where Akira got her PhD in astrophysics. Old-style speakers on wooden poles crackle, then play string-plucked native music. Music I remember playing at shuttle field gates back in the day while I waited to board for my trip to the continent.

Akeem looks up at the dome above us. "Fancy," he says. "Like lidded food."

"What?"

"You know, a silver-platter meal."

"You really are The Money."

"Stop it." Akeem playfully punches my shoulder.

I'm still facing the dive shop. Walking backward like my toddler, and I don't even realize it until I hear Akeem. "Hey," he says. "Stop getting distracted. There's nowhere to take a dip here."

I nod and turn around. We reach the end of the path. A modest, one-story pagoda-style house roofed with tiles that curve into arches, walled with sliding wood and paper doors. "Akira once told me these old houses were cut with perfect notches and puzzled together," I say. "That back then, they didn't use nails to build them."

Akeem nods. He's looking down. A line in the sand. "Man, I don't know," he says. "Do you see any lasers mounted on the roof? This is Akira Kimura we're talking about."

I shake my head. "She wanted me to find this." The line in the yellow-brownish sand is red.

And I can see it.

I think about all the conversations we had. Conversations about paintings. About music. About invisible light, and how we've known it has existed for years, even though our eyes can't see it. One of our very first conversations. Matisse. *Music*. A painting of red people on green grass. I told her I didn't like it much. Didn't like what most consider a masterpiece.

Then it occurs to me. She knew I was colorblind even though I never told her. Maybe from that first night we met. But how did she figure out when I saw green and red? I'm not sure, but I know now that she caught on. That red line in the sand. She *knew*. And worse, she figured out a way to manipulate it. This was a woman who has spent her entire life looking out. To light-years away, to the past. And when she couldn't see far enough, she built the tools to enable her to do so. Of course she saw me, a simple man with a sensory aberration, right in front of her. But how has she done this? Are the things I see and hear really just waves at certain frequencies? Is there some kind of scent or sight or sound that hits my brain and triggers the release of these chemicals?

A horrible thought hits me. *What if she set me up for it somehow?* The tour guide. I never caught his name. The tattoo. The gem. But I saw the green on his hands . . . I compartmentalize this, locking it away. There are other truths to dig up first.

"You okay?" Akeem asks.

I nod. I take a step over the red line. Akeem follows.

Our iEs drop dead behind us.

We both turn around and look at them. They're about as useful as marbles now. Akeem's beeps twice, then melts in the sand. All that's left of it is a swirl of silver and black.

"I think I'll head back," Akeem says.

I nod. "Do me a favor. Just give me an hour or so."

Akeem tells me no problem and heads back to the other end of the ghost town. I walk up to the sliding paper door and open it, then step in and flip on a light switch.

Unlike her penthouse at Volcano Vista, this place is furnished to the point that it looks lived in, much like my flotsam home. There's a couch, cushions crushed, pet hair stuck to them. A stack of old books on a mother-of-pearl inlaid coffee table. A pair of neon orange eight-pound dumbbells underneath. And baby toys, the kind that my generation used to play with. A turtle with wheels. A train. A rocket ship. Colorful rubber blocks imprinted with letters, numbers, animals, and dots like dice. Framed baby scribblings hang on the wall. An oblong ball that was used in a brutal sport now long gone.

I walk down the hall and enter a room floored with straw mats. It's empty except for a tiny electric piano built for a baby, the kind I had as a toddler that parents buy with Hail Mary hopes that their child will be a musical prodigy. It has only fifteen white keys. I know what I'm supposed to do. My knee and back cracking, I sit and rub my eyes. I tap a few notes. It's oddly in tune. Then I begin to play Ascalon's song. Backward, as it was meant to be played. At this point, I know it by heart.

I play the song through once. I've missed a few notes. This keyboard is so small. I take a breath and concentrate. I play again.

Nothing.

I calm myself. I take a breath, the same one I used to take before pressing a trigger and taking a shot at someone two miles away. I play it again. I see the words in red, again and again.

The one I gave up

In the middle of the room, the floor begins to groan open. I try not to watch. I just play. Both green and red wafts rise from between the keys. I fight to maintain my concentration. The greens and reds curl. I try not to watch them. I keep my eyes on the tiny keyboard and concentrate hard. I know I need to finish the song, and I know there's a run of tough notes and changes coming up. But I can't help but see them stream through my periphery. They drift to the now open pit in the middle of the room.

Find her for me and tell her that I'm sorry

The song ends. I take a breath. I am almost afraid to stand and look what's down there in the now open pit in the middle of the room. I watch the colors. The wafts dissipate. I get up and step to the edge of the square hole, hand on the hilt of my knife.

There are two coffins down there. Both open. One is adult-sized and empty. The other is the size of a shoe box and contains a ball and tiny sticks.

I climb down the hole. I crouch down in front of the tiny coffin. Inside is not a ball and sticks. It's the bones of a baby, small enough to be a newborn. They are twisted and deformed. One bone, or cartilage perhaps, is in the shape of a tail.

Ascalon Lee.

I hear the voice again.

She killed me.

And then I'm full of rage. I climb out of the pit and head to the front door. I've had enough of this—this game, this setup, whatever it is. I don't want to know the answers anymore. I stomp on the turtle with wheels on the way out. I kick the rocket ship through a paper wall. I turn around and take out my knife. I watch the blade as it heats and finally let in the terrible thought that I sealed away before stepping inside the house. And it's as simple as this: Akira can make me see green and red. It's possible she's played me before. I've killed people based on what I've sensed, so if she was able to manipulate that, I was just her murder weapon.

What was it she told me all those years ago? She worked on cloaking technology. Child's play for her. But it meant she could plant anything—even murder and death—where it didn't really exist.

I remember the dive shop. The tour guide. *She isn't who you think*, he said. Jerry is right. Akira Kimura was always using me and continues to even in death. If what I see is waves refracted through a prism, and she controlled that prism, there was no telling what she might do with it. This is the one ability of mine I've never doubted, that proved right so many times I never even considered it could be wrong. And she knew that.

Fuck Akira Kimura.

I throw the knife at the framed baby drawings hanging on the wall. Bullseye. The wood behind it begins to smoke.

As I step outside, I feel the heat behind me. Houses like this go up in flames quick. All that ingenuity, the light paper walls, the build without nails, the shingles that keep the roofs from collecting water. But they're structures of tinder.

Akeem is there, looking at the burning house, waiting for me. "I found another way into the place," he says. "Why'd you burn the house down?"

I don't answer.

"What is all this?" he asks.

"I don't give a shit."

"What is this all about?"

"Ego." I say.

"What do you mean?"

"She thought she was a god."

I stop walking. I look around the contents of the dome and open my arms. "All this. You know what it is?"

"What?" Akeem asks.

"It's Akira's mausoleum. Her tomb." I point to the house burning behind me. "This entire goddamn thing is her pyramid."

"What does she want you to do?"

I storm toward the beginning of the cobbled path. My iE rises from the dead and hovers above me. Akeem follows.

"She wants me to put her in it," I say, "then get rid of the evidence."

"What evidence?"

"So where's the exit?"

Akeem points west, and we head to a maw etched into a dark corner. I light it with my iE. A cave. "I guess we should've looked for the actual entrance instead of doing all that digging," Akeem says.

I barely register his words. "Did you know that the female giant octopus starves itself to death for six months while it nurses its eggs?" I ask.

"That's maternal instinct for you," Akeem says.

We walk through the cave. "Not all mothers have it."

"I don't blame them," Akeem says. "Sounds shitty."

I want to agree, but something primitive in me resists. And for some reason I'm having recollections of trying to build a fire as a kid.

"Hey," Akeem says, "before we go out there, there's something you should know."

"What?"

"There are islanders up there telling us we gotta leave now."

I crack a smile. "Of course there are."

"What do you mean?"

"She brokered the deal with the specific condition of letting the hippies live on the land, which everyone thought was altruistic. I never knew what she got out of it till now."

"And what's that?"

"They're there as a front for all of this. Maybe even to protect it."

Akeem nods. "Nothing's for free."

Spoken like a true member of The Money. And they're right. Nothing is, no matter who you are. As the black rock slopes up, I remember something, something I heard once ages ago. Something about looking up from the pit and thinking you're seeing god, when really all you're seeing is the reflection of the devil laughing at you from below. Nothing strikes me as truer now. And I don't need to see, hear, or feel it in green or red. Not that those should matter to me anymore. If it can be tricked, it ain't truth. I'd rather go blind than see those colors again.

Akeem and I emerge from the cave, and there are a good three-dozen islanders, all dyed as black as the frozen mounds of basalt we're standing on now. The wind is gusting hard, and up ahead, the earth sputters lava. Blue flames sparked by methane flare from the cracks. Tumbleweeds of bundled strands of blond lava glass roll past us. One of the islanders, tall with brown hair and blue eyes, steps forward. "We've been waiting for you," he says. He frowns at the hole in the ground, concerned about the smoke.

Akeem has already reattached the drill to my SEAL. He's looking at the islanders nervously, like they're the warriors that used to exist way back when, the ones that would kill a captain, boil him, and eat his big toe. These, they're just eco-crazy pacifists who crave the simple life. A life where picking food off the ground and breathing clean air is enough. I turn to Akeem. "Let's go," I say.

He nods. We head to my SEAL. The tall, blue-eyed islander follows. "But Ascalon?" he says.

I don't answer. We spot the SEAL, where another half-dozen islanders await us. When we get to it, Akeem ignores them and climbs in. I turn to the one that's been following us since the exit. "Where you from?"

He looks around at the rest of them then turns back to me, head down. "Carson City, southwest edge of The Great Leachate. But my great-great-grandfather used to have a timeshare here."

"Jesus Christ," I say, climbing in. "Well, you take care."

"But we have questions," he says.

"I don't got answers." I close the cockpit and take off, ascending over these ghosts still clawing at the cracks of the thing they already broke and conquered. My iE pings. Sabrina. Somehow she's pinging me from my own goddamn iE so I can't ignore the call. Fuck. I open the cockpit midair and direct my iE to float twenty feet in front. I pull out my rail gun and aim.

"Hey, should you be using that thing?" Akeem asks.

"Ever see one fire?" I ask.

"No," Akeem says. "Proceed, by all means. I wanna see."

I think for a second. About when I first started to see traces of green and red as a kid after years of being colorblind. In my adult years on the job, I saw them more and more, it occurs to me. Maybe they appear so strongly now because my brain is trying to spot them. Every moment. Every day I fed that appetite. The one for self-worth, for being right. I fed like a fucking crustacean at a Friday Night Prawn Bake. I want to stop feeding it. I wish I could starve my prediction machine, this psychodynamic merging. But I look around. Just one more time, I scan the air around me, knowing that there's usually no such thing as just one more time. *But*, I promise myself, *just once more.* One more bite before being boiled alive.

"Who gave you a license for that thing?" Akeem asks.

I'm looking. Where are they? "Who do you think?" I say.

"Akira." Akeem says.

There they are. I spot the slight green wafts to the right of my iE. If not for the gray vog behind, I might not have been able to see them. They're coming from something cloaked, a tiny orb shelled with a thousand mirrors.

"What are you pointing at?" Akeem asks.

"A cheap, second-rate magician's trick."

I press the trigger. The plasma projectile loops through the magnetic field and leaves the muzzle supersonic. The spherical drone is obliterated. Basically the same thing that should've happened to Earth all those years ago.

"How the hell did you see that?" Akeem asks. "It was invisible."

I put the rail gun down and sigh. "It was cloaked. And cloaked doesn't mean invisible. It means manipulated. It uses reflected light to fool the human eye."

"Was it for surveillance?" Akeem asks.

"No. My guess is it was packed with a chunk of ambergris."

"Ambergris? For what?"

I look up at the sky. A great frigate bird soars alone, heading to turbulence, where it can fly for months without landing. It disappears among the clouds. "Nothing," I say.

My iE floats back into the cockpit. We head back to Akeem's to drop him and his drill off. I try pinging Jerry again to apologize. No response. She must be pissed, and I don't blame her. On the way back, I start to remember the past, even though I don't want to. I recall Akira always going on about how most things are binary. They come in a set of two—she'd talk about how we always knew this. There was light and dark. Left, right. Up, down. Good, bad. Heaven, hell. Life, death. And we kept discovering and creating new things that were also binary, like numbers, like code. The Money, The Less Thans. In fact, she'd say, looking up at the sky on dark nights, most star systems are binary, too. I'm thinking about that on my way to Akeem's and determine that it might be the only true thing she'd ever told me. Because I start remembering a different past than the one I've thought was true all these years.

11

Back in 2102, no one was lighting holo lanterns for Akira and floating them out to sea. Being the one who discovered The Killing Rock, she was the ultimate bearer of bad news. And when it was announced that she would head up the team to build Ascalon, people didn't have faith in her. It wasn't because she wasn't qualified, because she was Japanese, or because she was a woman; it was because if someone told you they were going to build an intergalactic robot that would save us all, no matter who they were, wouldn't you call them crazy? Plus, she was awful in interviews. Once, when asked why she was trying to save the world, her response was: a simple calculation. She said that she estimated that .03 percent of the human population was worth saving. That .03 percent actually contributed something worthwhile to the planet or our species. If there were only a thousand, or even a million, of us in total, she wouldn't bother. But because there were eight billion, she figured saving 2.4 million productive lives was worth trying. I remember watching that interview in a bar and nearly spitting out my drink. It was right in the midst of the hysteria, and back then, after losing my third wife and second child forever, I was rooting for the goddamn Killing Rock. I laughed because .03 was one of those arbitrary numbers that sounded just about right to me.

My third wife, Kathy, had been one of Akira's .03 in my book. After we figured out that the ocean heals much more quickly than land, Kathy and her colleagues went to work. She was the captain of a plastic skimming vessel, one of many cleaning up the North Pacific Subtropical Gyre, trapping and recycling plastic efficiently enough to turn profit. It's what most of our float burbs and scrapers are made of today. A lot of plastic skimmers decided to give up the job after the world found out that Sessho-seki was coming, but not Kathy. Most jobs feel meaningless when the end of the world is coming, and recycling in particular seems especially futile. Why think long-term when time is short? Not only did people think Kathy was stupid and crazy, some were angry. They felt it was a waste of government resources with the coming of Sessho-seki, even though the government only funded about 1 percent of plastic skimming in those days. An organization calling itself the AWM, the Anti-Waste Mafia, was born, and it declared war on any government program that didn't relate to saving us from The Killing Rock. Its members tattooed "AWM" on their wrists. They had secret handshakes. They co-opted words like "omertà" and "goombah." I mean, these people were real American idiots. And most were harmless. But the death threats toward Kathy started coming in about three months after the Sessho-seki announcement. And she didn't care at all.

I was easy enough to push around when it came to Kathy. Her answer to life was refusing to take no for an answer. And sometimes with a person like that, even though you love them to death, you want them to be far away in the middle of the ocean for large chunks of time. I didn't protest her going back out there to skim plastic after the death threats. I even let her take our twelve-year-old son, John, with her, despite wanting to put my foot down. The ocean took my father, so a part of me was always scared of it, but I was weak. The thought of battling her in itself exhausted me, so I thought, what's the use? Besides, these guys weren't that dangerous.

The AWM fanatic's suicide bomb went off eight hundred miles from the coast of the island. The boat didn't just go down. No piece of it was left intact. I should've cuffed her and thrown her in a cell and made her stay. At least made John stay. But I didn't, and they became marine snow. It takes months for organic material like marine snow to reach the bottom. It took me a day to reach mine.

You would think that a person of my character, or lack thereof, would've instantly sought revenge, but for some reason I didn't, and that made the guilt even worse. I should've wanted to wipe AMW out. I had the skill set and means to at least track down and eliminate their leadership, plus maybe even their families. To inflict the same amount of pain they inflicted on me. But this agony I felt was an impossible weight strapped to my ankle, and no matter how hard I tried to swim up, it was drowning me. And as I went down atmosphere by atmosphere, eventually all I saw was existence flatbrushed in umbra. I thought about my father and the condition he was in after being pulled up from the depths. Forever crippled. Forever suffering. I didn't want to come back up and suffer the same lifelong misery. They won, I told myself. Once a person's will is shattered, there is only surrender. So I decided to turn tired metaphor into the end of my own reality. I was perched on the sea crane hovering thirty feet over what would become Volcano Vista's manmade beach and coral reef sanctuary, my wrists locked in the same cuffs I should've put on Kathy, and a cannonball on my lap.

I hated everyone. I saw a world where nobody gave a shit how people who weren't like them lived. I saw a world filled with people motivated by the fear of running out of shit. The man running out of virility. The woman running out of beauty. The addict running out of supply. The holy running out of faith. The Less Thans running out of money. And everyone, even The Money, running out of time. The Band-Aids: exclusives, memberships, flash feeds and flash sales, flashes to the point of perversion. Underwater cities to hide from sun flares no one could see coming. Grinders, freeloaders, con men, and self-cons taking advantage. A ping, another ping from Scam Likely. People using planetary alignment as an excuse for being an asshole. People looking up and envying manufactured celebrity. People looking down and shaking their heads with pity at the ordinary. A world mucked up with oversimplification. A piece of shit world, and I fit right in. I thought about my first wife, a space shuttle flight attendant, all lashes and curves. The kind you weren't supposed to marry and definitely shouldn't have kids with. But I was young, and hot and sultry were all I cared about. Until the kid came, a girl with a hairless body and impossibly long eyelashes like her mother. Then I ran off to the military. By the time the first wife left me, I had already become very good at writing people off. I had been sent off to war to kill, so it was pretty much my profession. Leaving wife two was even easier than losing wife one, and I'd tell people that divorce was one of the top three things that ever happened to me. They'd ask which divorce, and I'd say all of them. And now, I realize I'm the kind of person you shouldn't marry. Definitely not have kids with.

But then, with Kathy and John, things seemed different. It felt like they were the wife and kid I was supposed to have. Like the previous times had just been auditions filled with sweat, bad props, and complete lack of preparation. Each was a failure I saw coming. But this time was a success. Until they died and I wanted to die. I prayed that after my death, Sessho-seki would drop on everyone else like a fucking hammer. First wife, first kid, second wife, too. I was ready for everything to burn now that the most important people in my life were gone.

Then Akira came up to me. She was alone, wearing a white lab coat of all things, something that became a permanent uniform once people did the math and believed she was right. An asteroid was heading toward Earth and would destroy it in three and a half years. The one that offed the dinosaurs was the size of Manhattan. This one was twice as big.

The sun was setting, and the clouds above hung in the sky like frozen whitewash. Akira climbed up the ladder to the top of the crane and sat next to me. Seabirds dove into the water below to pick at a swirl of big-eyed scad. Volcano Vista was already a beacon to sea life that didn't know it didn't have much time left. "How'd you find me?" I asked.

Akira looked up. "Satellites."

"I like the coat," I said. "You look ready to turn hay into horseshit."

"Where did you get the cannonball?" Akira asked.

I looked down at it. A forty-two-pounder. "My dad. He

always brought things back when he dove to build the foundations of buildings like these."

"How did you get it up here?" she asked.

"If you don't break a sweat trying to kill yourself, you're not really trying."

She looked out at the deep, twilled water. Wind blew and sent the monkey pods into chatter. "This cliff," Akira said. "The ocean. The End of the World. It's quite beautiful, isn't it? Did you know it was named that two hundred years ago because it was so far off the beaten path? An old friend told me that."

"What do you want?"

"I want to make the end the beginning."

"It's not worth saving," I said. "To me, anyway."

"I need you to help me," Akira said.

"I'm kind of busy right now."

Akira nodded. "I saw what happened to your wife and child in the feed. Sorry I found out so late. You know I don't have an iE, and I've been busy."

"Well, if you'll excuse me," I said. I scooted closer to the edge.

Akira grabbed onto my arm. "Take me with you."

"No. Let go."

And I looked at her face and saw it. The pressure coming from all directions. Relentless, mashing pressure like the one the deep water was exerting on the behemoth of a building in progress beneath us. Akira had staked her entire career on the claim that the world was about to end. And the even riskier claim that she could save it. Talk about a tough promise to deliver. She'd barely gotten her feet wet on the saving part, and she was already feeling the squeeze. She was constantly beating back her own personal crush depth.

"Your hands are cuffed," she said. "You're holding a cannonball. You are in no position to stop me from hanging on."

"I'm tired, Akira. I'm just so fucking tired."

"I know. Me too."

"I can't do it anymore."

Her eyes began to well. "Listen. I worked around the clock to discover this asteroid," she said. "And now I'm working on a solution to save all this. I don't eat. I don't sleep. I just do the work of making the impossible possible. I do it for everyone. And can you believe people want to kill me? After what I have sacrificed for this—it's more than anyone could know. You want to take the plunge, let's go. I don't need this either." Her hands were still locked tightly around my arm.

"Stop messing around and let me go."

"No."

"Christ! What the hell do you want from me?"

"I want you to help me," she said. "These people who've been threatening me. They're terrifying. I cannot work. I cannot focus while worrying about them. I can't look through my telescope and make calculations and look back over my shoulder at the same time. I won't be able to save anyone without the feeling of security. That's where I need you."

"Find someone else," I said. "Put together an entire team. You have that kind of sway now."

"I wouldn't be able to trust them," she said. "I can only trust you. We both know that not one out there is better at this sort of thing." She grabbed my face and turned it to her. "You are part of the .03 percent. You know it, and I know it. Look around." She nodded out to the horizon, the sun on its slow plunge into the ocean. "We have not hit infinite density. Not yet."

"Stop with the terminology. Not everything is science or binary or invisible light."

She looked out at the setting sun. "See the green flash?"

"Yeah." I lied. I wanted to just tip over into the water and let drowning take care of the rest.

She smiled. "The atmosphere is splitting the sun's white light. It's—"

"Yeah, a prism or some shit. Let me go."

"No," she said. She yanked my arm. "Look at it. Just look."

I sighed and looked. And of course I couldn't see it. "It's a mirage," she said. She turned to me. "Everything is science. Do you know how I discovered the asteroid?"

"Yeah, through your big-ass telescope."

"No that's not how I first saw it. That's how I verified it."

"How then?"

"I looked up and saw a halo in the sky."

"What?"

"I was five years old when I first saw it." She paused and looked at me. "It was the day of the Great Sun Storm. I spent the next thirty years of my life proving its existence."

"You're crazy," I said.

She looked down at the water. "My father used to work until very late. Asian market crypto finance. Every night I would sit on the porch, waiting for him to come home. Sometimes he would. Sometimes he wouldn't. Sometimes, I would sit out there for hours, just waiting and looking up at the stars."

"On that night, the sky was very clear. By this time, I'd learned all my constellations. And every night I would look up and count them. I would look up and make sure they were all still there. And on this night, just like every night before it, I did not see anything disappear. Instead, I saw a flash and all the lights went off, then something new showed up. Another spot on what I called the tail of the dragon. It was very faint at first. Like the aura around a lit candle. Physically impossible, really. Preposterous. For me to be able to see it." She turned to me. "But sometimes I see things that are impossible to see. I knew the halo was death coming from very far away."

I kept quiet and looked out at the skyline. The sun had set, and the limbo between day and night began. I related to her words in a way she couldn't even know.

"I've never told anyone this," she said. "In fact, if you told anyone, I'm sure I would be ostracized and removed from this project. But I know it exists. I know it's coming."

I nodded. She looked at me. "You never . . . see things?"

"No. If anything, I see less than the average person."

Akira grinned. She looked out to the ocean. "Your first two wives and firstborn are still somewhere out there, aren't they?"

I nod. "My first wife took off with our daughter when she was one," I said. "I haven't seen them since, so I'm not sure. My second wife, well, I'd rather forget about her anyway."

Akira nodded. "You never wonder about your first child?"

"Sure I do. But when I got back from deployment and they were gone, a part of me was relieved."

Akira sighed. "I know that guilt too. It drives me."

I turn to her. "I came back a monster."

She grabbed my shoulders. "Listen to me," she said.

"What?"

"We're both in the business of discovering what we don't know. And failure is not an option."

"Failure needs to be an option," I said. "Or whatever we find won't necessarily be the truth."

"Now there's the person I came to talk to," she said. "If you do this for me, I can promise you revenge for your wife and child."

"I don't got revenge in me."

"Protection, then," Akira said. "You'll be protecting your closest friend. Do you have that in you?"

I thought about that and looked over at Akira, who stuck her tongue out in the rain and let tiny drizzles fall onto it. It was the first time I'd ever seen her do something childlike, an action so slight but so telling: she enjoyed being alive.

She stopped and turned to me. "Look," she said, gesturing.

I looked down. The cannonball was gone.

"The night I saw the halo for the first time and discovered Sessho-seki, my father didn't come home."

"What happened?"

At first, silence. Then she said, "My father was in an airplane. A small one, a puddle jumper coming in from Seoul. He never made it back."

She knew my pain. How I saw things. I wondered if she blamed the universe itself for her father's death. And for a moment, I looked at her and couldn't tell the difference between us.

She stood up and extended her hand. "Now come," she said. "Help me save these last droplets of humanity."

When I think about it now, I still have no idea how Akira Kimura made a forty-two-pound cannonball drop from my lap without me noticing all those years ago. Like an idiot, I never once wondered how she did it. I got caught up when it came to her and forgot about my belief in history. Working a criminal case is largely a study of existing patterns. A natural-born liar doesn't stop lying. A person with a violent itch that started from childhood won't stop scratching it once he or she starts. Behavior is consistent, nearly impossible to change. Anyone who says don't dwell on the past and only look forward is a self-deluded dimwit blinded by pixie dust of guilt and regret. Looking at the past is the only way to accurately predict the future.

Akira knew that well. She was aware of my patterns and my personal tragedies. She knew that what had happened had filled me with a paralyzing rage. So she shared her own pain, confessed an impossible secret, and I believed her. In the weakest moment of my life, this sharing made her more than a friend. We became binary, like asteroid and weapon—one a killer, the other a savior. When I uncuffed myself and followed her down that sea crane ladder, I became something new. Something that snuffed out the light around me. It was my event horizon, not that I knew it at the time. Most of me figured I'd just climb down from the steel perch, then come back tomorrow and try again.

But I didn't. Instead, I let myself be put through the battery of background checks and debriefings. Once I passed, my job, as it was first explained to me, was to simply watch Akira's back. Shadow her, protect her. This felt too passive to me. I didn't have it in me to just wait for another tragedy to strike. So instead, while she pored over the math that made the creation of Ascalon possible, I pored through the threats. By then, Akira had already obtained complete government and financial backing. The top brass wanted her to get an iE, a state-of-the-art one to help her compute and document the saving of the world. But she told them it would just be a distraction that ultimately hindered her progress. When they forced other top scientists on her to help create Ascalon, most didn't last longer than a month. She would fire them, accusing them of being incompetent dolts to whom she had to explain too much. Even though there always seemed to be people around, Akira worked primarily alone. As did I.

I examined every threat with utmost gravity. Even though I knew the chances were that all of them had been sent by cowards blasting their idiocy off into the ether, I never took a chance. I told myself that never again in my life would I not take a threat seriously. Every single person who posted a threat was identified, arrested, and detained. It was an easy job at first, except for the volume. In just a little over two months, I had over five hundred people plucked from their basements, hourly wage jobs, and bored retirements. I had some extradited. People all over the world got the message, and the crackpots, for the most part, started keeping their mouths shut.

But other threats still arrived in less public forms. Handwritten letters. Graffiti. People sneaking past military security and throwing rotten seaweed at the telescope, since eggs had become precious. With basic surveillance and evidence analysis, these were easy enough to catch, just like the first batch. But these I didn't only arrest—I had them incarcerated. To me, their brashness made them actual threats. Some of them grew old in those cells. Most don't remember, their memories wiped clean by salvation.

After that, things settled down for a couple of months, and I began to look at the short list of people allowed to get close to Akira. A handful of senior scientists helping construct Ascalon, each with a large team serving under them. Jerry, her lawyer at the time. Her SEAL pilot, Dave, who had grown up on the island and knew his way around better than anyone else. Director Parker, Idris Eshana. Chief of Staff Chang. And his head scientist, Karlin Brum. Of everyone, she was the most unsettling. Skin a little too smooth, eyes a little too big, face a little too expressionless, like someone grown in the deepest point of the uncanny valley. She was the one who demanded the full-body scan everyone had to submit themselves to when they entered the telescope, even Akira. In fact, Brum picked the contractor who installed it. As individuals, each of these people were brilliant, except for maybe Chief of Staff Chang. But together, their egos, fear, envy, and ambition were a toxic stew that made me think that they'd get us all killed before Sessho-seki even got here.

Then the first odd threat Akira received came by the way of a note tucked into her handwritten journal. It wasn't a note, really, just a doodle of a completed game of hangman. The word. Five letters. Akira. We rummaged through past body scans. We ran human genome sweeps. Swept the telescope, the residence she had there, the home she never went to, her SEAL, the note itself, everything for DNA. The note went through every law enforcement scan on earth. Nothing. The president begged her to step up her security, but she refused. Just another distraction. More people who posed potential threats. The president threatened to force the Secret Service on her. She said that if he did so, she'd walk away from the entire thing. So they struck a compromise. I would be granted the authority to do anything necessary to protect her. It was put in writing. Executive order. Akira and I were there when he came to the telescope to sign it. After he left, I asked Akira something.

"What are your chances of beating this thing?" She never answered this question publicly.

"It doesn't matter," she said. "Don't you see? The world is already changing." And she was right. Before the discovery of Sessho-seki, apathy had hit such an all-time high that people were entering virtual reality arcades to be reminded what certain emotions felt like. But as The Killing Rock sped toward Earth, they didn't need to be reminded anymore. People started to feel everything again. Everyone except me, or so I thought at the time. I was in a passionless state of seek and destroy. And I didn't realize that people were watching me, too. Even the most powerful people in the world were afraid I might investigate them. Fewer people started showing up at the telescope, which to me meant lower threat levels. Some nights, it was just Akira and me on top of that damn mountain in the scope that people had started calling The Savior's Eye. Her sipping her ginger tea and trying to figure out how to engineer a weapon that could produce—and aim—the energy of an exploding star. A cosmic ray that would inevitably slash the sky as particles accelerated and collided. And me, like the rest of the world, patching together a cursory half-assed knowledge of physics without really understanding anything, giving up when we hit the impenetrable wall of Too Fucking Hard. With the world ending, and the last thing most of us wanted was to go back to school.

So, while Akira was bashing particles together and trying to add some weight to those tiny suckers without slowing them down, I kept looking for greens and reds. I studied the island and its population of about 300,000. Too many. I began shipping people off for relocation. This caused a real shitstorm, civil liberties and all that, but we were in a state of martial law given the pending apocalypse, so even if I didn't detect a speck of murder on them, I sent most of them packing before they could protest. I tried to be nice about it, telling them as they were being rounded up that they don't want to be here anyway with a woman on top of that mountain juggling high mass particles and supernovas. Years later, after it was all done, Akira said she felt bad and began repopulating the place with those who wanted to come back. But only those who agreed to care for the island like it was the Garden of Eden. And back when I'd been shipping them out hundreds at a time, and Akira hadn't seemed to notice, I'd cut the population of the island in half by the time the next threat came.

This one was bad. It was inside The Savior's Eye. Not many people had unrestricted access to this place, not even Idris Eshana, Jerry, Chief of Staff Chang, or his chosen scientist. I was surprised I had access, and on the first day I went in, Akira showed me around. It was just us two in there, and she started spouting scientific language I couldn't comprehend, a series of letters and numbers. I had a good memory, but like most people, I was trained to memorize either letters *or* numbers, not a combination of both. She turned and saw that I was confused, so she ripped a page from her journal and drew a bunch of circles connected to a different bunch of circles and started folding the piece of paper. She talked about forks, mirrors, dimensions, expansion, and infinity, and I'd never felt so stupid in my life. She handed me the folded-up piece of paper, and I put it in my pocket. She said maybe I could try to understand later. When we got to the eyepiece, Akira asked if I wanted to look through it. I said no. She looked a bit surprised. "You're the first," she said.

"The first what?"

"The first person who's declined the opportunity to see the asteroid that might destroy humanity."

I shrugged. "I've seen humanity destroy itself enough times already."

She nodded and went back to work. I headed to my desk and looked through the stats on the island's residents. I scanned through surnames that don't exist much anymore, with an eye to registered weapon owners and their private psych records. It was tedious work, but soothing in a way. It distracted me from picturing Kathy and John's faces. Sometimes, I'd see them during the good times, like when John won three gold medals at his very first swim meet, and Kathy and I sat by the pool, swelling with pride. Other times, I imagined their faces melted when the skim boat was incinerated. It didn't matter which I pictured. The result was the same. White-hot rage. Hotter than the supernovas Akira was mimicking. But on this day, at this time, I was scanning mindlessly. Then I started to smell it. It was the first time in a long time.

I looked around the huge room. Nothing. I looked back at the eyepiece. And I saw them. Faint traces of green. The next thing I saw was Akira's face approaching the eyepiece. I practically charged her. She saw me coming and looked confused, though not alarmed. I grabbed her arm and pulled her back. "Wait," I said.

"What is it?"

"Something's wrong with that eyepiece."

"You're just being paranoid."

She bent to look through. This time, I gripped her even harder and dragged her halfway across the room.

"Have you lost your mind?" she said.

"You told me you wanted me to do this job because I'm the only one you trust. So trust me."

She nodded.

When we got forensics in there, we found out that the eyepiece had been laced with enough VX to kill a whale.

The president himself sent his team to the island. Just a few hours after finding the VX, everyone was interrogated. Including me. Including Akira herself. A couple of scientists and military personnel were detained because they were the only ones who might have access to the most powerful chemical weapon on the face of the earth or know how to make it, but in the end, even they were cleared. Nobody had any clue how getting VX on the eyepiece was even possible. I barely knew what VX was, so I was in the dark more so than most. I needed to learn about threats like this. After Akira sent the president's team back, he signed off on another executive order, granting me even more power and access to classified information. I began to study. Not physics, but hacking security entries and deadly nerve agents. I crammed in research on invisible ways to kill. All the while, I was very much on alert for that smell and any hint of green. My computer and chemistry knowledge capped out pretty quickly, considering I'd only taken as much math as I'd needed to get a college degree and hardly remembered any of it. I started pestering Akira with questions, which she said she would gladly answer. And it made us both laugh, because the only way I could understand a goddamn thing was if she explained it in analogies. "Imagine if I poured cement into a barrel of a gun," she said. "What would happen?"

"It would blow up."

"That's what VX does. It directs the body to block its barrels."

I apologized to her for being an idiot. She told me it made her happy to see me look alive again.

And I felt alive. Electric. I wanted to find out who was trying to kill my friend. I was in no shape to let someone I cared about die again. I blazed through all the information I could. I saw images of dolls in Russia wearing gas masks. Piles of dead pigeons in Syria. And molecule formulas that resembled military maps. In some cases, they kind of were. It went on for a couple weeks like this, and then I saw them again. The wafts. Faint. Even fainter than before. And they were coming from Akira. My first instinct was to grab her and stick her under a decon shower. And I marched toward her to do just that. But then I started thinking. The wafts, they don't only come from victims. They lead me to murderers as well.

Was it possible that Akira was planning to kill someone? Could her playing with those nova simulators and colliders all day be her planning to murder the entire goddamn world by way of Sessho-seki, or even before then? My march slowed to a walk. I always had everything that came into contact with Akira inspected thoroughly. A bottle of shampoo had a harder time getting in here than it would to fucking Mars. I stopped walking.

That day, I watched her closely. Followed her movements more than usual. Nothing out of the ordinary. She pulled her usual twenty-hour day, then headed to her private quarters and shut the door. She'd spend a couple hours in her AMP chamber, then get back to work. I went to the surveillance room and watched her door from there. About two hours later, just as I was nodding off, she stepped out and headed to the SEAL docks. I got up and followed at a distance. At the docks, she and Dave were standing outside her SEAL arguing. He finally threw his hands up and got into his pilot's seat.

I wasn't sure what to do. It'd be impossible to follow them

without being spotted. I thought maybe I should wait and put a tracker on her SEAL once they got back, but security swept that SEAL every day. I couldn't get into her private quarters to look around. No one could. It was against the rules even for Akira to let anyone else in there. All the new rules that had been put in place to protect her made it harder to do.

Helpless, I shook my head and sat down. I was exhausted. This woman was a machine, and when it came down to it, my job was basically to watch her while she worked. Considering what she was doing, it was pathetic that I felt gassed. She was painting a technological masterpiece every waking moment. Even when she briefly slept in her AMP chamber, she was probably dreaming about the next touches she would make to Ascalon. All I had to do was ensure nobody interfered.

I pulled the piece of folded paper out of my pocket and looked at it. All those circles and lines and folds, all of it just an attempt to oversimplify a single concept to me, a buffoon. I couldn't even imagine how complicated her work really was, because I couldn't even understand the premise in its most distilled form from the person who had created it. My job was straightforward, and I was failing. I felt like I was still carrying that forty-two-pound cannonball while chasing after the fastest woman in the world.

And that's when it happened. I looked and the paper and saw something recognizable on it. Dyads. Two-note Möbius strips. Music.

The circles floated from the page in red. At first, they were just red puffs that ascended, bounced once, and disappeared. Then they rose with sound, and the bounces became notes. I began to hear them. Red notes stretched from the page, clipped by flats and sharps. I put them together in my head, these puffs gasped from the lips of a singing caterpillar. A plucky three-chorder about a place. An old place on an island long forgotten. I stood up and headed to my SEAL so quickly, it never occurred to me that she was never trying to explain a physics theory to me. She was leaving me a clue for something else. Could she know how I perceived things? No way. No one did. It didn't even occur to *me* as possible. She was manipulating me? It had never happened before. I'd solved every case that ever crossed my desk.

Why didn't I even consider her capable of this back when it happened? Because she'd once told me a story about her failure as a musician, a story about her childhood that I simply accepted as fact. Akira being able to write music? Ridiculous. And I always liked believing she had no musical talent. I wanted her to have a weakness, or at least be worse at something than me. It was pure ego. Because as smart as I knew she was—the smartest person in the world, in fact—at the end of the day, I never really thought anyone was smarter than me.

So, without question, I went to the place in the drawing's song, never suspecting that she could be the second incarnation of Mozart. Never wondering why she couldn't be. She was Mozart in everything else. *There's an icon for you, Jerry.*

I was so relieved that the circles had sung out to me, that I could finally help her, that I jumped in my SEAL to go to this place without thinking. Maybe I thought no one else could puzzle it out except me.

And not for a moment had it crossed my mind that Akira had scribbled the hangman note. That she was the one who put VX on her eyepiece. That she wanted me to have the power to do what I was about to do.

12

Akeem's place is a huge, floating swirl ten klicks off the coast. The center is an ecodome that grows all sorts of food, and from there the complex expands out, first into freshwater catchers, then docks, and finally a series of high-rises shaped like giant seashells. It looks like what the float burbs were first marketed as when they came out, back when state colleges finally went under. No one who bought that early realized that whatever floats pretty much always starts to sink at some point. That seawater mixed with air ends up damaging everything pretty quickly. Or that it's hot as fuck living under the sun in the middle of the ocean.

So people who bought the first float burbs sold soon after and moved to seascrapers. The price of the burbs plummeted, becoming affordable to people like me. But Akeem's floater doesn't suffer the same problems as the originals. No cost was spared on preventative measures. Akeem spent so much time underwater for his geothermal work that he didn't want to live at the very bottom of the ocean like the rest of The Money. But he loves the ocean, too, and couldn't bear to live without it right under his feet.

I still feel terrible and figure talking might help, so I ask. "Why'd you build so many high-rises?"

"For my kids and grandkids."

"How many grandkids are you up to?"

"Seven grandchildren from my four kids. Even three great-grandchildren now." That's how you know you're The Money—when you build so many rooms it's impossible to fill them, no matter how much you procreate.

"Let's dock under," Akeem says.

My hands are shaking. Med withdrawals, maybe. Getting off pharma is like being born again. Day two is the worst. "It's been a while since I took her under," I say. "Not sure if she'll hold up."

"It's only one story down," Akeem says.

I try my best to steady my hands and navigate us beneath the ocean's surface. The SEAL makes a predator's splash. I take her underwater and see the dock, a ramp up ahead. I speed toward it and lower the wheels. "Why under?" I ask.

"I'm a simple man," Akeem says. "Sometimes I just like hearing the splash."

As we go up the ramp, it folds in on itself behind us. "You don't want anyone to know I'm here."

"I've been breeding Maran chickens in the dome," Akeem says, ignoring me. "Let's go eat some eggs."

Akeem Buhari is one of my more recent friends, which when you're eighty, means I've known him for over a decade. I met him at a crypto fundraiser for cancer research—that disease is one of the few blights we still ain't managed to beat. A giant asteroid hurling toward Earth? No problem. Cells that uncontrollably multiply and spread until they snatch the life out of us? We gotta kill part of ourselves to get rid of them, but they never stop growing. Even The Money with all their farmed organ transplants eventually succumb. It was how my mom went. She hit that fork in the road at Hayflick's limit where cells either panic or wither. And they tried everything. Chemo. Gene therapy. By the end, they were cutting her in half and putting her back together like some sick magic trick. I was at the fundraiser representing law enforcement in my ceremonial blues, resenting that I felt like I'd been made to volunteer because I had personal experience with cancer, while Akeem, whose mom had been taken by cancer as well, stood behind the bar serving drinks with a giant smile on his face. Highballs looked like shot glasses in his giant mitts. He was in the middle of a voluntary double shift. His absurd, flower-printed shirt was drenched in sweat. I knew he was a better man than me right off the bat.

I think about that now, seeing him pour behind his horse-shoe-shaped bar. His customers are his wife, two of his children, and three of his grandchildren, all of whom live here with him. They spend most of the time ribbing each other. Akeem's kids tell their kids that Akeem was the worst cook when they were growing up. They laugh and talk about a dish called Seaweed Surprise. One of his grandkids tells another about leaving her baby out in the living room once and rushing to pee. She came back and her daughter was sitting next to a pile of pet vomit, pointing at it. "Uh oh," the baby said. Everyone laughs. Akeem's wife, dressed in a fluorescent foam-fit sarong, talks about the last trip she took with one of the kids who isn't present. The flowers on her sarong bloom as she reminisces about trips to Rome, Athens, and Istanbul together. Akeem's wife is in her sixties. The child she speaks of is in his forties. They went on a trip together. Alone. Most kids can't conjure up the willpower to spend Thanksgiving with their parents. These people go on long vacations together all the time by choice and seem to enjoy the hell out of it. Of the hundreds of families I've come across, I've seen maybe three others like this one. And I'm eighty. I start thinking that maybe only people like Akeem and his wife should live this long.

Akeem puts a prairie oyster in front of me. The yellow yolk floats in the middle of a puddle of tomato juice that looks like beige slop to me. I realize I can't remember the last time I ate, so I gulp it down. After Akeem's wife, kids, grandkids, and great-grandkids head to their rooms for the night, Akeem and I stay at the bar. After a drawn-out pause where we pretend we're thinking about what to say but are actually just afraid to say it, Akeem finally speaks. "I only met her a few times. I don't even know that she qualifies as an acquaintance."

"She kept to herself for the most part."

"When did she go crazy?"

"What do you mean?"

Akeem gulps down his drink. "That place you took me to today could only have been the work of someone who's completely lost their mind."

"I used to think she was the sanest person I knew."

"And now?"

"You know how they used to treat gunshot wounds back in the day?" I ask.

Akeem shakes his head.

"Docs would pour gallons of .09 percent saltwater solution in the wound. Just over and over. That's how thinking about this makes me feel."

Akeem nods, fixing another prairie oyster and putting it in

front of me. As I gulp it down, he steps out from the bar, strips off his foam-fit top, and dumps it in the eager laundry bot. It wheels off down the hall. Akeem heads to the elevator. He notices me turn to watch and says, "Go see your family," over his shoulder before disappearing through the open doors.

I look out the window. The sunlight is blaring. It's tough to see the island from way out here, but I spot its peak through the haze, where Akira's Telescope sits. On these islands, invasive species and structures have always strangled and thrived. I suppose that's common, but it happens fast here, the islands a drooped neck already weakened by generations of cozy solitude. Isolation breeds vulnerability. Maybe that's what happened to Akira Kimura all those years ago. It could be what's happening to me now. Akeem is right. It's time to see my family with a clear head—without the sound of whistling on a carefree stroll through the woods, which is usually what astronaut-grade antidepressants sound like.

I turn on my iE's feed. Every law enforcement agency in the world is on the island now. I think about how the population was only about 300,000 back when Akira was building Ascalon. Counting the float burbs and the scrapers, it's about eight million now. Add to that the cops that have come in force, I imagine a packed stadium for the Friday Night Prawn Bake. But among this teeming mess is a baby, long gone, our savior's innocent, tailed, mystery child. I head for my iE. Suddenly, I'm scared and want to see my own baby again.

13

When I was a kid, I had this toy. A doll named Life Coach Teddy whose buttons you could press for him to tell you what you wanted to hear. If I was sad and pressed the heart button, he'd tell me a parable about hope and how everything would get better. If I was scared and pressed the right-arm button, the arm would inflate, and Teddy would tell me that he would protect me. A button for every mood. My dad was already dead by then, and my mom was busy working. I'm not bitching and moaning about that. She was a deep-water glass engineer who supported the two of us on her own. So Life Coach Teddy was just nice to have around when I was by myself. Once, I confided to Life Coach Teddy that I wanted to grow up to be a time hacker so I could travel back to the right moment and save my dad. Teddy said it was a great idea, even though the job didn't and probably will never exist. Or at least, that's what Akira told me once.

I'm heading home, wondering what I learned from Life Coach Teddy. He did everything I wanted him to, and it made me happy. In turn, I grew and became a real people-pleaser. *Need me to do something for you? I'm on it. Oh, you love me and want to marry me? No problem, I got you. Kids, you say? You want kids? No problem. Want me to train you and show you the ropes? Sure. Need me to exterminate all your potential threats while you're trying to save the world? Press here, on my right arm. I'll protect you.* Looks like Life Coach Teddy was my role model.

I dock at the float burb. Home sweet home. The wharf lights flicker. The flags are at half-mast. The moors creak, but at least there's no tilt under my feet. It's late, and except for the occasional pulse of iE light dancing behind closed drapes, everything is still. My thighs itch, my dry skin getting worse with age. I scratch at the scales and think that this is what getting old is, becoming something more reptilian. Sometimes, I crave sugar like an old lady detective in a cozy mystery.

I head to my unit. It's quiet here, too. I have no idea what I'm going to tell Sabrina. She used to say, half-jokingly or not, that Akira Kimura was the love of my life. That there was no way I'd be able to shake that kind of love when reminders of her were all over the place. Books, statues, biopics. I would respond by saying that the books and documentaries were missing most of it, or had just gotten the whole thing wrong, and the statues were looking less and less like Akira—I didn't even recognize her in the newer ones. If Akira had been the love of my life, I argued, the reminders certainly weren't working on me. Sabrina would smirk and tell me that as real memory of her faded, all that was left was how people wanted and imagined Akira to be, me included. And she was right.

I want to tell her that. It's the least I can do.

I set the lights on dim, in case Sabrina and Ascalon are sleeping. I take the elevator down to the second of our two floors and head to Ascalon's room. I tell my iE to open the door just a crack, trying not to wake her. I peep inside. Nothing. Maybe they've gone to stay at a friend's. There are no in-laws. Sabrina's parents died when she was three, found among the cloudscraper jumpers whose feet I skimmed out of the ocean after the days of Ascalon. God, she hated them for that. She once told me that not only were her parents cowards, but their conviction was weak. If they'd truly believed the world was ending, they should have had the conviction to take her with them. That was when I told her about my first wife and child and the guilt I felt. Not because they left while I was in the military, but because I hardly ever thought about them, and even less so after what had happened to Kathy and John. I told Sabrina that involving your kid in your conviction was overrated.

Creeping around my own house like a burglar, I think about the fact that John would've been in his forties right now, probably a better man than me. I dream about an alternate reality where he doesn't die. Where I'm an old man with a son. Maybe we go on trips together like Akeem and his kids. I envy that fantasy version of me.

I enter Ascalon's bedroom. Empty crib. No replacement changing table. Maybe Sabrina decided we didn't need one anymore? Is my kid completely potty-trained, and I don't even know it? I look down at my hand. I'm holding my rail gun, and I don't know why. I need to eat and sleep. I've been at this for more hours than my tired mind can count. I rub my eyes and tell myself that Sabrina and Ascalon are just away for the night, maybe at Judy's. Judy has a son around Ascalon's age, and they do a sleepover playdate once every couple of weeks. Yeah, probably that. But I've gotta make sure. I ping Sabrina. No answer. I try Judy. Nothing.

Then I realize again how late it is. Everyone's sleeping, like I should be.

I look up at the wall to my right. A frame. I think Sabrina put it up a week or two ago. I'm embarrassed I can't remember. A framed picture of Ascalon's doodles. Nothing coherent. Definitely not watershed. Just evidence that shows an eighteen-month-old can jerk orange, purple, and blue watercolor onto paper.

An eighteen-month-old. I think about Akira's self-made tomb. The box of newborn bones. *Newborn.* Not old enough to have made the drawings I threw my knife at before setting everything on fire.

She killed me.

I spin around. No one is there. I check my iE. Again, no recording of the voice. I must be losing my mind. I want to crawl into an AMP chamber and crank it up, maybe get a month or two of sleep. I remember the first time I hibernated in one. The tech told me that every cell in our bodies contain mitochondria, which at one time, eons ago, were a separate organism. At some point, they invaded other living organisms, and a symbiotic relationship was born. They produce the electricity we need to exert energy. We, in turn, provide them a nice, cozy place to live. Now we're inseparable. They're wrapped in our RNA, passed down only from our mothers. Sabrina passed hers down to Ascalon, Akira to her daughter.

The picture. Her daughter. There's something I'm missing. My mind is lumbering in slow circles right now.

Another sound behind me. I turn and raise my rail gun. It's heavy. A PD drone is looking right back at me. Its LED pupil expands and brightens. I squint, and the drone instructs me to lay down my weapon and put my hands up. If I don't, it'll hit me with ninety-five decibels of paralyzing sound. I sigh. I crouch and put the gun down and my hands up in the air. Another drone floats in and cuffs me. Then the chief and a corporal walk in. The chief picks up my gun with a gloved hand.

"This is getting ridiculous, Chief," I say.

He inspects it. "You look awful. Maybe I should put you out of your misery."

"It's illegal for you to hold that. You aren't licensed."

The chief nods. He hands the corporal my gun.

"I'm pinging my lawyer," I say. But I pause—Jerry's probably still rightfully mad and won't take the call. I'm also so tired. Maybe I won't ping. I feel like my mitochondria are on low-power mode, about to flicker off.

"Jerry Caldwell?" the chief asks.

"Yeah, Chief. Jerry Caldwell," I say.

"You're a pathetic old man, you know that?"

"What?"

The chief's iE projects a 3D vid above the bars of the crib. Footage from Jerry Caldwell's iE.

It's me walking into Jerry's bedroom, then marching toward her. I'm holding a knife. I look angry, so angry. Almost unrecognizable, even to myself. I put my hand around Jerry's throat. Of course, on vid, there's no green wafting from my hand or her neck. There's just the hand of a murderous man looking to snatch the breath out of one of his friends. Jerry slaps me twice, and then the vid flickers off.

"She's dead?" I say.

"You're done, old man," the chief says.

Oddly, I think of something Akira once told me. There are

two types of sunlight, and most creatures on Earth absorb one kind of light to repair damage from the other. Somewhere along the line, humans lost the ability to do this. Maybe because we spent most of our existence hiding out in the dark. Fuck. I should've seen Jerry's murder coming. The greens were there. It was all there except me. I got caught up in Akira's mess and didn't even hang back to protect my friend.

"No comment?" the chief asks.

I try my best to pull it together. "You don't have the rest," I say. "Or you'd know I didn't kill her."

"We have enough," his corporal says.

Damn Jerry for her lawyer's reflexes. Once she figured the conversation was about to turn privileged, she cut recording on her iE. And she had complete faith that I wasn't gonna hurt her. That's the kind of stand-up person she was. That's the kind of friend she was. And I somehow got her killed. I begin to worry about Sabrina and Ascalon. "Where are my wife and kid?" I say.

He ignores the question and pulls on his beard, then whispers orders into the corporal's ear. I think of Kathy and John. And I'm beside myself. "Tell me where!"

"You don't deserve to know," the chief hisses at me.

"What the hell is your problem, anyway?" I ask.

"You remember when you were in charge of Akira Kimura's security? All those people you had arrested?"

"I don't know what you're talking about," I say.

"My mother was one of them, you fucking asshole. And your protector's dead now." He grabs me by the arm and pulls my ear to his lips. "It's open season on you, old man."

I should've figured Akira had my back all these years without me even knowing it. A lot of people probably remember the things I did and have been lining up, waiting for her to die so they could get their shot at me. But I'm not worried about them right now. "Where in the hell are my wife and kid!" I yell, my wrists becoming bruised and scraped as I struggle against the cuffs. Just more pain I'm causing myself.

"Tell me what happened."

I stop fighting the cuffs. "Fine. I'll tell you what happened," I say to the chief.

"What?"

"Come closer."

His face inches toward mine. I can smell the musky shampoo he's used on his ridiculous beard. I try to be careful with my aim because at this point, I'm seeing double from all this fatigue. I smash into his face with my forehead.

Ninety-five decibels crackle in my ears, so I can barely hear the chief's screams. I'm on my knees now, and through the pain, hope rises. Hope that Sabrina and Ascalon are okay. That I'll never be able to see or hear green or red again. The pain puts my vision back in focus, and the last thing I see as I'm dragged out of the room is Ascalon's framed drawing. I wish I'd been there when she drew it. I'm proud in a way only a parent can be of something so wholly commonplace.

Was Akira like this, too? Why did she keep those drawings that—if those bones don't lie—never should have existed?

The corporal pushes me into the elevator, and we go up to the living room. When we get to the front door, it doesn't slide open. Like a child, the chief repeatedly stomps his left foot in front of the three stairs leading to the door. Nothing. He finally turns to me. "Stop screwing around and open it."

I can barely hear him. I see the elevator going back down from the corner of my eye. "It should open fine," I say.

The chief touches his bleeding nose, then stomps in front of the door again. "Open!" he says.

The elevator comes back up. Must be on the fritz, like the plank outside. The door slides open. Ascalon's remote-controlled ball rolls from the elevator and into the room. It stops at our feet. I wonder if Ascalon was sleeping with Sabrina in our room. I didn't even think to check. I look down at the ball. I spent a fortune on it, and it captured my daughter's full attention for all of one week. Why, all my life, have I coveted expensive things? Building my entire life on debt for this impractical shit. The stupid curved, hyper-ergonomic furniture that surrounds me. Who the hell needs a sofa that can turn itself into a tent? Always gotta buy the latest gadgets. In that way, I've always been truly American.

The chief picks up the ball. He looks at me. Ears ringing, I look right back. My cuffs and the PD drone drop to the floor.

"What the—?" the chief says.

The ball swells in his hands. Its bright pink hisses as it transforms into translucent flesh. Me, the chief, and the corporal can't keep our eyes off it as it grows and grows. Words begin to form on the sphere in red. Am I the only one who can see them?

I am still here.

This is not Akira's work. I hear laughter coming from the elevator. It sounds like Akira's laughter, which is surprising because Akira almost never laughed. I glance at the elevator doors, but don't see anyone there. I turn back to the ball. Something pulses beneath the stretching letters. Something that smells green. "Sabrina!" I yell. "Ascalon!"

The hiss becomes a scream. The explosion that follows is tough to describe. Skin-peeling heat. A thump that shorts all the human circuitry inside me. I don't know if I'm still alive. I'm sliding down the continental slope into the midnight zone. I feel my heels digging into the cold, deep sand. I wonder if Kathy and John felt the same thing all those years ago. I wonder if they're together now, waiting for me to join them. I plant my heels hard into the cold, briny sea mud and reach out to grab onto something, anything, that will stop my descent beyond the abyss and into the trenches. I feel alive. So alive that I know I'm not dead, even if I'm not conscious. Maybe a person doesn't truly feel alive until he fights to stay that way.

14

When I come to, I'm cuffed to a gurney, and my first thought is: *handcuffs*. That means I've still got hands. I look down to check if the rest of me is still there, and incredibly, all of it seems intact. I look out of the SEAL window. I get my bearings and immediately know where we're heading. Must've been there hundreds of times. It's a rough part of the ocean, about thirty klicks off the coast. Shaped like a giant top, it's kept afloat by a hydro propulsion system almost as old as me. Its official name is the North Pacific Correctional Facility, but because of its slow spin and inconsistent bobbing in the water's undercurrents, everyone calls it Vomit Island. Only about five to ten percent of people are impervious to seasickness, and the rest suffer it in varying degrees. On Vomit Island, prisoners make bets on which new inmate will throw up first. The food ain't bad here, so they can't even use that as an excuse.

I turn to the cop guarding me. I don't recognize him— might be a Fed. "Are my wife and daughter okay?"

He ignores me. I feel something wet on my face. "Shouldn't you assholes be taking me to the hospital first?"

No response. I stick my tongue out and rub it against the edge of my mouth to see what the liquid stuff is. The prickle of iron. Blood.

The guard frowns. "Don't do that," he says.

"Am I bleeding?" I ask.

He shakes his head. "You're licking all that's left of Captain Kashogi and Corporal Barns."

I spit that out. "But I'm alive. How?"

The guard looks at me. "I'm pretty sure the superintendent is wondering the same thing."

"Where are my wife and kid?" I ask again. He just ignores me. I pass out.

When we land and get to the top level, I'm shaken awake, pulled from my gurney, still cuffed, and escorted into an interrogation room. The guard from the transport, who's on his feet now, is a mountain of a man, jacked on super-protein. He's not a Fed. He's Correctional. He stays close to me the entire time. I look around the nearly bare room—not a friendly one, now that I've got human flesh and blood all over my face. They're gonna go old school on old me. I'm pushed into a chair, my cuffs attached to the table.

The superintendent steps in and sits across from me. He's in his rumpled dress blues, probably been in them all day. He sees me looking at his coat. He rubs his hands over it, and the wrinkles disappear. I haven't spoken to the superintendent in years, but he's still got the beady eyes of a political animal caged by wheel-and-deal steel. "I can let you stew here for the rest of your life," the superintendent says. He holds up my now deactivated iE. "Or you can give consent to let us look at your iE. I'm surprised you turned it off. Your rights and all. But if you're innocent, your data can prove it."

"Want to tell me where my wife and kid are?" I ask.

"Give us your consent first," the superintendent says. "Sign over your iE data. Just the past two days."

"How about some medical attention?" I say, although shockingly, I feel fine. Great, in fact.

"This is Akira Kimura we're talking about," the superintendent says. "Even if you say no now, we're gonna get those rights eventually."

I know exactly what he's saying. "Fine. Let me talk to the Feds," I say.

The superintendent stands and sighs. "We lost two good men today," he says. "Forensics says the IED was crafted to charge in a conical radius."

"It wasn't me," I say. "I never liked the chief, and I feel fucking horrible about the kid, but I didn't do it. I didn't kill Jerry either. She was my friend. One of my best. Now, where the fuck are my wife and kid?"

The superintendent steps out the room.

Sabrina steps in. Her sleeves are retracted, her forearms still jacked from years of returning 200-mile-per-hour pulse serves. Her biceps shapely too, from all that Ascalon-carrying. Her eyes are bright as airglow. She looks strong, and I'm so relieved to see her, I want to cry. I try to stand and hug her, but the cuffs keep me in my seat. "How's Ascalon?" I ask.

"She's fine. Why would you think she wouldn't be?"

All the relief I've just felt chills into the same old hard feelings. "After I heard about Jerry," I say. "I went home. The house was empty. I was worried."

"So, is Jerry's death related to you in some way?"

It takes me a few ticks to put the pieces together, but I realize that Sabrina's on the job. The superintendent has activated her and called her in just to fuck with me. And the worst part is, she agreed to it. "You must really hate me," I say. "To come back to work and throw my ass in jail forever as the first case you work."

"We don't choose our cases," she says. "You know that."

I nod and look at her. She looks fantastic. Sharp gray vest and slacks. Like the superintendent's coat, everything made of smart fabric and 3D-printed to fit. It's the suit of a corporate dominatrix, meant to intimidate. I'm trying to hide the fact that I'm a little turned on. And I wonder if there's something fucked up in me, or maybe all men, that finds a woman more attractive when there isn't a child tethered to her. I know it ain't right. Everyone's always jumping on evolution as an excuse for terrible human behavior. We were *meant* to be this way. We've survived this long because we *are* this way. We're getting closer and closer to perfection, people say. Always sounded made up to me.

Sabrina sits down across from me. "Where's Ascalon?" I ask.

"Not that you give a shit, but daycare."

I look at her hands. She's even done her nails. Maybe I'm staring at them now so I don't have to think about whether what she's just said is true.

"Akira's funeral is tomorrow," Sabrina says. Then she looks at the time. "Or technically, today, I guess. They'll vid-cast it live here."

"That seems fast. It's only been two days since she died."

Sabrina shrugs, then changes the subject. "No seasickness, I presume?"

She's my wife, so she knows I don't get seasick. My father loved the ocean. He always complained about how much time was spent studying stuff light-years away compared to what was right around us. The thing that made life possible. I spent half my weekends in childhood out in the water with him. Dove to depths other children couldn't even imagine. Once stroked the ears of a Dumbo octopus in the midnight zone. Whatever seasickness I might have been capable of was drowned out by the time I was seven.

"What was her cause of death? Jerry," I ask.

"The superintendent seems to think it's an old man's rage."

I look out the window again. Night has turned to morning. Shallow water full of sediment splashing against the glass. It's supposed to give suspects the feeling of treading water. That way, when they've been in here long enough that the tide rises, they start to feel like they're drowning. This is the closest thing law enforcement has to a seascraper. It doesn't come close to reaching the bottom, but like most seascrapers, the true celebrities live on the lowest levels, which are the coldest and hardest to escape from. It's where they'll put me if I'm convicted of this. I'm so tired at this point, I'm not even sure that I'm innocent. I try to pull myself together. "I guess they put you in charge of this," I say. "Brought you back because the real brain power's being spent on Akira? Just pass this up to the Feds. There are a few too many hard feelings here."

"You killing the captain didn't help. Blowing the dome off our home didn't help either."

"You and I both know I'm no bombmaker," I say.

"Who, then?"

It can only be Akira. Even from the grave, she's protecting me, not for my sake, but to ensure that I can complete one final mission. But she's not a god. And she's *dead*. I can't believe I keep having to remind myself of this.

"It's looking more and more like Akira's death was a suicide," Sabrina says, as if she's read my mind.

They're stalling. They can't figure it out. Maybe that's the reason for her rushed funeral. To take the pressure off. Then again, JFK was buried three days after he was shot in Texas, and that didn't seem to get his assassination out of the public eye.

I remember the day I was about to plunge into the deep holding a forty-two-pound cannonball. Akira holding my arm, telling me that she was tired too. Then I remember that Sabrina's always been good at mind games. It's what makes her so sexy and so hard to live with. My wife, the one-time great collegiate pulse racket player, never stopped playing the game. This whole conversation, like so many conversations before it, goes serve, volley, point. Serve, volley, point, and as usual, she's winning.

"But you're right," Sabrina says. "Until they confirm anything about Akira, Jerry's death is a blip, even as powerful as the Caldwell family is."

And that makes me sad. Jerry Caldwell wasn't just impressive on paper. The most impressive thing about her might just have been that despite how privileged and cynical she was, she managed to remain honest and good. A person who always had something to teach. Like when she told me in all of human history, three things never went out of style. Graffiti, keep-out signs, and statues of ourselves. She'd use this rule to explain human nature: we desecrate in protest, we're afraid of people taking our stuff, and we worship ourselves. All that dark belief, and she still let me crash over whenever I wanted—still remained a true friend. Even the last time I saw her, she was trying to help me. But because I didn't like what she was trying to say, I threw a tantrum and left. I deserve to end up at the bottom of this slow-spinning top with the worst of the worst. I'll fit right in.

"A blip," Sabrina repeats. "The captain's and corporal's, too."

"Open casket?" I ask Sabrina.

"Akira? Nobody knows. Just rumors. Some think they'll shoot her up into space, so she can orbit Earth forever and ever." Sabrina's eyes narrow. "It's ironic," she says, "because for years now, Earth has revolved around her."

"I was asking about Jerry," I say.

She sighs. "I don't know."

Dad, Mom, Kathy, John, Jerry, even Akira. It's the worst, realizing that pretty much all the people you loved most are dead. I wonder if Akira felt the same way—if like me, she felt responsible for any of those deaths. Especially her baby's.

I keep thinking back to her tomb. The row on the right is her past. It stands to reason that the row on the left is another's. The end of that path is the dive shop. A good-looking man runs a small tour business there and lives his life like most of us, under the radar not by choice, but by being unremarkable. Maybe a curious, lonely girl who has moved to a new place, tired of being cooped up in the lab day and night, decides to see more of the world around her. Maybe she goes to a dive shop at a secret, picturesque dive spot miles from shore and steeped in ancient myth. He shows her marvels she has never seen before and becomes her only friend. They get closer and closer. Then comes a mistake that turns into a false blessing—the oldest story in the world. Over the past couple of days, I've come to understand how little I knew about the real Akira Kimura. But the one thing I will never doubt is that she could never bring herself to love anything outside of the top .03 percent.

Not even her own daughter, whom she killed for having a birth defect.

Back then, I followed the music like a mindless bot, one of those awful plastic automatons lonely men once used to learn how to foxtrot. Those years we worked so closely together were just me following the map Akira had drawn for me. The circles. The music. The red. That day, when I followed Dave and Akira from the mountain to the flotilla out in the middle of nowhere, I landed my SEAL on the ocean surface a klick away. I sent my iE in to pick up audio and watched from a distance through my rail scope. I felt like a sniper again.

The tour guide stood next to Akira. Dave was still in his SEAL, which was moored to the floating dive shop. It barely seemed seaworthy: barnacles clung to its rusty hulls, and the old lithium batteries it probably ran on based on the generator out back were no longer produced. Akira and the tour guide were arguing. Akira slammed something on the counter between them, a patterned blue silk jewelry pouch. Zooming in, I saw that it had a button and zipper, so old it was probably an antique. The tour guide opened it and poured its contents out. The sparkle of cut gemstones hurt my eyes. An under-the-table bribe? Blackmail?

The tour guide brushed them off the table and started to yell. My iE finally got to the scene. I sent it under the dive shop's hull for audio, their voices coming low through the polymer planks painted to look like wood.

Akira got on her hands and knees and began collecting the spilled gems. I felt an unexpected surge of anger—my friend, who was trying to save the world, was reduced to scrambling around on her hands and knees like some feeding beast. The tour guide laughed, leaned down, and picked up one of the gems. A big one, the size of a baby's fist. Red, maybe because I couldn't quite see it in detail. He tossed it overboard, and it splashed into the deep. Akira, now in tears, collected the remaining gems that she could find and stumbled through the door and climbed on the SEAL wing. The only thing my iE picked up was, "You can take your bribe and shove it up your ass, Aki. You're a fucking lying, murdering, selfish bitch, and you know it. The rest of the world might think you're some kind of saint, but they'll find out the truth. You killed her with your bare hands."

Akira turned around. "You didn't stop me."

"Make no mistake," he said. "I'm going to hell for this, too."

Akira began to cry. It was the only time I ever saw this happen. She quickly wiped any traces from her face and returned to the SEAL. It rose above the water and bolted off. I wondered what this guy was talking about. I had known Akira for years at this point, and while she could definitely be standoffish or careless, she was in no way a murderer. I'd busted enough of those to know how emotional the vast majority were, hardwired to rationalize an immoral act before they could carry it out. Not only that, but they were terrified, convinced that every trouble they encountered was life threatening, when really, it only triggered their pride or rage or frustration. Most murderers had these terrible weaknesses, and the Akira Kimura I knew had none of them. In this moment, I failed to consider that I might be a murderer myself.

Before approaching this guy, I wanted to talk to Akira. To

find out what the hell was going on. But before pinging her, I took one last look through my scope. I looked at the lines at the edges of the tour guide's eyes, the salt and pepper in his beard. He had about ten years on Akira. Maybe this was where he first brought her, telling her how this was where the natives of old believed spirits entered the underworld. The kind of stories she missed from back home. Maybe she didn't want to dive at first, but he promised her it'd be safe. He might even have given her a bit of liquor to calm her nerves. He would've taken her hand and told her she was safe with him. And they would've walked to the edge, taken a breath, and followed the path of the spirits into the deep blue, down to black.

The tour guide crouched down to the floor and picked up a gem that Akira had somehow missed—another big one, emitting a fierce green.

It refracted rays of sunlight onto his wrist, which bore a tattoo.

AWM.

So he was a member of the Anti-Waste Mafia, which had proudly claimed responsibility for the deaths of my wife and child.

I pulled the trigger and took out his iE. He turned around in a panic, his eyes searching for where the shot came from. He squinted and spotted me. Before I could squeeze off another round, he grabbed a pair of fins and dove into the water. *Fuck.* I throttled up my SEAL, flew, and docked at his floating hovel. I switched scope optics and pointed the rail at the water. I couldn't spot him. I pulled an old scuba tank off the wall, threw on a mask and fins, and dove into the water. He had no gear on. This was going to be easy.

It wasn't.

I was in no hurry, so I frog-kicked my way to the bottom. I was surprised how deep it was, a hundred feet at least. I helicopter-turned. Nothing. Where the hell did he go? I turned again. And that was when I spotted it. A line of bubbles, floating from a cavern. I kicked my way in. It was dark, and I was tempted to light up the place with my iE, but I didn't want him to see me coming. Pushing myself through the rocks in pursuit of more signs of movement, I imagined him wrapping his hands around Akira's neck and squeezing. I pictured her eyes watering, the blood vessels in her head bulging, her face eventually beginning to darken and the capillaries in her eyes popping until even the whites turned the color of blood. And in those two pools of blood, I saw Kathy on one side and John on the other. I had to fight to regain concentration. Another left. Another right. Something slithered quickly beneath me.

It was starting to become obvious that this was some sort of underwater labyrinth I might not be able to find my way out of. But I didn't care. I just kept chasing my own goddamn tail. It began to slope upward. That was when I saw a hand shoot out of a hole above me and yank my regulator so hard, it detached from the tank.

I turned my feet to the rocks and kicked off. I fired. I put so many rounds through the rock ceiling that it began to collapse. I had to bail. I pulled myself though a tunnel on my left and kicked as hard as I could. The tunnel began to narrow. I jerked out my harness and dropped the tank. I squeezed through the gap, tearing up my arms and thighs on the way. But I held onto the rail. Not that it did me much good. I hadn't free-dived in years and was running out of air. I was also lost. It occurred to me as long as this guy could hold his breath, it wasn't forever. He had to head to the surface. I pointed the rail at the rocks above me and blasted away until I carved out a hole big enough to swim through. I crawled through the hole and finally broke through and looked up. Fins fluttering. I aimed. For a brief moment, I wondered why I didn't see greens and red twisting together. In fact, there was no green or red at all. The lack of their presence made me even more eager to fire.

The first shot of plasma shredded him in half. The second split his torso in two. Desperate for air, I wanted to swim up with all I had. But my father taught me better than that. I exhaled all the air out of my lungs and began my ascent, careful not to rise faster than the bubbles. I kept my head up and tried my best to breathe out anything else left in my body. The gem sank toward me. I snatched it and continued to kick. I made it, barely.

Sprawled across the wing of my SEAL, I gulped down air. Once my breathing eased, I turned my eyes to my hand and looked at the gem. It was now colorless. Confident that I wasn't bent, I stood and entered my SEAL. I'd never been more grateful to my father for the things he taught me. During liftoff, a weird thought struck me. I never caught the tour guide's name.

The next day, I put the gem on Akira's desk. She eyed it and placed it in a drawer. We never spoke about it again, or the others that followed. Five, to be exact. But with the rest, at least I knew their names. Now, I knew that his probably ended in Lee.

So here I am, being processed at Vomit Island. Being interrogated by my own wife. And it's where I'm supposed to be.

I run through my past wives, my personal failures. With the first wife, we were both too young. Definitely not ready to have a kid. I don't even know what she looks like. I wonder if she has other kids, maybe even grandkids. The second wife, a short-lived mistake. The third, a tragedy that I try to avoid thinking about. And now this. How will my fourth marriage end? Does it even matter? As years pass, disasters all start to blend together.

What Sabrina says next shakes me. "Akira left you something."

"What?"

"It was in her will," Sabrina says. "I can show it to you, but you can't keep it here."

"How old was the will?" I ask.

"Doesn't matter," Sabrina says.

"When did she write it?"

Sabrina sighs. "A week ago."

I look at Sabrina. "Around when she reached out to me. Do people know about the will?"

Sabrina shakes her head. "Not yet. But you know it'll break." Sabrina pulls a small velvet pouch from her bag. She slides it across the table.

I pick it up, afraid to open it. "Don't worry," Sabrina says. "We scanned it for anything hazardous."

I stick my hand in the sack and pull out the item. A giant gem. The same one I handed back to her all those years ago.

"It's worth a fortune," Sabrina says.

I inspect it closely. It really is beautiful, even though I can't see its real color. The sort of family artifact that should be passed down to someone's children. I think of the newborn in Akira's tomb, who I now understand Akira killed. I wonder how she did it. Her own child? I know why she led me to that dive shop. But why only tell me now?

Ascalon is not only the name of the savior
It's the name of the daughter
The one I gave up
Find her for me and tell her that I'm sorry

The song replays itself in my head. I put the gem back in the pouch and hand it over to Sabrina. My days of playing pulse racket with her are over. Game, set, match. She wins. "It's yours," I say. "Yours and Ascalon's. I'm sorry, Sabrina. I really am. You can let me rot here. But I'm not giving you access to my iE data."

Sabrina stands. It's only been a few days, but somehow, I forgot how tall she was. Athletic. The kind of woman whose features should be digitized in some action/adventure holo game. It's funny—most people I know who've remarried several times tend to stick to the same type. My wife and ex-wives have all been so different from one another. An impulsive space waitress into some anti-grav kink. A meticulously vain woman whose literal occupation and identity were based on her good looks, destined to be lost with age even with the help of the best, most expensive tech. She's probably pretty unhappy right now, her holo-influencer status having faded away. A fiery badass whose judgment I trusted entirely, even when it came to our son. I wondered if I had been as bad a father as usual to John. Distant, impatient.

And now there's Sabrina, her every move perfectly calcu-lated. When she was a pulse racket champ, she was known as a counterpuncher. Error-free, high-octane swings that frustrated her opponents into mistakes.

"I'm sure whatever you did in the past will be forgiven," Sabrina says. "It was permitted by the president's executive order, which gave you the authority to do whatever you had to. And I know you didn't kill Jerry. Or the chief and corporal."

"Thanks," I say.

Sabrina thinks for a moment. She closes her eyes and puts the pouch back in her bag. "Mind if I cash this in?" she says. "Daycare's expensive, and there's the matter of our blown-up front door and roof."

I nod. "It's yours. Do whatever you want with it."

"By the way, your bail's been set," she says.

"I can only imagine."

"Take what you're imagining, then double it."

"Don't let Akeem try to get me out," I say. "Or any of my other friends. I know I'm not in the position to ask you for anything, but if you could honor this as a last request."

She nods, then exits interrogation. Good. She doesn't need this anymore. It's a crap job for crap pay. That gem might not be quite enough to make Sabrina and Ascalon part of The Money, but it should bring them pretty damn close. I'll be glad never to see it again. It's just a reminder of what I've done. I know now that the chief was probably right, for once in his prematurely ended life—I try not to think about the years of happy bureaucracy he won't get now. Like he said, Akira being alive was the only thing that kept me safe all these years, kept me untouchable. The executive order won't hold up—if I give them access to my iE, I'll go down for the tour guide and the others. Akira's legacy will be questioned. Worse, I could put Sabrina and Ascalon in danger. Whoever it was that rubbed out the chief doesn't want this looked into and doesn't believe I will betray a dead woman. Their goal is probably for me to be locked away safely on this puke vessel for the rest of my days.

I think about the mourners throughout the world, rushing to the nearest coast to float their holo lanterns in tribute. I imagine the water slurping up the dim light of their collective sorrow. I picture myself standing there with them, floating my own lantern. I look behind me, and there are children building sandcastles on the beach. I see my Ascalon back there building with another toddler I can't make out.

Two children.

Shocked, I stand, but the cuffs pull me back down. I feel like I've dislocated both my wrists. The big guard appears, uncuffs me from the table, stands me up, and re-cuffs my hands together behind my back. "We're moving you to holding," he says.

But I'm not listening as he leads me down a hallway that bends in an arc.

The one I gave up

Saying "the one" means there is another.

I remember the voice I heard when I was leaving Jerry's. And again in the paper-walled house in the cavern. Then . . . right before the ball exploded.

She killed me. But I am still here.

The words stop me in my tracks. The guard tugs at me. "You're not gonna give me a hard time, are you?" he asks.

The child whose remains I found in Akira's Tomb isn't the one I'm supposed to say sorry to. I'm supposed to find the one who made the scribblings on the wall of that Japanese house. The one who played with those re-created toys. She must be about sixty now, the daughter Akira managed to hide from the world. I was sure now that it was her laugh, not Akira's, that had come from the bedroom.

Two coffins. One filled with a baby's bones, the other adult-sized, empty. Akira didn't want me to put *her* in there. She wanted me to find her other daughter, Ascalon Lee, and bury her next to her sister. But why?

"Move!" the guard says, shoving the small of my back.

I stumble forward. He uncuffs me and puts me in my cell. "You actually knew her?" he asks.

And it's the first time I look at him. He's young, maybe thirty, the wife and kid type. He's got some major years ahead of him. But . . . years of what? We live longer now. We age a little better. But what do we do with that extra time? Me, on my fourth marriage, I've just put my thirties and forties on repeat. Jerry worked on an art piece with no end. Akira, who used to hibernate so she could work twenty-hour days, started to hibernate herself for so long she could stay the same age she was when she saved the world, without doing much with or for what she had saved. None of us were any smarter. We were just like my old neighbor Fred, fishing out there in the float burbs with all the wrong gear. "Yeah, I knew her," I say.

"What was she like?"

I think of Jerry and say, "She was a bitch."

He's taken aback. He stands in front of the cell for a moment, not knowing how to respond, then continues down the arced hallway. He'll probably spend the rest of his shift, the rest of his working life, walking that spiral deeper and deeper into the ocean.

Saying "the one" means there is another.

Akira Kimura had two daughters. Twins. I see that now in black and white.

15

For obvious reasons, as Earth rotated, no single telescope could watch Sessho-seki at all times. There were other super-telescopes spread around the world. Arizona, China, South Africa, Chile, Spain. Not to mention the ones in space, ion-drive probes with cryogen-refrigerated sensors. The problem with telescopes is that they need light to see. And Sessho-seki, a spectral-class rock to begin with, was sneaking through the spaces between galaxies, evading vapor, stardust, and light. It was coming at us from so far that infrared couldn't spot it at first. The only way Akira saw it was by building a telescope so sharp that it could pick up the bend of space-time. There was something out there bending it. Something enormous that she couldn't see. But after studying its giant space-time footprints, she knew it was heading to us. It was massive. And fast. This meant it couldn't be nudged off course. And in just a few years, it would hit us with the energy of all the nuclear weapons we ever had times a million. The one that took out the dinosaurs killed seventy-five percent of life on Earth. This one would hit so hard that it would permanently tilt the planet's upright spin. It would kill everything. And we couldn't even see it.

These circumstances meant Sessho-seki was the greatest horror story there ever was. It caused chills, screams, and heart attacks in the first months after its existence was announced. Questions and theories regarding this monster impact event abounded. What was the asteroid made of? Was it a chunk from another planet, a rogue planet itself, or a celestial body that through gravity had become bigger and bigger through the eons by attracting more space junk? How was it moving so quickly? It must have orbited *something* at some point. Had something else knocked it out of its orbit with enough force to rip it from the gravitational pull of its solar system and send it our way ever since? Some started questioning the very existence of gravity.

Thought camps began to form. Consciousness nuts. Multiverse kooks. Religious zealots. Alien invasion conspiracy theorists. Gravity haters. Dozens of them. And no matter what camp, all it took was a fifteen-minute holo to sell a kid on a camp for fucking life. After watching a random fifteen-minute spiel on something they knew nothing about, performed by someone who barely knew more than they did, the kid would defend that camp's theory to the death.

The reason it only takes fifteen minutes of pizazz to convert people into true believers is that somewhere deep inside, they want to believe. Even though I didn't know it at the time and judged the hell out of those crackpots, I had always been the same way. In my own personal midnight zone, I was waiting to be told I saw things more clearly than everyone else even though I was colorblind. *Because* I was colorblind. And the day my dad brought home that chunk of ambergris, the first time I saw green, there was the confirmation I'd been seeking. Look long enough for something, and you'll find it, whether it actually exists or not. And once you find it, you'll feel less scared.

But Akira didn't think about things like this while she was building Ascalon. She didn't care about the crackpots or humanity's mental condition. The only dissenters who pissed her off were the ones with just as much science cred as she had who were saying one of two things: that Sessho-seki would not hit. Or worse, that Sessho-seki did not exist. She refused to debate either point. Time was too short, she'd always say. Instead, she responded with this simple notion: Let's say they're right and it won't hit. Or that they're right and it doesn't exist. Fine. So we do nothing?

Most shut their mouths after that. They would bite their tongues and leave her to her work. Begrudgingly support it. It was worth the time, money, and effort, just in case. At the very least, we were learning more about what was out there, they'd say.

Most. But several didn't.

Several appeared on any media program that would have them and denounce her. They would yank at the ear of those with power and whisper or scream that Akira Kimura was wrong.

And that was when she responded with me. Akira had left something in the desk that I kept at the telescope. It was a device, a small, handheld thing that looked like a taser. She left a paper note saying it would shock any iE into sleep mode. Under that, a scribbled list of names. The dissenters. I turned off my own iE and took the list to Akira, checking to make sure no one else was in the room. "Why?" I asked.

Her eye was looking through the telescope. "They could defund this project."

"Could?"

"They're dangerous," she said.

"What if they're harmless?"

Akira stepped to me and put her hand on my shoulder. "You are simply removing threats," she said. "Something you've no doubt done in your military career. And you're protecting this project. Indirectly saving all of us."

I nodded. She put her eye back on her telescope. "Did you know that two observers can watch the same photon at the same time and disagree on how it behaves?" she asked.

I squeezed the crumpled list in my hand. "No," I said.

"The interesting thing is that both can be right."

I thought for a second, then opened the list and added a name. After one last look, I burned it, took the device out of the drawer, and left.

It wasn't until years later that Idris Eshana told me that he'd made the device for her. He winked and said he was in the loop. He was proud of it, even though it was a secret. I guess those of us closest to Akira were proud to orbit around her. Micro moons making their own contributions to her noble mission.

The first scientist I silenced was a celebrity of sorts. An advocate of science education for decades, he was a persistently happy man with a quick wit and an impressive mustache, who appeared on all kinds of programs—vids, pods, and late-night roundtables. He liked to wear neckties printed with something from space—planets, pulsars, or swirls of galaxies. He would never directly attack Akira on vid. Instead, he'd talk about the fact that we have identified well over twenty-thousand asteroids out there whose orbits passed in the vicinity of Earth. That we had an arsenal of telescopes, gamma, infrared, X-ray, radio, and ultraviolet that could detect just about everything heading toward us, and years ago, we already identified 99.8957 percent of the big ones, the ones as large or larger than the dinosaur-killer, these the easiest to spot by far for obvious reasons. The man spoke with grandfatherly common sense. When I left him in his tentacle-lighted Emerald City suite, I think it was the pulsar tie that dangled from the doorknob, his two hundred pounds slumped on the other end of the taut fabric. His iE lay next to him like a toy that had rolled out of his hand. I took the black ops military shuttle back home, staring at the hair of some unidentifiable creature stuck to the seat in front of me the entire way. No record of my round trip.

The second and third scientists were a married Chinese couple. One would think they'd be the most difficult to get to, but the 610 Office in China practically escorted me to them. China's president, a sturdy-looking man who seemed to almost take pride in his premature balding, as if it were a symptom of his tireless leadership, had minored in astronomy in college and was arguably Akira's strongest supporter. Nothing brought him more joy than sort of understanding what Akira was saying when she explained Ascalon to him. With this couple, I staged an at-home murder-suicide. Plausible that one would turn off both their iE's before such an act. After it was done, the 610 Office insisted they give me a ride back home. I watched the feed on my way back to the island. The Xinhua Media and PR Agency tucked the report of their deaths beyond the fifteen-minute mark of their evening broadcast.

With each of these three, the moment after I was done, I waited for confirmation that what they had planned would cost lives. I waited for green. And the green wafts would rise and curl, and I would breathe them in through my nose. They were going to cause all of our deaths if I didn't stop them. I would force my heart to fill with hate as I looked at their still faces. I would stare until the perfume became choking. I was certain I was doing the right thing.

But still, I walked around paranoid during those days. I felt like all eyes were on me, like I was constantly being judged. The worst was when I walked in public spaces. People watching public tourneys of virtual dragon mount duels would pause and eye me as I passed. Others were on their way home after work, their tired eyes wandering in my direction under the float lights. Even the rare dog, the descendants of the handful that survived the 2030-something dog plague, would sniff at me and whimper. Who were these people and these dogs who had the fucking nerve to judge me? They probably knew even less about astrophysics than I did. Bellmen, salespeople, and desk jockeys who hadn't done a hard thing their entire lives, which was why they existed in the permanent middle, where nothing they did garnered notice. In space terms, they were meaningless trojans, tiny planets and moons that stayed in their predestined orbits.

And then there were the radicals. Fuck the radicals. Try talking to one. I could guarantee you that you'd be interrupted within five seconds by rants on why they were right and you were wrong. If you stated an opinion, a defensive, contrarian outburst would be volleyed back in less than .05 ticks. Watching radicals talk was like watching a pair of starving dogs fight over an imaginary bone. Fuck what they think. Besides, these were the types who killed Kathy and

John. A part of me still hoped Sessho-seki would hit just to wipe them out.

All of them, normal or radical, I could feel them judging. But after every contentious scientist I silenced, I smelled ambergris and saw green. It never once occurred to me that this stain had been left by me. That I had become the radical.

By the time I paid a visit to the next one, it was easy. An asteroid hunter in Spain who believed in Sessho-seki's existence, but unlike Akira, believed it could be nudged off its trajectory. She advocated the Keyhole Theory—that when it got close, we could disrupt its course slightly, so that it would just sling by Earth. It would maintain its universal orbit and return again in a few years, pulled dangerously close by Earth's gravity, but this would buy us more time to perfect the Ascalon Project or maybe even come up with a better savior plan. I tased her iE and nudged her off a cloudscraper. I leaned over the edge and watched as she fell. Green ribbons fluttered like suspension lines cut from a parachute.

I was so single-mindedly focused on this target that it barely entered my mind that my first wife and kid lived in Portugal, one country over. I had the sway to easily locate them, and I could see how my eldest child, a teenager by now, was doing. I wondered if my ex ended up cheating on her second husband, too, with some rich space tourist on one of her shuttle runs. Maybe she was on her third or fourth marriage too. My mind went to judgment and insults, so I jumped back on the military shuttle, its itinerary wiped permanently from the system. I calmed down and told myself it was selfish and impolite to pop in on these two. The world was ending, and the last thing they needed was another complication. Plus, I was the last person in the world who should be anywhere near an innocent kid. Looking back now, I think I was ashamed.

I never reached out. It was easy to stop thinking about them, because my last target would take some planning. This was the one I'd added to Akira's list myself. I was the only one who knew what I was about to do, and I'd get no support, no ghost transport, no 610 Office, no access. The ones before this were easy to get away with. Akira signed off on them, and the world was so busy looking upward in dread that they almost never stopped to see what was going on around them. But this next one was tough. And I promised myself it would be my last.

She was the worst of the bunch. Broadcasting her doubt every chance she got, going over her math in public again and again until eyes glazed over. But some people understood her math and started agreeing with her. I needed to stop this before it threatened Akira. I needed to silence Dr. Karlin Brum, Chief of Staff Chang's scientist. She had the president's and the cabinet's ear, for Christ's sake. I was shocked her name wasn't at the top of the list.

But she was hard to get to because she was always with Chang, a big, tall man with supposedly bad knees who seemed to wince whenever he sat or stood. She was constantly piloting him by the arm into or out of one chair or another. People speculated that they were an item, but whatever was between them, they kept private. I had to somehow get to her without touching a hair on Chang. He was the president's chief of staff so if I got caught, I was done. And if I was connected to this in any way, people would accuse Akira of being behind it.

Brum was in permanent attack mode. She began simplifying

her message, maybe under the direction of Chief Chang. He knew politics, and that the key to swaying minds was keeping it simple. In the weeks after my trip to Spain, Brum opened every interview with these words: *Akira Kimura is dead wrong.* She said Akira was operating in the realm of theory, and therefore had zero proof that Sessho-seki was coming or even existed. When interviewers would hold in their scoffs and ask how it was possible that a person could fool the entire world, including thousands who wielded expertise in the same field she did, Brum stopped answering with math and started answering with this: The Greeks still believed in Zeus during the age of Aristotle. Catholics still believed that Earth was the center of the universe during the age of Galileo. That during the twenty-first century, there were still people who believed Earth was flat five hundred years after Magellan sailed around it. Fooling the world, Brum would say, has always been possible, because people think they're smarter than they really are. A confidence that, ironically, stems from their fear of seeming stupid.

And if an interviewer asked Brum about the Ascalon Project, she'd basically flip out. Recreating the energy of a supernova and concentrating its power into a beam? Not only was it insane, it was impossible. She was an ear-piercing boom of relentless doubt. At one point, the president wanted to fire his chief of staff just for Akira's sake. But she actually demanded that he didn't. She told him that skepticism was a healthy, vital part of science, and that if Chang were fired, some might speculate that Dr. Brum's claims had credibility. The act of firing or the demand of resignation would validate this crazy woman who was making a spectacle of herself.

But I couldn't stand watching her. It filled me with rage,

even though I didn't understand the science. There was something so plastic about her. She had the look of a natural-born model who meticulously mutilated her symmetrical good looks with ill-fitted clothes over her always matte-black generic foam fit, bad makeup, and a hairstyle that made one wonder whether she actually woke up every morning, walked to the nearest mirror, and tried to pull all her hair out. It was like she was uglying herself to gain credibility. She was manipulative. She was dangerous.

But now I think maybe I had it wrong. Maybe she dressed that way because it didn't matter to her. Maybe she was so frustrated that people weren't listening to her that she actually woke up in the morning and tried to pull all her hair out. Maybe she was genuine, even if she was wrong. What if I was the one guilty of mutilating myself, not Brum? Deforming myself so badly that there was no coming back, all to prove my worth to Akira?

But I didn't see things like that back then. All I knew was that when it came to silencing Dr. Brum, there was no off-the-record black ops round trip to Washington. She hung on the arm of arguably the third most powerful man in the world. I had to wait until she came to the island herself. I needed to study the chief's Secret Service team and its procedures before then. So when word came that they would be paying Akira a visit in three-and-a-half weeks, I used that time to plan. I used my executive order privileges to learn everything about those two, which was standard security procedure for anyone coming to the island by now anyway. And going through Brum's file, I noticed something very interesting. Despite her perfect grades in high school, she hadn't been named valedictorian. Despite her standardized test scores, which were off the charts, she couldn't pass a simple test required for graduation. In fact, the elite institution almost didn't allow her to graduate. Why?

Karlin Brum didn't know how to swim.

And so, when Akira and I picked up Chief of Staff Chang and Dr. Brum in my SEAL from the shuttleport that night, with the Secret Service team in another SEAL following, I took the normal path over the ocean. That was when the malfunction occurred. The ratchets spun and hit the pawl. The vehicle twisted out of control. I fought with everything I had, really putting on a show for the three iEs hovering in the cabin above us. But the flat spin was too much for any pilot. *Physics*, I imagined Akira saying with a smile. The chief and Dr. Brum were screaming in the back. Even our iEs jostled in the cabin, looking like they were in a panic. "Eject! Eject!" I yelled.

"No!" Brum shrieked, looking out the window down at the black water.

"Don't worry, darling!" Chang said. "I'll get you!"

I looked over at Akira. She was calm, with a hint of a smile on her face.

"Don't touch anything!" I said. "The 'chutes will self-deploy! And remember, light your flares!"

"No!" Brum shrieked again.

I pressed eject. The strongest wind I'd ever felt swept off the canopy. Then the four of us popped out of the SEAL like corks. All four of us sent in different directions so we wouldn't hit each other. Four 'chutes blossomed at the same time.

When I hit the water, I lit a flare. Three other flares lit the sky. Everyone was alive. The team of Secret Service in the SEAL behind us went for Akira first. Of course they would. That, I found out during my research, was part of their mandated protocol. In the event of an emergency, keep Akira Kimura safe at all costs.

I went for Dr. Brum, hoping I wouldn't have to finish the job. After fighting through at least a quarter mile of chop and bent, corrugated tubed remains of the SEAL, heading in the direction of Brum's light, I was surprised to see that Chief Chang, bad knees and all, had beaten me to her. He was sobbing. A giant swell lifted and separated us. It began to rain. I fought toward the chief and Brum again. He was still holding her. It looked, oddly, like he was hugging a deflated floatation device. I lit another flare. "Help will be here soon!" I said.

"Get away from us!" he screamed.

I looked up, waiting to see the if the Secret Service SEAL was heading our way through all that flare light. At first, the light was colorless to me. Then it burst into a blinding green and red. I squinted and looked away. I spotted saw another green light treading to the shore. It left a trail that looked like an endless green snake, its head rested on shore and its tail slithered all the way to the invisible horizon. I'd never seen green that strong before.

I treaded and waited and watched the green light reflecting off the black water. The tides began moving the light's tail. It began to shrink and drift toward us. It moved naturally in the water. By the time the green reached us, I could see that the tail had split. One side drifted to the screaming chief and the motionless Brum. The other wafted to me. I looked at the chief and swear that for a moment, he saw it, too. He knew what I had done. That moment before the Secret Service SEAL broke the tail with its blinding hover lights, while

Brum's brain shut down from lack of oxygen, the chief saw his own greens and reds stitched together, leading back to me.

When we got back, more interrogations. I played the accident on my iE for the Secret Service. My SEAL was deemed irreparable. It had been ripped to pieces on impact, junk spread out three hundred atmospheres under the sea.

Two hours later, I was cleared of any wrongdoing and given another SEAL, top of the line. I'd executed my plan perfectly. Chang lost his shit. He lost his power, his job, and the hopes of getting one ever again. He went on every outlet that would have him, none credible, and screamed that Karlin Brum was murdered. That she was killed to cover up the fact that Sessho-seki was a lie. He embarrassed himself so completely that Congress passed a bill that changed the title of Chief of Staff to White House Director. The funny thing was that in all his public rantings, he never once mentioned my name. Akira Kimura killed Karlin Brum, he'd say. And the public would collectively laugh and say, yes, all ninety pounds of Akira Kimura sabotaged a military-grade transport and risked her own life to off a dissenter who hardly anyone was buying at the time anyway. The actual funny thing to me was that even though people completely dismissed that scenario, they had zero problems believing this same ninety-pound woman was going to smash a state-sized rock that was heading our way.

And now I know that during those years of Sessho-seki and Ascalon, there may have been a girl around twenty years old watching all this craziness. Maybe she was in college, maybe not. Maybe she was working the abyss mines, helping to plug our underwater cities into the earth's core. Or maybe she was a black-market bullet runner, servicing all the crazies stockpiling primitive ammo as preparation for the end of the world, thinking their bunkers could protect them from what was coming. No, she would probably have been more than that. She would've been the only one in the world not looking up. If she knew who she was, she would have been watching her mother. And if she were nearly as clever as Akira Kimura, she would've known what me and her mother had conspired to do.

I'm falling asleep on my first day in the holding cell on Vomit Island. I'm still at the shallow end of the prison, not yet convicted. My floor is filled with smugglers, flower poachers, polluters, and iE hackers awaiting trial. It's a rough morning, and the moors strain to hold the structure in one spot. I can imagine what it's like for the prisoners on the bottom. Even from up here, my ears are filled with the sound of creaking moors. That sound is soon overtaken by the retching of prisoners. I finally drift into sleep.

But then I start dreaming, and like most of my dreams, this one's not giving me the relief I seek. I'm at Jerry's cloudscraper, and I can smell and hear the color scheme of her furniture, vibrant greens and reds. This is the first time I remember seeing these colors in a dream. I look around. Her sculpture is only one image: Ascalon the ray, sitting in a deep-space satellite, about to fire into the dark places between stars.

I turn and notice where I'm standing. I'm in front of that painting hung in the alcove, the one with children playing around a giant banyan tree. It's the only thing in the room that isn't green or red. Two children have managed to climb the tree: the boy hugging a branch and looking down at the children beneath him, and a girl, casually sitting on a branch and looking down too.

Another girl with blond hair in a white sweater is looking up at the two, emitting jealousy, while two girls on the ground smile for the artist, oblivious to the kids above them. The last girl is in the sweater that I know is red, even if I can't see it.

I smell perfume and look to the side. Akira is standing next to me. I turn to the other side, and there is another identical Akira, pointing at the picture. Right at the girl in the red sweater. Music in the background begins to play. Ascalon's song.

The one I gave up

I look at the last child, who is standing on the left side of the tree, facing away from the painting's viewer. She's gripping one of the thinner sinews of the banyan with her left hand. She seems to be looking at something else entirely. Gray-brown smudges . . . A river, maybe? But with all the grass under the foot of the children and the tree, I can't really tell. All I know is that even if I can't see her face, she has no interest in being a subject of the artist. Her right foot is slightly raised, like she's tempted to step either around to the other side of the tree or into the river.

That's when I see them. Wafts of green and red curl from both Akiras' eyes and drift to the painting. First, the green slowly colors in the grass. Then the dark patch becomes clearer to me. It isn't a river. It's a pond. A darker swamp-green, murky with unknown.

Then the red starts filling the painting. There is only one red object in the whole thing. The girl's sweater. Dot by dot, it becomes redder and redder. A real, aria red. Then the girl ages in front of my eyes. She grows taller. Her hips begin to flare slightly. Her chestnut hair darkens into a brown that is close to black. She is no longer a child like the rest of the people in the painting. She is a young woman, still refusing to look at the artist. Still far away from the rest of her classmates. I see her take a step. Then another. She strips off her jeans and her red sweater and dives into the pond. After the splash, the pond's surface settles into a taffy twist of green and red. The girl does not come up for air. She is gone forever.

I already know who she is. I feel it in my old, creaking bones. *Everything is binary*, as Akira used to say. Even Ascalon the Savior was part-satellite, part-neutrino stream, which scarred the sky forever. I look around. Both Akiras are gone. I look back at the painting. The daughter who survived.

They were twins, orbiting each other like in most star systems. After they were born, Akira killed one and hid the other, who was in her twenties when the world-saving cosmic ray was named after her instead of the other way around. She would be in the shallow end of her sixties now. But all those years ago, she was just the girl in the red sweater in Jerry's painting with her back turned to the artist. Could she have been under the charge of Jerry Caldwell? It would explain so much about her falling out with Akira. Ascalon may not even have known her parentage. But something tells me she knows now.

And that's when I wake up. My toes are clenched in an arthritic curl. The rough waves have passed, and the only sound is the opening of cell doors for chow time. How could I have missed it all these years? There was that gap in her young life while she pursued her many PhDs. Everyone, including myself, assumed she'd just studied twenty hours a day, every day, for years. Such a ludicrous thought. Someone who functioned like a machine with no social interaction, no personal curiosity. No one was like that.

How could she have killed her own daughter?

Even now, I'm reluctant to dig up the darkest parts of her life. We all wanted to bask in her light.

I stand up and wash my hands. The water is as cold as the walls in this place. I splash some on my face to wake up. I think about all the enemies I've made within the department alone over the years, like the late chief. I'm guessing there are way more in the cafeteria, waiting for me with cereal-spoon shanks and dental-floss garrotes. But at least Sabrina and Ascalon are safe.

I splash more water on my face when I notice my hands are turning green. I try to scrub it off, but the friction darkens my palms. I inspect the water shooting from the spout. It runs clear. Green water drips down my wrists. Images form on each palm: an adult-sized hangman on my left, and a child-sized one on my right. Seven dashes under each. I rub my hands together again, and when they come apart, the dashes are filled with letters and each illustration with a full corpse.

Sabrina. Ascalon.

I need to get off Vomit Island. I yell for a guard. Instead comes a prison drone. I hold out my hands. The drone's eye pans down. It's a machine, but I can almost hear it breathe an exasperated sigh before it flies off. I look down at my hands.

There's nothing there.

16

During lunch in the cafeteria, prisoners dressed in old, broken orange foam fits attack their food since the sea is calm for now, and they know that, for at least part of the afternoon, they'll be able to hold down their chow. I find that I'm hungry, too, but I'm worried and can't eat. The half-life of my space-grade anti-anxiety and sleep pills has passed, and I'm wondering if I'm experiencing hallucinations as a result. What I saw just now is impossible. I know Vomit Island isn't the most secure on the inside, but breaching the plumbing with some kind of magic ink? Only Akira could come up with a trick like that, but she's dead. Maybe I saw it because I'm surrounded by murderers. Like the small man about my age that I'm sitting next to, the white roots of his hair coming up against the dyed black strands. Not salt and pepper, exactly, just the real color beneath cracking tar. His eyes match his hair, cloudy lenses spreading over his dark pupils. He is jarred by the crackle of incoming feed.

I follow his eyes to the vid being projected so strongly on the wall that it renders the graffiti underneath it invisible. It's prison, so we only get 2D. It's a recap of Akira's funeral.

The procession. The six pallbearers, each an old person of notable importance, guiding the floating, closed coffin down Santa Monica Boulevard. Row upon row of people in formal dress, some with synthetically feathered hats, others wearing kimonos in her honor, heads down, almost bowing. Everyone polished in this rich, rich world. The prisoners mindlessly watch. The cafeteria looks like an emergency room after a three-day holiday, packed with the idiots who overindulged past a reasonable, healthy point.

Onscreen, the talking heads explain that Akira will be pushed coast-to-coast across each continent like the Olympic torch. California to New York. Paris to New Alexandria. The casket will be decorated in full splendor from India to Southeast Asia. And finally, a boat to her home country of Japan, where she will spend thirty days before being shipped to the island. She was a world treasure after all, the one who saved it. Every human on Earth should be given the opportunity to thank her before she arrives at her final resting place. This journey around the world will take months and end at the island, at The Savior's Eye, where she will be laid to rest at the feet of a giant statue of her now under construction.

But then begin the tears and the audible sobbing arising from this pomp and circumstance. This turns into full-blown mourners' wails. It makes me think of what Akira once told me: everything acts differently when it's being observed. On a primitive level, we have always known this. The zoologist who needs to observe animals from afar to prevent altering behavior. The botanist who discovered that plants act differently under our gaze. Even subatomic particles will change trajectory under the watch of the human eye. Some amateur scientists were even scared to look at Sessho-seki, thinking that we could change it for the worse if we kept looking at it. Its energy could grow. Its mass. Its velocity. Some blamed Akira for looking at it in the first place. Like she was the one who caused it to head toward Earth.

Me, I'm just watching a funeral where people are putting on a show for the cameras that they know are there. Some start chanting, "Show us the body! Show us the body!"

Military guards push back the chanters who are rushing the casket.

Commentators chime in. There are reports of groups who doubt how she died, even though it was made clear that she froze in her cryobath. They ask, was she poisoned, murdered by the government, or did she commit suicide? Some cultish groups are claiming that she's not really dead. Others are saying she's crossed over to another reality to save the world again. And must do so over and over into infinity. Others claim that she's just in a state of cryosleep and will rise again one day. A third theory is that she left on a spaceship of her own creation and is flying along the path of Ascalon's Scar. She will follow it to the very end, where she has already discovered an inhabitable planet on which to start a new colony. And both our worlds will be forever linked by the scar streaking millions of light-years through space-time. The scar will serve as a bridge between both our worlds when we are ready to be united.

"Show us the body! Show us the body!"

All this from a group of people who probably can't tell you why a ball rolls or where the seven new stars are on a Milky Way map. By the time the feed announces the construction of a water statue of Akira Kimura, the biggest in the world, that will spout from the tallest mountain in the world, I want to start a prison riot and bust out of here. In fifteen minutes, the vid is over. Now the prisoners, stirred by the chant, are screaming, "Show us the body!" too. I remember that, back in the day, fifteen minutes was the average lifespan of a plastic bag.

The old guy sitting next to me leans over. "A spaceship," he says. "It makes perfect sense." Then he yells, "Show us the body!"

Fuck me, I think. I'm starting to figure out the worst part of being in prison real quick. All anyone really wants is a break from their shitty existence. Whether it's Jerry with her art or Akeem with his family or me working a case and popping astronaut pills, we all seek it, that state of flow. We're all that aviophobe who does sudoku puzzles during shuttle liftoff, pressing stylus to screen so hard we might put a hole through synth glass. All the cons in the cafeteria are evading their own miserable existences right now with their "Show us the body!" chants.

But there ain't no flow in prison unless you can make it. Only violence. The nervous sweat, the high of fear, the bulge of lungs, pupils, and muscles. And I realize a disturbing truth about myself after being on this earth for eighty years: violence is when I'm the most in tune with my flow.

I think about Sabrina and Ascalon and how I'll never get to hold them again, the incisors of prison gum deep in my ankles. The old man stops chanting and turns to me. His eyes begin to swirl with a vivid green. "She killed me," he says. "But I am still here."

I take my thumb and jab it into the old man's eye. The guy on the other side of me grabs my shoulder. I slam my elbow into his face. I turn back to the first guy, but he's gone. No green or red trail, no nothing. After that, I'm in the thick of it. I get blindsided by "fuck the law" tattoo guy. Two more bodies pile on top of me. I'm fighting for my life. Fighting anyone who's on me, anyone who steps in front of me. I was taught a long time ago that when you punch, you're not supposed to try to just hit something, you're supposed to try to punch through it, like Ascalon the Savior did. So I'm at it. Trying to punch right through every face that appears, like I'm in some sick VR game. I'll show every one of these motherfuckers. I punch and howl for Sabrina and Ascalon. I try to punch myself back to sanity.

When the guards finally get to me, I knock the first one out. The second is smarter. He pulls out his taser, and high voltage rips through my body. I'm writhing on the floor, thinking about what happened after Akira saved the world. When it was confirmed that Sessho-seki was split in half by Ascalon and was now two asteroids heading in opposite directions on an x-axis instead of a y, I'm remembering how that very night, the president pinged my iE and revoked the powers that he'd granted me under martial law. Just like that. Like it was on his top ten list of things to do once the world survived. At the time, I was upset. How could my reward for being Akira's sentinel be getting demoted to regular cop again? There was no severance. No "thank you for your service." But then I calmed down, went home, and found I couldn't sleep. The next morning while the rest of the world was still celebrating, I went back to the station and found it empty. So I plugged into the system to see what kind of cases were open. Not much except a collection of suicide feet that needed to be matched with names and faces. I started working on it. This became my flow. My escape from space-time. I barely even noticed the weeks of celebration around me.

The guard who zapped me cuffs me and drags me to my feet. "Listen, you idiot," he says. "We were gonna come get you right after you finished lunch."

I try to respond with thanks, but I can only babble. Right now, my toddler can probably speak more eloquently than me. But the guard senses that whatever nonsense I'm expressing ends with a question mark. "You made bail," he says.

Goddamn Akeem. What a beautiful human being. The two guards pull me along, my feet dragging behind me across the grated floor. Now I know I won't stop. I think of those tiny bones left in the coffin in Akira's tomb. I think of Jerry, who was a good person. Why her? I think back to that painting again. Akira's daughter in the red sweater. I know in my core that Akira wanted me to put that girl in the coffin next to her disfigured sister. I think of Kathy and John. I will never let that happen again. I will protect Sabrina and Ascalon. Something is supercharging in my body. My new mitochondria, high-powered electric.

I remember one last thing Akira told me. There's more dark matter out there than light. Some people believe dark matter is made up of all the dead souls in the history of the universe. That supposed twenty-one grams lost in death, a 250-year-old myth attempting to link science to the mystic. Akira laughed at the notion. Not me, though. I imagined the pound of dark matter I'd put out there and could never take back. Now I'm considering adding to it. The first step that I must take will be the hardest one I've taken in my life.

But it's the only way to see.

17

When I was a kid, my mom took me to this magic show. The performer, just a kid my age, did a bunch of miraculous things with a deck of old-school cards and his seven-fingered hands. He made cards levitate. He changed the five random cards I was holding into a royal flush. It's not so much the specific tricks I remember, but being so thoroughly deceived. I could not, and to this day cannot guess at how this twelve-year-old did these things. It wasn't that cheap magic that was all the rage back then. Not like the wizards pairing smoke and mirrors with money and tech to split rivers, turns staves into snakes, and make pack of locusts appear. "Bible magic shows" was what they called them. This kid, his tricks weren't theater. They were simple. All he needed was a deck of fifty-two and hands so fast that I couldn't see them. On my way out of the show, he called out to me. Told me to check my back pocket. I stuck my hand inside and pulled out an ace of spades. He winked at me and told me to keep it. He cut his deck in half and showed me another ace of spades. Said he had a spare.

There's a magician just like him hoodwinking me now. That, or I'm losing my mind.

As I'm waiting to be processed, looking down at my swollen hands, a guard walks over and hands me my iE. I boot it up and see the first automated message. Conditions of my bail. I'm informed that my SEAL and rail gun have been confiscated. That I now face new charges, which include assault and battery and the arson of private trust property—Akira's tomb. The island leader from Carson City ratted me out on that one, no doubt. I'm also notified that even though my resignation hasn't been officially processed yet, I no longer hold any law enforcement privileges. And finally, that I cannot leave the state under any circumstances. I check "Agree" on my iE, and the guard removes my magnetic cuffs. I'm free to go.

When I step outside, it's pouring rain. My iE tells me a tropical storm is coming, one that might grow into a hurricane. I walk along the gimbal and head for the docks, squinting through all the splash, looking for Akeem. I don't even want to know what the computer set my bail at. I doubt even my old age mitigating the danger or flight risk shrank the financial hit. I definitely owe Akeem the rest of my life for this one.

It's a slow day at the docks because of the weather. Not many heli-taxis out to visit inmates in general, and they definitely don't do it in weather like this. I look up at the spin axis, a two-hundred-foot lighted structure and the only still thing on the prison's rotating gyro frame. I'm half hoping one of the turrets up there will open fire on me. I'm feeling beat down, my hands are killing me, and worse, I'm gonna owe big-time for this. But I forge on. There are important things to do and people to protect, sore hands or no.

When I get close to public docking, I see only one transport and I recognize it immediately, even through the storm. It's Sabrina's hover. I stop for a second, and she steps out. She's wearing sleek black rain gear, and her dark hair whips across her face. A swell comes, and the pitch of Vomit Island almost pushes me forward. I walk to my wife.

We are face-to-face now, and her youth makes me self-conscious about my age. I'm such a sad cliché—an old man who chases women too young for him. Or worse yet, an old man out of farmed organs who will one day need round-the-clock care so that he doesn't accidentally burn the house down or manage to fall and break a titanium hip.

"You were expecting Akeem, I assume?" she practically yells. I can't tell if it's because of the wind or because she thinks I'm deaf. I just nod.

"Disappointed?" she asks.

"No," I say. "Relieved. Did he pay the whole thing?" I ask.

"I did," she says.

And with that, I'm furious. I know how she got the money. "I told you to sell that gem for you and Ascalon!"

She comes at me with the same high volume. "I did. I used it to get my husband out of jail."

The wind howls. The sun is setting. My hands shiver. I glance at the glowing axis again. Sabrina brushes my elbow. "Get inside," she says.

I mop my face with my sleeve, and we both step into the hover. Sabrina, who has always been a good pilot, lifts off easily in the chop. We sit quietly side by side. As we get closer to shore, we glide over the underwater city below. The seascrapers, with their lights, rings, and tubes, look like endless rows of bright plastic toys under all this chop. I look over at Sabrina. In contrast to all the vibrancy below us, she's got the look of a seahorse tugging at a dirty Q-tip. "If it makes you feel any better, Akeem did help," she says.

"How?"

"He gave me ten percent above market value for the gem."

I nod. "That's a real pal."

Sabrina turns to me. "You really thought he was going to save the day?"

"If I asked him to," I say.

"Did you?"

I shake my head.

"Well there you go," she says.

I look at her, and I can see it. All the compromises she thinks she's made. All the other choices she's rejected to be with me. Everything she thinks she's sacrificed; I can see it in that one look. I know that look well. Maybe because it's the same look I'm shooting back at her in this very moment. I've been through this four times now.

It's the look of marriage.

I turn to face forward. "Thank you," I say.

She turns forward as well. "You're welcome," she says.

The lighted float burbs bounce near the horizon. "How's Ascalon?" I ask.

"She's out of control. Just like you."

Sabrina brings us down to the docks, masterfully in the dark and all this bad weather. Without making a single splash, she brings us back home. We get out of the hover and run through the rain to our unit. The docks are clear of people because of the weather, and it's an easy run because the teetering isn't nearly as bad as it was on Vomit Island. The moors in the float burbs hold strong and steady compared to there. I see our place. New 3D-printed dome already grafted and fitted with insta-insurance. A crime scene, sanitized in one day. We clean up too fast nowadays—maybe that's why we forget so easily. The chief and corporal were probably replaced as quickly as the dome.

When we get inside, I notice some of the overpriced furniture is gone, probably damaged from the blast, and I like the place better already. The babysitter, an undyed teen who's just gotten some natural sun, is hopping up and down for Ascalon, who thinks it's hilarious. Ascalon tries to hop, too, but can't manage to get both feet off the floor at the same time. But she doesn't care. And her joy is pure. "Hop!" she says. "Hop, hop, hop!" The babysitter obeys, and bunny hops to the elevator, which is also already fixed. I think this hopping game is something I should've been doing with Ascalon months ago, that and a few other things that bring her pure joy. I never did those things with my other children either. I'm a shit father. The proof is that Ascalon doesn't even notice that I'm home. She screams in delight and follows the babysitter. They go downstairs.

"Who's the sitter?" I ask Sabrina.

"The Esperito kid from three units over," she says. "We've only been their neighbors for three years now."

I nod. "Sorry, I never noticed."

"Yeah, you've always been good at ignoring kids," she says.

I keep my mouth shut. I don't want to fight. Plus, she's probably right. Kids are like harmless aliens I have no interest in understanding. Can't fend for themselves, cry when their basic needs aren't fulfilled. And as they get older, the talking, the boundless energy. As teens, there are the skin dyes, hairstyles, and trick-or-treat fashion, plus those fleeting moments of pure elation or disdain in between chasms of boredom. Trying to pretend they're cool or smart when they're not. Always faking it. But the young ones like Ascalon, they aren't even irritating yet. I should take joy when it comes to her. I should have done that with the ones before. But she's just so nonstop. Once, I watched her for three hours straight, and it zapped me so badly I slept for twelve hours afterward.

I wonder if it's because I was so young when my dad died that I never learned what a father was supposed to be. My own adolescent and teenage years were marked by tons of fights, shotgunning a wedding, going off to war, coming back to nothing, and trying to bed anything in sight as some sort of ridiculous revenge against women. Sure, I had to figure out on my own what a man was supposed to be. But that's a bullshit excuse after this many decades. I've gotta start trying. Gotta put in the work. And when it comes to Sabrina, the woman who just gambled her own and her daughter's financial future on me, I've gotta close the book on this so I can start grinding on something new. Akira Kimura killed one of her daughters and gave up the other. It disgusts me, but the worst part is, I can't even spend more than three hours alone with my own kid. When it comes to parenthood, I'm barely better than Akira.

I start thinking about the explosion, the voice I heard coming from the elevator, and I feel nervous about Ascalon not being within view, so Sabrina and I head downstairs. We go down the hall and step into her bedroom. The babysitter is pretending to look for her. "Hmm, are you in the closet?" the babysitter says slowly. "Are you in the drawer?"

No, Ascalon is standing behind the curtain, trying to stay as quiet as possible. Her tiny feet are sticking out from the bottom of the drapes, and she has no idea we can all see them. Her toes are curled. The whole thing is so fucking cute, it makes me want to cry.

Sabrina steps beside me and holds in a laugh. This little girl who resembles us both fills our hearts in this moment. Sabrina takes my hand. I wince. "Are you okay?" she asks, inspecting it.

"Yeah, I'm just thinking about who planted the bomb. Who was in our home?"

"I checked everything myself. I even scanned through hours of security footage of the entire complex. Whoever it was left no evidence."

I nod. "I'll go see the doc tomorrow," I say.

"Take the hover."

I turn to Sabrina. "Someone's after me."

"Us," she says.

I nod. "And here I thought you were taking your old job back and trying to keep me on Vomit Island."

"After the interrogation, I turned it down," she says.

"Conflict of interest?"

"No," she says. She nods at the tiny figure behind the curtain. The babysitter yanks it back. "There you are!" she says.

Ascalon squeals, then runs out of the room right between us. The babysitter gives chase. "I'm selfish," Sabrina says. "I don't want to spend a day without her."

In this moment, I know that Sabrina was right. I loved Akira Kimura. Not only did I worship her along with most of the world, but I killed for her without hesitation. And much of that is earned. She saved the goddamn world, after all. And I was grateful that she trusted me to be a part of it.

That gratitude blinded me, the man who thought he could see everything.

But the woman who saved the world didn't trust me to make my own choices. And despite my wounded pride, I don't blame her. She might never have finished Ascalon if I'd turned her down, and the stakes were global extinction. But now it's time to set right what I've done. I will find Akira's other daughter and discover who killed Jerry. Maybe this is just Akira playing me like a puppet again, but I'm gonna have a little more faith than that. Because right now, I see for the first time that in more than one way, Akira Kimura ain't half the woman my wife is.

"After I take care of this mess, I'll make sure you can spend every damn day with that kid for as long as you want," I say.

Sabrina smiles. "You already gave me that. And I traded it to get you back."

"I know."

Sabrina turns to me. She grabs both my arms. "Go do the thing you're best at. Put an end to this."

"I'm worried about you two," I say.

Ascalon and the babysitter run past us down the hall. Sabrina and I both turn and watch. "You can't stop this by staying here," Sabrina says. "Nothing will happen to us."

I nod. I want to believe this.

"She wasn't everything you thought she was, huh?" Sabrina asks.

"Akira?"

Sabrina nods.

"How'd you know?"

"We're all human," she says. "Even if we somehow manage convince the entire world we're a god."

Sabrina scoops up Ascalon, and they twirl, Sabrina in her slick black raingear and Ascalon in a quilted pink dress permanently stained at the collar with dozens of clumsy meals. Ascalon is laughing so infectiously that Sabrina follows. The twirling continues. They twirl till they're dizzy, till Sabrina can barely stand. To me, this is art. An iconic moment forever crystallized in my history.

The sitter goes home, and we spend the night watching Ascalon fight sleep like she does almost every night. She hasn't got much hair for an eighteen-month-old, and dressed differently, she might pass as a boy, but those insanely long lashes give her big eyes a feminine quality. She charges to her toy area and brings us back a puzzle, an artifact my mother once saved for me. It's a simple puzzle, one where you fit each letter of the alphabet into its correct spot among twenty-six holes. Each letter is a different color, and Ascalon's bumbling hands are having a tough time with Q. I can't see it, but I know it's green. Sabrina helps Ascalon fit the letter in, and Ascalon picks up her pacifier and rubs her eye with the nub. She's exhausted.

I take the letter Q out of its notch, hold it up, and inspect it. "I'm colorblind," I say.

Sabrina looks surprised. "Let me put her down. Be right back," she says.

She picks up Ascalon and takes her, along with her two pacifiers, her stuffed sloth, and her stuffed bunny, to her crib. I wait, nervous. I've never had this talk with anyone.

Sabrina comes back and sits next to me. We put our iEs on sleep mode, and I tell her everything. About ambergris and greens and reds and Akira Kimura and Ascalon Lee. I even tell her about the voices and the old man in the prison cafeteria, and how I might be going insane.

Sabrina begins to tear up. She tells me I must've felt so alone, seeing and hearing things the way I did. Not telling anyone. Not having someone who understood. I tell her one person did, but I don't want that running my life anymore.

Sabrina leads me to the bedroom. And we end the night the same way we used to, although it's been a while. Sabrina dozes off and says she wonders why we don't end all our evenings like this.

But life never lets you end things the way you want.

18

The next morning, I'm at the doctor's office. The doc is overbooked and running late—I've never met a doctor who wasn't. I spend this time distracting myself with useless information. The table in front of me is round, emitting a soft yellow light that makes patients feel like they're outdoors. My childhood was the tip-tail end of "the age of the magazine," when it was normal for a deck of them to be spread out on a waiting room table. Actual glossy pages, end to end, bound by glue. And when new issues arrived to replace the old, the previous ones would inevitably find their way, like all trash back then, into the ocean.

Now, most waiting room tables are like this one, skirted with twelve tiny half-domes that make the table look like a clock. Each half-dome can project a holographic vid, which one can patch directly into his or her iE. But the selections aren't the same as what people choose out there while they're living. These informational holo vids cover topics ranging from science to interior design to gourmet cooking. At my age, I've racked up so much doc wait room time that it occurs to me that I may have accumulated more useless knowledge in these places than all of my formal education. Makes sense. I select a holo vid on precious gems. A geologist talks about how the diamond was the most valuable stone in the world until we found out there were a quadrillion tons of them under our feet. Seems like a human thing to place great value on something we think is rare, only to find out nothing is.

I'm called up via my iE. I stand, nervous. A part of me wants to walk out on my appointment and forget this whole thing. The procedure itself isn't scary at all. Zero risk, though doctors refuse to call anything that for legal reasons. Fifteen minutes, and I walk out a new man. I don't wanna go in, but once I commit to something, I follow through—it's part of my code, or whatever you want to call it. Even if I'm the only person who knows about that commitment.

I head inside. The hum of chakra bowls fills the hall, and I think about the dream I had where I'm standing in front of the painting with the girl in the red sweater with two Akiras standing next to me. How vivid those reds and greens were, and why it took a dream to see that behind the giant banyan tree was a swamp. Considering my affliction, I've done research on the human eye. I know its parts: iris, pupil, cornea, retina. It has six muscles, which, like all muscles, create tension and torque. There are millions of cone cells floating around in the orbs we see through, and those cones are what show us color. Humans aren't even the best at it. Butterflies, for example, have five times as many cones as we do, and fifteen different types to our three. This means that they can see things we don't. I used to tell myself I was like a butterfly, and that was why I saw more than everybody else. But now I'm thinking that all this time, I was seeing less. I'm more like the bumblebee, which ignores all colors except the ones left by trails of nectar, lighting up like shuttle runways to what will satisfy their single-minded appetites.

The last thing I know about the human eye is that it should've taken millions of years for it to evolve as it has, when we certainly aren't millions of years old as a species. When it comes to sight, we were fast-tracked. Some think it's proof we're more recently descended from aliens. Others just shrug and figure we'll learn why later. I personally wonder if our ability to imagine sped up the process, but that's probably my half-assed logic and a hope that I'm not the only one who's seeing things in this way.

I walk into the procedure room, where I'm greeted by a doctor. He's a happy-looking fella who talks with his hands. They flutter while he explains the procedure. He tells me he's never tried this on someone so old before. When he says it, he gets so excited, he shifts to his tiptoes and lets out an uncomfortable squeal of laughter. I sit in the chair and tell him to strap me in before I change my mind.

Then he gets somber and apologizes. He meant no insult with the comment about me being old. I tell him it's fine. I *am* old. And on the rare occasion that I forget, my body reminds me. My hands are killing me. My ears ring with fluid, bringing the chakra hum down to a gurgle. Maybe I'm sick, or maybe it's just nerves. I don't know. I know I'm thinking about Sabrina and Ascalon—I hope they're okay.

The doc studies my worried face and looks hesitant. He asks, "You sure about this? Why after all these years?"

I think about that. I picture my dad the day he brought home the chunk of ambergris. That first time I saw and smelled green. I think about my mom and those piano lessons. At first I ran through the basics: "Twinkle, Twinkle,

Little Star," "Drops of Jupiter," "Für Elise." It wasn't until I played "Somewhere over the Rainbow" that I saw it. I'd seen hundreds of rainbows by that point, both real and on vid, the top of the spectrum always a muddled yellow and the midpoint only slightly clearer, where yellowish-brown broke to blue. As I played the song, red appeared in my head for the first time. The color shocked my eyes open, and I saw the red notes. They floated up from the keyboard and coiled gracefully around the lid prop to the strings and hammers inside.

I stopped playing and pulled the lid up. The red let me see piano hammers for the first time. All this time playing, and I'd never even known how a piano worked. I wondered what else red would show me. I didn't see it again until the day my dad died. And after that, I never wanted to see it again. Of course, years later, I found myself in the midst of the war and saw it every day. During my time as a rail gun sniper, my affliction helped me. Each target was a cloud of greens, and I could even spot them behind walls. Too easy. We're all murderers in war.

I think about the dozens of cases I've closed. The greens leading me from clue to clue. Terrorists, hitmen, men who regretted their affairs going after innocents, high-profile marks, mistresses, and unwanted children. All solved. Except one.

Akira's.

I'm now seeing my life up till this as a sort of parabola. And Akira cuts through the middle like a laser. An axis of symmetry. There is my life before her, and my life after. Entirely separate. I can finally see that, even if I had to walk backward like my toddler to bump into it. Some would call the second half of my time more impressive than the first.

When I ran with Akira, the most famous person on earth. With Idris Eshana. And was granted absolute power by the president himself. Bringing down Akira's enemies made me a player during the biggest event in human history. Some would say it was a role in saving the world. Even if the dangers were communicating silently, people standing still like trees and warning each other through their roots, otherwise powerless, it all worked out. Though I understand why no one must know.

Akira and her .03 percent. Her philosophy that it's what's to the right of the decimal that counts. I no longer agree. I've realized that .03 percent of a person isn't a person. Thinking in percentages like that might make us smarter, but it also makes us worse. When it comes to human beings, it makes accepted casualties and extermination easier because all we're getting rid of is a number.

I look up at the doctor. "Because there's things I gotta do. And I gotta be able to see to get them done. I need to be normal for once in my life."

"Well, you are," the doctor says. "You just can't see every color."

"I've gotta start seeing like everyone else in order to understand them."

The doctor nods. I don't think he gets it.

In fact, I wonder if anybody gets how much I need this. This thing I've always thought of as a gift has become a liability. An unwrapped plaything that someone out there is having fun with. The doc starts the procedure. I listen to the muddled croon of the chakra bowls and close my eyes.

Fifteen minutes later, I open my eyes. The doc is standing over me, looking satisfied. I sit up and look at him, almost expecting to see something green or red. Maybe green eyes or a red tie. But his snug foam fit is a shimmery yellow and blue, like the scales of a damselfish. When I came in, I didn't even notice that. It occurs to me that I've been looking for green and red so long that I stopped seeing the other colors in front of me.

"Success," he says.

"How do you know?" I ask. "I haven't looked at anything yet."

The doctor pulls a lab-grown guava out of his pocket and tosses it to me. I slap it away. The doctor laughs. "Well, what color is it?" he asks.

I look down at the floor. It rolls to the wall. "It's green," I say.

The doctor nods. He leans down and picks up the piece of fruit. He pulls a pocketknife out and slices it open. "And the inside?" he says.

The fruit juice drips from his hand. "Red," I say.

The doc shrugs. "Like I said, success." He sucks at the inside of the guava. "Want one?" he asks. "It's the latest mutation."

I stare at him. This guy is sucking down a mouthful of music, but I don't see them. I don't see anything rise. I'm waiting for them, but they do not come. In the end, all I see is a doc with bad bedside manner sucking on a piece of fruit that, to me, always had too many seeds.

Before I leave, the doc tells me I should take it easy. It might take some adjusting to my newly repaired eyes. But as much as I'd love to take his advice, I just don't have the time. I've been charged with the murder of one of my dearest friends, which I'm out on bail for. And that won't last forever. So I'm back in Sabrina's hover, heading to Jerry's cloudscraper island. I've gotta figure out who killed her. Who the hell is threatening my family and messing with my mind. And when I find out, I might get charged for murder all over again.

Akira had so much control over me that part of me is scared I *am* the one who killed Jerry. That the threats are figments of my imagination. If I did do it, I deserve to fry for it.

I ping my wife. She answers. "How'd it go?" she asks.

"Swell."

"All this time, and I didn't know."

"No one did," I say.

"She did."

I look down from the hover. What I see is almost blinding. The island. Green. So green. So many different shades. Then there's the lava. Bright red. I blink hard and look again. It's like I'm looking at a giant sea turtle strangled by ribbons of red garrote. "This is pretty jarring," I say.

"I can imagine."

"I'm heading over to Jerry's now."

"You need to be careful. If anyone catches you snooping around the scene of the murder you're accused of."

"Right back to Vomit Island," I say. "I'll be careful. Besides, it's like you said. They're focused on Akira's death right now."

"Watch the chop. The storm moved west, but we're still going to catch some bad weather. The hover can't muscle through turbulence like the SEAL can."

"Noted. How's Ascalon?"

"Well, I turned my back on her for one second this morning, and she scribbled all over the walls. We might just be raising a future anarchist or vandal."

I elevate the hover, and the turbulence shakes me. It's been a while since I piloted one of these. Newer, smaller, nimbler, but lacking the old-school heft of a SEAL—it glides more than charges. I stop myself from yanking on the stick. I cannot push my way through this pocket where hot and cold meet. I drift back down. "A chip off the old block," I say. "Remember, I'm being charged with burning down private estate property too."

"Go get whoever killed her," Sabrina says.

"I will. And hey."

"What?" Sabrina asks.

"I love you," I say.

"Sometimes that's all I want to hear," she says. We let the note hang there for a second. Then her tone changes. "Look under the seat. It's no rail gun, but stay safe."

I reach under the seat. It's a loaded handgun, no charge required. .45-caliber 1911. Steel—heavy, which helps with the recoil. Fifteen in the mag. Red-dot aiming, which I can actually see now. Besides the rail gun, we ain't done much to advance the tech of personal weapons. Outside of military use, we never needed to. And since beat cops converted to nonlethal weapons even before I was born, guns like these have become rare, illegal in the hands of anyone except SWAT and high-ranking police. Making detective and getting a handgun is like earning a medal. That's why this sucker is so shiny. And for short-range self-defense, it can't be improved upon. "You have the other one?" I ask.

"I do," she says. "Sorry, but Ascalon's gone suspiciously quiet. Keep me posted."

Sabrina can take care of herself, maybe better than I can, but I'm still worried. A gun's no match against some of the things I've seen in this investigation. Akira, frozen and carved up. Jerry, viciously strangled. Flying orbs cloaked in invisibility. A massive underground tomb with the body of a newborn inside. And my own chief and his corporal, vaporized by a toy ball. I'm still trying to figure out how that old guy somehow became a conduit to deliver that brief message, the most likely answer being my imagination. I'm nervous. But I'm also happy that I don't feel so alone now. Sabrina. I'm not saying we're completely fixed. But at least we're trying instead of just pressing our fingertips white on the things that irritate us about each other. There's enough we respect in each other for us to fight for this. Maybe we hit a point where we both realized it's not about who's right or wrong, but what we can live with. She put it all on the line to get me out of prison even though I've been an asshole for the last year. My wife is fucking down. And she deserves for me to never forget it.

I look down. I'm crossing the ocean. A bridgeless blue gap between two islands that's deeper than it is wide. A place where I once found myself skimming feet and matching them with their rightful owners. I think about how the dead can sometimes wield stronger voices than the living. Maybe that's why, even now, in the twenty-second century, so many of us still believe in ghosts. The dead are apparitions that both haunt and guide us. And maybe they've earned it. Most times, they can teach us our own history better than any book. I'm sure Jerry left me something, one last message, in that penthouse. It's worth the risk to find out. The towers break through clouds in the distance. I head for her building.

Guest parking is an outdoor ring of landing lilies at the midpoint of the building, so I'm glad the rain has broken. I glance ahead through the briny, overcast air and see a rainbow. I pause to really look at it. I'm eighty, and it's the first time I've seen one in full. Nearly every culture has a myth surrounding rainbows. For the Norse, it was a bridge from Asgard to Earth. For the Greeks, it was a message to humans from the gods. For the Indians, it was the bow belonging to the god of war. For Christians, it's god's promise that he'll never flood the earth again. And for us, it's just an optical illusion caused by light split into its full spectrum as it's refracted by water in the air. For me, a test of colorblindness. I pass the test and wonder whether it will be something different in another two thousand years. I force myself to look at all the colors one last time. Then I press a few buttons for a hood to appear over my head, a mask over my mouth, and a thin trench over my shoulders, and head to Jerry's.

As I take the elevator up, I know I'm taking a huge risk by even being here. I don't know if anyone's still watching Jerry's place. For all I know, the superintendent or the Feds could be up there waiting for me, or worse, some assassin hired by Jerry's father, who last I heard is still hanging in there at 130 years old. Still running his corn syrup empire. His heir apparent, Jerry's older brother, has been hanging in there at senior VP for the last ninety years. Probably the longest wait in human history for the scepter to be passed down. When we live too long, our children have no choice but to become our enemies. This makes me laugh for some reason, and I need it, because if Jerry's father is after me, it's no joke. Corporations are like their own city-states, operating largely outside Federal jurisdiction. And Jerry's dad is the emperor of his corporation. The murder of my own son stirred a rage in me that seethes to this day, so if Caldwell believes I killed his favorite child, I'm in real trouble. I take out the gun Sabrina left me, just in case.

The elevator stops at the top floor. I take a breath and punch in the entry code I've known for decades. The code that Jerry trusted me with. And this feels funny, because it's the first time I've ever come by unannounced. Throughout our entire friendship, I always gave her a heads-up out of respect. I wish I could do that now. I wouldn't blame her father for wanting my head. When I find out who did her in, I'm gonna want their head, too.

The elevator opens, and I step inside. It looks exactly the same as the last time I was here. *Procedure.* When you investigate a murder within The Money, you don't mess their shit up while you look for evidence. You close the case quickly, or The Money will send every exorbitantly priced PI and lawyer in existence to breathe down your neck until you choke on your failure.

I know the other reason nothing has been touched. As far as the chief was concerned, this case was closed. I murdered Jerry Caldwell. Fuck it. I put my gun on the bar and pour myself a drink. My prints are all over the goddamn place anyway. I take a sip and look around. Still black and rose gold, a place of antiquity. It's funny—ever since the operation, I'm consciously trying to soak in the colors I could always see. The ones that were already in front of my face. When did I just stop looking at the things around me? I've gotta re-teach myself if I'm going to solve this. I eye the floor. Its shimmering pink-gold ocean surface that gives one the feeling that they're walking on water.

I take another sip and watch Jerry's sculpture. Ascalon. I remember when Akira shot Ascalon into outer space. How unimpressive it looked packed up. Like a giant shipping container with stupid satellite ears. People got real scared the first time they saw the ray upon completion. It looked like Akira's plan had been to deliver furniture to The Killing Rock. Even I laughed and a part of me thought, *Oh boy, we're fucked.*

But then she explained. A cosmic ray cannot be shot from the earth's surface; it would be severely weakened by atmosphere. Ascalon was taking a six-month journey past Mars, near Saturn, where this giant metal can would unfold into a weapon that would unleash the aimed energy of an exploding star at Sessho-seki. The Killing Rock, she said, had no chance. People listened, but with a skeptical eye at the giant box, which didn't look like it could fly over a puddle, much less to Saturn. *What if doesn't make the trip?* some asked. *What if it misses?* asked others. *What if it's too close to us when it fires and destroys the entire solar system? Can't we test it first?* Honestly, that one popped into my mind more than once. Few doubted Akira until time was too short and they saw what cynics had begun calling The Spam Can and The Mystical Flying Lunch Pail.

Akira lost her patience with this and refused to appear in public. Then people started speculating that she knew she'd failed and was hiding out of humiliation. Others thought the packed ray was shaped like a box because Akira's master plan was to save herself and live in it as a condominium in the far reaches of space. The president did his best to reassure everyone, but no one trusted presidents anymore. The unimpressive man was just another in a long line of entertainers and influencers who had enough name recognition to get elected and were more than willing to tell people what they wanted to hear. Everyone knew politicians got their jobs because no one smart wanted them. Someone like Akira or Jerry should have been president, but the slick got recruited by corporations. So the president was almost impeached.

And it occurred to me then that the people I'd silenced, I'd silenced just in time. If the dissenters had been around when the box was revealed, the entire Ascalon Project could have been ripped apart at the hands of billions who in an earlier lifetime couldn't fathom that a large object hits the ground at the same time as a smaller one. That the earth is round, or that it isn't the center of the universe. They never saw such a telescope in their goddamn lives. And I couldn't blame them too much. Hell, looking at that box, I wasn't too sure myself.

But nobody remembers that version of Ascalon anymore. They remember the image playing in Jerry's sculpture. The bright spear of a saint that slayed a flaming dragon. The one that cut across the sky. The people old enough to remember deny that they ever felt doubt. They claim to have been the level-headed ones who did a little hobby astrophysics studying to confirm Ascalon would work. Others claim they beat some sense into neighbors who didn't have faith. Me, I remember the looting. The marching of soldiers through cities to squash mobs. The resurrection of every kind of church. The mass suicides. I remember watching all this with Akira. By this time, she and Jerry had had their falling out. It was just me and Akira at her telescope, a battalion of soldiers surrounding us. She didn't appear nervous for a single moment.

I step up to Jerry's sculpture, lean down, and turn it off. When I stand back up and look around, I notice for the first time how damn distracting the piece is. Which makes sense, since it's a series of iconic images, which people can't take their eyes off.

Now, with the holo sculpture off, I look around the room at the other works of art. Some I recognize, others I don't. One, I'm pretty sure is an original Monet. A bridge with floating pink and purple lilies beneath it. But it's the grass in the backdrop I'm looking at, seeing it for the first time. Another painting, a Dalí, the one with the melting clocks, has always seemed a little too forcefully symbolic to me. But now that I can see the red clock, it strikes me as more interesting. I remind myself to stop concentrating on the greens and reds. But it's tough. I force myself to look at the pink and purple lilies, too, and the black ants infesting the orange clock and the monster almost seeming to take a nap in the middle of the painting. I look, but these aren't the ones that interest me. The one I want to see is the one I've always looked at first.

The only one I have ever dreamed about. It's the one of the girl in the red sweater.

I have always, always looked at this painting and hunted for green, never knowing why. But looking at it now without that hang-up, I'm just admiring the richness of the colors. The tree, its giant, brown twisted branches giving the impression that I'm not looking at one tree, but a hundred melding together. The children with their dated, dirty clothes. Focused on their brave expressions, I've never noticed that the kids who climbed the tree had to get dirty to get up there. I look at the children smiling in front of the twisted trunk and see a brightness in their skin that suggests the artist enhanced their vanity more than their fake smiles do. I see the girl in white off to the side, indecisive about which group to join. She wants to belong so badly but doesn't know where.

Then the girl in the red sweater. I still can't see her face, but her sweater is such a striking red that I don't see how the paint didn't bleed through the canvas. Why her? Why always her? Maybe it's because I can't see her face.

The next thing I know, I'm doing the unthinkable to what might be a priceless masterpiece. Like gods, these aren't supposed to be touched, just worshipped. But I need to look closer. I need to see what the red sweater feels like, smells like. I smash the locked glass case with my elbow and pause. Good. No alarm. Carefully, I remove the painting from the wall and flip it over, expecting to see a red stain behind it. What I see instead almost makes me drop the canvas.

It is the exact same painting. But from the opposite point of view.

Four of the children, the two in the tree, and the two smiling in front of it, are no longer visible. The giant banyan obscures them. The other girl, the indecisive one, now has her back turned to me. I can see from the dirt on her denim shorts that she, at some point, sat on the ground. This suggests that she got tired of standing there all day and sat down, but the artist asked her to get back up. There she was, forced to look at her classmates all day long, not knowing which group to choose. In fact, once the artist started the painting, she could never choose. She would be rendered alone forever.

I see the pond now. Green, depicted in such detail that I even spot slivers of tadpoles under the water. I also see what looks like a tiny piece of bright candy at its muddy bottom. But these aren't the things I'm supposed to be paying attention to. Clearly what the viewer is supposed to look at from this side is the face of the girl in the red sweater. So I do. I study her closely. The first thing is something anyone would notice, colorblind or not. A deep scar runs down her forehead to her right eye—straight, as if it were carved with a scalpel down the edge of a ruler. The scar leads to an eyeless socket, its lid held open with a small right hand without a pinky finger. The crater is black and endless, and I immediately feel horrified for this child. Who would do this to her? Of course she didn't want to face the artist for the front side. Then why would she do so for the back? I tell myself to not get stuck on the missing eye and step back to look at everything. I rehang the painting with the new side facing out and take another step back.

It's a very recognizable face. Parts of it, I've seen thousands of times. She has Akira's eyes and lips. Her ears are even pinned close to her head, just like Akira's. Her hair isn't black like her mother's, but the brown of the tour guide's. Her skin, a touch darker, and nose, more broad than pointy, are her father's too.

Then I see another thing I missed in front.

The girl is holding a green bird in her left hand. Its drooped neck is clearly twisted. It's dead.

I look away and take a breath. I have no doubt. This is Akira Kimura's daughter. Whether Ascalon is her or the one in the tomb doesn't matter. She's the twin who survived. She must still be alive. I look at the painting again, hoping to see red or green, but I stop myself. No, I'll never be tricked by those colors again. I don't need them. I look back at the girl, who is familiar somehow. Not just because of the features she shares with her mother, or because I see a bit of her father in her even though I've only met him once. No, I've seen this person before. But she's a child, and I rarely deal with children in my work. I've never been around any of my own children at this age—maybe my Ascalon will be the first.

I tell my iE to shine a light on the painting, but it doesn't help to jar my memory. I instruct it to zoom in on the face of the girl and project it on the wall. It's tough to resist fixating on the one eyeless socket, but I try. Still nothing. This definitely isn't a person I've met. If anything, it's a person I've glimpsed. Maybe in a crowd. Walking along a dock, holding her father's hand. At one of Akeem's Friday Night Prawn Bakes? A girl with her family, watching the prawns climb over each other while being boiled by their own moisture. How could I forget a face so distinctive, a face so sad? I stare at the picture and slowly walk my memory backward. I project a holo of my recorded experiences, rewinding everything I have seen from the present back. I watch carefully.

I find I don't need to go that far back.

I tell my iE to layer blue over the girl's face.

When was the last time I actually looked at a teenager? For

years, I've seen them as ignorant life forms with no respect for or memory of the past. Like the red ones hanging out in the float burbs, alternating boredom and mock indifference. They've interested me zero for decades. I'm an old man, for Christ's sake. And I've never really cared about kids.

But maybe it's more than that. Maybe I've never found find them worth looking at because they didn't live through the end of the world. I despised them because they weren't there when we were taught that life should be appreciated. So I clumped them into a group I thought appreciated nothing at all. And maybe I didn't realize that looking at them reminded me of my own dead son.

I look back down at the girl's face, now tinged with blue. I tell my iE to darken the tones even further. To give her pink hair.

I take the painting off the wall. I put my thumb over the scarred forehead and empty socket.

It's him. It's the blue boy I saw in the elevator the day I found Akira's body. The one with pink hair covering the right half of his face. He was getting out of the elevator I stepped into and took 177 atmospheres down. He even had a tail, like the baby in Akira's tomb. I missed it.

He passed me in a color I could see. Why didn't I see green? Because I wasn't looking then. I was preoccupied with the reflection of an old man failing his family. I was too busy looking at myself.

I recall that day: my mood, my exhaustion, not from a bad day, but from what I saw as a bad life. I was about to pander for a job I didn't want but knew I needed. I was being needled by my wife, who resented the closeness I shared with the woman I was about to see, which perhaps made me resent Sabrina even more. I wanted the elevator going down

177 atmospheres to implode from the atmospheric pressure with me in it.

I ignored that teenage boy, as she knew I would. It was the perfect disguise for a woman who'd just killed her own mother. And right at the moment I might have instinctively done a double take, the woman, the weary renter, her skirt malfunctioned. Was that deliberate too?

The lights shut off, leaving only the paused projection. I try to turn, but my hands are stuck to the painting. I try to pull them off what feels like some kind of powerful adhesive, but other parts of me are getting stuck while I fight. I strain until my muscles shake. I can feel my skin tearing. If I've got a phobia, it's this. Not being able to move.

As I struggle, my iE goes to sleep, and soon I'm collapsed onto the painting, my chest and the right side of my face stuck to it. I strain to get up but can't. The only muscle moving now is my heart, which is beating so hard that I can't breathe. Pain creeps from my back up to my neck. The trembling spreads to my jaw and my teeth, even the fake ones. If I could move, I'd rip all of them out.

Then comes a woman's voice, right next to me.

"You have a lovely family."

I tremble slightly. She's here.

I feel warm breath brush my earlobe. "Hello."

I try to turn my head but can't. She runs her hand through my hair. "Did you love her?" she asks.

I don't answer.

A pause. "I was six when she painted that," the voice says. "My first year at boarding school. I remember missing my father, wondering why he sent me away. What I had done wrong. This was, of course, years before you murdered him."

The last sentence makes me shiver. But the presence of the person I've been looking for breathes a second wind into me—I've still got some fight left. But I don't use it to try to peel myself off the painting. I concentrate. I calm down and try to listen.

"Don't worry," she says. "I understand why you did it. Sometimes it's necessary."

"You look lonely there," I say.

"I was. Jerry Caldwell only visited from time to time. They told me she was my 'benefactor.' I didn't talk much during those days. Then came the hospital after I took my eye out. The therapists tried to get me to speak. But what's wrong with not speaking?"

I hear footsteps head behind the bar. I try to imagine her feet. Small, like Akira's? I remember that the girl in the painting is barefoot. She had her father's feet: big, good for swimming. Blades of grass choked between her toes.

The footsteps stop. "This painting was from the first day I met Akira."

"She showed up because of what you did to yourself," I say. The pain in my mouth eases. The straight-line ache from my tailbone to my neck fades into spasms. The talking soothes my body.

"Yes," the voice says. "She was disgusted when she showed up and looked at me. But even worse, she tried to convince me she wasn't, and to prove it, she said she wanted a keepsake. She asked me to pose with five other children in front of the giant banyan tree."

"And you refused," I say.

"I refused to look at her. She gave all of us candy. While the other children ate theirs, I threw mine in the pond. She actually begged. Can you imagine that? The great Akira Kimura, begging? But I wouldn't budge. Then she screamed at me and called me ungrateful. When I still refused, she asked Jerry to paint from the other side of the tree. For some reason, I didn't have a problem with that. I just wouldn't face her."

"You were angry," I say. My eyes are adjusting to the dark.

"I *am* angry."

"Even then, you knew she was your mother, even if she didn't admit it."

"Of course. I knew the first time I saw her. Has that ever happened to you? You take one look at a person and just know who they are? Her sullen insomniac eyes, broad shoulders like a swimmer's, hands and feet so small and different from mine except for the curvature of her nail beds. I asked her if she was my mother. She said no, that she was Aunt Akira. She was a beautiful liar, even back then. But she was ashamed of me."

"Why now?" I ask, the tension in my body easing as I accept oneness with the ground.

"You don't know?" she says. "My mother spent her entire life trying to become a god. Gods don't grow old and decrepit and slip into a state of pleasant dementia. The infirmed cannot be worshipped. Like Jerry said, people will remember Ascalon and forget Akira. I'm here to make sure they remember Akira."

I don't know if I buy that. "She was still sharp," I say. "She was only my age. She had so much time."

A laugh as the blue tail passes in front of my face. "Time for what? The world has been saved, has it not?"

I think about the iE snapshot of that blue teenager. I remove the tat dye, the hair, in order to picture the person standing above me, but can't quite get there. "Not neces-sarily," I say.

"You don't understand," she says. "What she would've become. Every true god needs to be martyred at the end. I'm the force that has ended my mother's reign."

And there it is. She wanted so much to matter in Akira's life that she's spent her own plotting this.

"You're crazy," I say. She's stopped pacing, and I feel her warmth now, still close behind me. "That old guy on Vomit Island. Was that—"

"Did you see how her body slid apart?" she interrupts, whispering. "Wasn't it beautiful? The most iconic thing in history. Jerry Caldwell saw it and didn't understand. She, of all people, should have. She's the artist. But instead of appreciating it, she threatened me."

Jerry's holo art flickers on. At first, it's too bright. I squint and wait for my eyes to adjust. Each of Jerry's images has been replaced with pieces of frozen Akira. Arms separated from shoulders. Calves from knees. Head from neck. Torso from torso. They play on loop until I'm numb. I struggle again to see who I'm talking to. I somehow manage to get to my knees, but it's as high as I can go.

And suddenly, there she is, squatting in front of me in an onryō white kimono. One lidless eye a glimmering yellow. Her face quilted together like stained glass with grafted skin, some patches blue and others a pale tone, the same as her mother's. An arched, reptilian mouth, as if someone grabbed the skin on the back of her head and pulled. Her hair is no longer pink, but a glossy, untamed black. It's all so unfinished, I don't know if she's in the process of turning herself into a normal-looking person or the other way around.

The rest of her looks so young, though. Athletic. Maybe years sleeping in an AMP chamber and out at the gym. She has, in a brilliant way, made herself inconspicuous. She is noticeable, but a person whose appearance causes such discomfort that a stranger would immediately look away, like a carnival freak of old.

"Don't you see?" she says again. "It's our job to protect Akira's legacy."

"And Jerry?" I ask. I look into black pupil of the yellow eye, which is clearly the replacement one from all those years ago.

She sighs, sounding regretful for the first time. "Jerry was a mistake."

"What happened?"

She stands and walks around me. I try to twist to keep her in sight but can't. "I built this security system for Jerry Caldwell. We're in a room full of her priceless art, and she wanted to protect it."

"Is this painting a glue trap?" I ask.

"Bio-engineered suction cups, like you would find on the arms of an octopus or squid, but of course, far smaller and stronger." She circles around me and squats again. She looks so much like her mother, but distorted.

The sharp tip of her tail splits like a lizard's tongue. It slithers toward my face. She watches me steadily with her yellow eye while the points extend and move to my nostrils. I try to pull away, but she plunges the prongs up my nose.

I'm hyperventilating now. Frozen. Prone. The painting suddenly releases its hold on me, and the floor beneath me rises to form a bed. Or maybe a sacrificial altar. Ascalon Lee stands at my bedside. "Akira Kimura wasn't the first great Japanese scientist," she says.

I flail, trying to regain control of my breath.

"For example, Hanaoka Seishū was the first person in history to administer general anesthesia for surgery. He created a substance called tsusensan. That's what's flowing through your veins now."

The name rings a bell. Akira mentioned him once. Seishū used tsusensan on his wife. She went blind.

"I can fix you," she says. "Make you what you were before."

For the first time in my old age, I do not want to feel younger. I do not want to be as fast as I was, or to be able to see and do as I have done before. I try to say something but can't. I just want to survive this, but I doubt that's gonna happen.

She slowly lowers her head toward mine. I'm afraid one of those lidless eyes will come rolling out of her face and plop on mine. She presses her forehead against mine. I feel something seep from the seams in her skin.

"Do you feel sorry for me?" she says.

"Yes," I say. And I mean it.

She drives the points of her tail further up my nasal cavity. I snarl as my eyes begin to tear.

The anesthesia she dosed me with is probably the only thing keeping me alive. I can barely feel anything except vibrating anxiety for when it stops working. "There is hardly the living organism in this world that I haven't dissected," she says. "Taken apart, pieced back together for the better. Your sight, for example. Yes, I've been watching you for years. I know about that."

Despite the anesthesia, the pain under each eye is blinding. "Curious, isn't it? The pain you're experiencing now feels closer to your eyes than your nose. The brain is magnificently complex."

I expect a fog of green to rise before me. It doesn't. "I don't see it," I say. "I don't see green."

"Correct," she says. Her head snaps away from mine. "You don't see it. You *smell* it."

A projection beams from her eye and settles on the ceiling above. It's a nose. *My* nose. The lights dim. The image splits, and the nose is pulled inside out. Now, the ceiling is specked with green and magenta. The image stretches from 2D to 3, and the specks begin to take shape into something galactic looking. I close my eyes and think about the ambergris all those years ago. I smelled it before I saw it. A scent so vivid that to this day, I feel like the perfume is here in the room. I open my eyes and am forced to stare at the perinuclear colors.

She continues. "The eyes and ears detect waves," she says. "The nose detects particles." The holo above me is magnified. Now, all I see are two crooked strands, one green, one magenta, that bulb at their ends.

"Every particle in existence is chemical," she says. "From the sun to blood to excreted hormones, it's all chemical matter. Don't you understand?" The image pans back to the neural panorama. "The relationship between murderer and victim is revealed on a particle level. It's entangled. You can sense this. It's what makes you remarkable. The fact that you see it instead of smelling it is simply a result of your synesthesia. That you are colorblind makes it more distinct. Let me ask you—when was the first time you sensed it?"

I stare up at lit scatter and begin to see patterns. "If it's chemical," I whisper, evading her question, "I can be fooled."

"Yes," she says. "Now. I need my mother's iE."

This request puzzles me. What the hell is she talking about? "Akira didn't have an iE. Never has."

The prongs go further up, and I resist the urge to scream. "Don't lie to me. Do you really think she just sat around and did nothing for the last four decades like you?" The 3D image of my nose flickers back on. Not the microscopic view, but a much simpler one that expands to more than just my nose. It's a floating MRI of my entire head, my own lidless eyes staring back at me. "Do you see, there?"

The prongs probing my inner nose glow, as does a spot on the holo. "I can pierce straight through to your prefrontal cortex. Taking into consideration your former occupations, I imagine you know what that would do. Now I'll ask you one more time. She had an iE. You're the only person she would give it to. Where is it?"

I grit my teeth. "I'm not lying. She didn't have an iE! She would've told me."

A pause follows, both of us in quiet stillness. Time stretches. Unlike any of my own targets, I'll see the bullet coming. What was it that I told the chief when I found Akira's body? At least she succeeded. At least she did well in life. I can't say the fucking same.

Time snaps back in an instant. I gasp as she withdraws her tail from my nose and the holo MRI flickers off. Now I'm able to turn away, which I do, praying that I'll wake up if I pass out. Only I turn the wrong way. I fade to unconsciousness as Akira is cut up again and again on Jerry's installation, the only god I know being sliced apart on repeat.

20

When I come to, the first thing I see is the glimmer of the 1911 on the bar. I roll off the bed, grab the gun, and struggle to stand. The second thing I check is whether my iE is online. It is. I breathe both suspicion and relief. Next, I touch my nose. It feels normal. No pain. Was it all an illusion? Nothing about the encounter on my iE history. I try to get my bearings. I look up at the shelves of liquor. Each one is aquarium-tubed, subtly backlit, and filled with a convoy of tiny glow-in-the-dark jellyfish. I snatch the opened bottle off the bar and take a swig, hoping it will calm me down.

But I'm still here.

Lightheaded, I look up at the chandeliers, each one a real tree stunted and trained to hold giant bulbs containing genetically engineered fireflies. I grab a clean towel from behind the bar and wet it, then press it against my face. I wonder if these things, the shelf tubes and chandeliers, were here the last time I came to visit Jerry. I'm not sure. As usual, I wasn't paying attention. But as I see these now, I think about how looking at nice things has a weird effect. At first, you admire them. Then you start wanting them. By the end of the day, you start thinking you deserve them, even if you ain't worked to get them. That woman who just crammed her tail up my nose. All her life, she watched her mother. And apparently me, too. She feels I owe her something, and I can't give it to her because it doesn't exist. Akira Kimura never had an iE—she hated the things. What the hell is her daughter after?

I recall more of what she said, trying to piece the whole encounter back together without external replay. Is it really smell that makes me see these reds and greens? I've just been coming up with half-assed theories most of my life, never having anyone to ask or bounce ideas off of because I was so afraid to share what I saw. She's probably right—she's certainly qualified to theorize. What was it that Enrico Fermi once said while frying a bunch of onions? It would be nice if we could understand the sense of smell, he said. I laugh inside. This coming from the genius who built the first nuclear reactor.

I look down at the bar and see something that wasn't there before. It's a real book, paper and all. I open the leather-bound cover with my shaking hand and see the title.

There it is, meticulously handwritten, like a medieval monk-scribed bible. Some letters boxed and emblazed in gold. I think that I should be seeing all kinds of green and red floating up from this thing. Or smelling them, according to Ascalon Lee. But I don't see or smell any of that. All I see is the title right on page one.

The Book of Ascalon.

She's got her mother's handwriting. I take the book and head to the hover. Trembling, I ping Sabrina. No answer. I ping her again. I touch my nose and wonder if she planted something inside me. Some kind of surveillance device or an explosive. I crawl into the hover and lift off. The wind knocks into the vehicle, and I almost crash into the building. *Steady, old man*, I say. *Steady. You're alive.* I take a breath and ping Sabrina a third time. Again, no answer. I bank and head full throttle to the ocean. For the first time that I can remember, speed scares me. But I've gotta get back quick. I take another breath and keep the hover going at full speed. I ask my iE to run through the basics on our sense of smell. There are about four hundred different receptors on the surface of olfactory neurons, which dangle from the brain like tentacles. It's the only part of the central nervous system constantly exposed to the outside world. I dig for more and am slung over to reality and theoretical evolution. Some theorize that the brain may have evolved to hide the true nature of reality, not reveal it. Like an interface—widgets that simplify so that we can interact with something more complex. The water is lit up with city lights beneath me. For some idiotic reason, I'm relieved I can still see green and red. It's probably just the general relief of being alive. I glance at my iE. How the hell can we make this device and the underwater sprawl below us, but not know how our own noses work, these things literally attached to our faces? I fly above the saddle between the two great mountains and pass The Savior's Eye. It's turning dark, and it begins to snow up there.

After I land, I stumble out of the hover and run to our unit. I'm stripping things off along the way: the 1911, my coat, even my iE. Anything she could have cursed with her scientific magic I drop into the ocean. The last thing I have is the book. I think about tossing it, but I can't bring myself to do it. No, she put too much work into this. It's not gonna self-destruct. I hope this applies to me as well, especially after being manipulated for days and framed for two murders.

I get to the door and bust through it, nearly falling on my face. My body responds to the sudden imbalance well. The last thing it wants is to be stuck on a floor again. I look around. Everything is like I left it. A holo plays dimly in the living room.

A gun muzzle presses against my temple.

It's Sabrina, her cop's finger still well trained. The finger never on the trigger unless she's about to fire. "I tried to ping you," I say.

She puts the gun down. "I was putting Ascalon to bed," she says. "She had me playing her a holo vid for the last thirty minutes."

I look over at the holo vid in the center of the room. It's one I've seen before. I turn up the brightness and sound. It's talking about how some scientists believe that we all started off as bright pink microorganisms so great in number that we tinted the ancient oceans and could be seen collectively from outer space. The image of the pink and blue planet is beautiful, and it makes me wonder what the fuck happened to us. The vibrant pinks of our existence have darkened, and we've become so shattered that we gaze at each other's chipped reflections to make excuses for being so dark and ugly. We're cut from the same master glass, which can never be fixed. Or maybe that's what Sessho-seki was supposed to be. Our reset button. Our way back to becoming the breathtaking, swirling image I see on vid.

"She was watching this?" I ask.

"Yeah, she liked the colors." Sabrina touches my face. "Where'd you go?"

"You wouldn't believe me if I told you."

"Try me."

I take *The Book of Ascalon* out of my pocket and hand it to her. She reads the first page. "My god," she says.

"That's the idea."

"Did you read it yet?"

"Didn't get the chance," I say. "I was worried."

"Let's read it together."

We grab a couple of chairs and drag them to Ascalon's door. Sabrina armed and vigilant. We sit side by side and open the book. Sabrina's hair brushes my cheek. Then she tilts her head slightly away, leaving the feel of something pleasantly phantom on my skin. I finally feel alive again. My entire body hums with energy at an eighth octave C. I try to settle down.

Sabrina's iE hovers above us and beams down light. Sabrina reads the first page out loud. I begin to calm. We read the second page silently together. I think I'm okay now. I turn the pages while she points at certain words or phrases and gasps. It's just the two of us, huddled outside our baby's room under a dim wedge of light.

21

THE TALE OF ASCALON BEGINS SOME SIXTY YEARS AGO
with a young pregnant scientist and a man in the
mountains preparing for a live water birth. It was a
long-abandoned technique, passed down to him in family
stories. No hospital, no certificate, no confirmation. Just
life jettisoned into a pond cleansed by a waterfall, the
flowing hair of some forgotten goddess. Why the young
woman agreed to such a birth, the man had no clue. He
was just happy she had. So they hiked the mountain, him
carrying blankets, towels, and such, her toting a basket
filled with envy apples and local ginger. Shortly after they
arrived at the secluded spot, she went into labor.

Ascalon came first. A beautiful, healthy baby girl. The
woman handed the man her first child, and he attempted
to swaddle her in a blanket. It was his first time trying to
swaddle a baby, so he struggled as the baby's cries fraz-
zled his nerves. When he finally finished, he noticed that
the woman was quiet. She had, in fact, been quiet the
entire time he folded and re-folded. There was a second

baby in her arms, this one neither beautiful nor healthy, but twisted, tailed, and eyeless. The woman looked up at the man and put the quiet baby underwater. She twisted its neck to speed up its death. At first, he objected. But the woman reminded him that when it came to deformity, his people used to do this, too.

She stepped from the pond and rinsed herself in the goddess's flowing hair. The man, still holding Ascalon, stepped into the pond and scooped up her dead sister. He cried and called the woman mad. She stepped over to him to take Ascalon. He told her she would have nothing to do with this child. He didn't trust her. She was a murderer. If she challenged his wishes, he would tell people about the dead child he was holding alongside the living one. She agreed to leave both of them. These are the sacrifices this woman made, as told to Ascalon by her father. A loving, devoted man. But ultimately a weak man. He wanted his daughter to hate her mother. The first time he took Ascalon into the ocean, she feared it. The tug of its current, its unthinkable depth. "Just like your mother," he said. When the girl taught herself to read at two, the father looked on, furious. He imbibed every night after the last tourist departed, and on one of these nights, when she was three, a sweltering September afternoon filled with dead wind, he told her the story of her drowned twin. She nodded. Somehow, she already knew. She had always felt incomplete, not just from her mother's absence, but from something else. Her father cried as he told her about her eyeless, twisted, tailed twin. The girl felt a prickle in her tailbone.

Now, upon confirmation, the girl ached for her twin, and she thought to herself, maybe she would have been able to fix her. She could learn how to do it. She could study. Those around her marveled at the ease with which she learned. She could read before she could talk. She could imagine as easily as she could remember. And it was easy for her to imagine her mother. All she had to do was look in the mirror and guess which parts came from her. She wanted to amputate these things, but she was no fool. She knew that before she cut herself apart, she had to learn how. And it was hard. She was always alone. She had no friends her age in her small, cold tourist town beneath the mountain. And even the adults, both the ones from other places who imagined moving to tropical paradise and the others whose families had lived here for generations and were now relegated to jobs servicing the newcomers, both types whispered behind her back that she was a freak. It was the one thing they could agree upon.

No one would teach her, so she taught herself. She started with animals—like the true offspring of a scientific giant, lab rats first. She begged her father for two from the same litter. The softhearted man felt badly for the child and bought them for her. When he found them flayed in her bedroom, one eyeless with parts everywhere, he was horrified. Looking back on it now, she thinks he should have been proud. The girl was only four years old, but her hands were steady enough to remove the eyes with such precision.

He vowed never to buy her a pet again. She didn't

mind. Alone, she enjoyed the challenge of catching life out in the wild. Birds, fish, the occasional vermin. She wished her sister were there trapping these things with her, though. Even if she'd had to be her twin's caregiver, leading the frail, blind girl by the hand, she would have been able to teach her. To enjoy this with her. Together, they could have learned how to fix her.

When the father caught the girl clipping the entrails of one of the last remaining dogs on the island, he trembled. *Why?* he asked. *You shouldn't have let her die*, she said, her bloody hands stitching the dog back up. The man said he had no choice. *You are no man*, the girl said. She hadn't said this to hurt him. She just believed it to be true. She'd tried furiously to stitch the dog up before its heart stopped beating, but of course, it was always easier to take something apart than to put it together.

After the canine incident, her father contacted her mother, who was on the East Coast at the time. He couldn't handle Ascalon anymore, he said. He told her that his business was failing as technology outpaced him and the new gear became too expensive for him to buy. He could no longer maintain the houseboat that he used as his dive shop because no one made the parts he needed any longer. She replied that a friend of hers would pick up the girl and enroll her in boarding school. She reminded the man of his promise. She would take the girl if he kept their secrets. There was no twin. And the child was not hers. She would send him some money. The man agreed, though his daughter did not understand why she had to leave. She was learning for him, trying to show him that she could repair life. That she could cut off the things he hated about her. Once at boarding school, she would hasten the project in order to get back home to him. Then he would love her. But he ended up not loving anything except alcohol, drinking away the money that her mother sent.

The woman who picked her up claimed to be an aunt named Jerry Caldwell. After her father signed the papers presented to him by the woman, she and the girl left him standing in a puddle of his own tears. During the shuttle run from the island to the continent, the girl cried so hard, she couldn't breathe. Jerry was patient and kind, but the girl was nonetheless blinded by tears. When they arrived, Jerry brought her clothes, sheets, blankets, and a new identity. The girl was no longer Ascalon Lee. Her new name was Tamamo Nomae. The girl asked what it meant. Jerry said she was named after the Fox with Nine Tails, a very clever woman in Japanese mythology. Tamamo liked the idea, but she never forgot her real name.

When enrolled in boarding school, the surgical cutting wasn't as difficult as she imagined. The institution's tools, like its lessons, were among the best in the world. First came the pinky finger. A laser saw in the lab meant for etching out decorative figurines out of polymer glass. Oops, a finger gone. One girl screamed. Another fainted. The girl still didn't understand her mother's horror at her sister's tail. Amputation was painful, but easy enough.

Then came the cut down her forehead to her right

eye. In her dormitory, with a mirror and scalpel. A steady hand and an exquisite pain that encouraged her to sustain the perfect separation of flesh. On arrival, she had looked into the mirror and hated the tears that ran down her cheeks. She remembered her father, always crying. She hated the eyes that produced these tears, eyes that she knew were her mother's. She did not know she was going to pluck the eye until she did it. This blindness was what her twin would have felt if she'd survived. And it was awful. But it felt fixable. Just about every organ could be transplanted and cloned for generations now, but eye transplants were close to impossible: too many muscles, vessels, nerves, and most importantly, the eyes weren't just connected to the brain, they were part of it. An eye transplant was as impossible as transplanting another part of the brain. But perhaps she could create something artificial to replace it. Perhaps this was the first step to recreating the brain itself. Her roommate screamed and screamed after walking into the room. What she didn't know was that the girl had considered performing this surgery on her the night before, after weeks of being ridiculed by her and her friends. While the roommate had slept, Tamamo's scalpel had hovered above her forehead, but in the end, she'd decided against it. So really, her roommate should be grateful. The ambulance arrived. Her roommate, traumatized, ended up at a psychiatric hospital and wasn't allowed to return, even though the girl was. Why had they allowed her back? Akira Kimura had paid them a visit.

"Accursed creator," the girl said.

"Shelley?" her mother said back. She looked the girl over and turned to Jerry Caldwell. "Possibly body integrity identity disorder."

The seven-year-old looked up at the mother. "That is neurobiological reductionism."

Her mother smirked. "Explain."

"My cortical body matrix does not see *less*. It sees more. There's something missing that I must replace."

Her mother frowned. "That is nonsense."

I am just as intelligent as she is, the girl thought. Then she decided to test something. "I'm not only missing my eye. You know what it is, the other thing I miss."

"Shut your mouth," her mother hissed.

Jerry, visibly taken aback by the mother's response, began to speak, but the woman interrupted her. "I would like to paint you," she said to her daughter.

"Paint me as I will be."

"No. I will paint you as you are."

Days after the girl met the goddess Akira Kimura and posed for that painting, she asked Jerry for her mother's academic records. Jerry first said no, but when the girl threatened to carve out another part of herself, Jerry relented, on the condition that there would be no more cutting. The girl received the records and focused her energy on smashing every single one. Over the next four years, she completed all of her elementary, middle, and secondary education at the institution. When Jerry took her out to dinner for graduation, she looked more scared than proud. But she told the girl about her trust fund, banked on a Caribbean island. She mentioned college and begged her to wear a false finger and false eye. The girl replied, "This isn't my mother's face or my father's, it is mine, and I will not be false like them. I will do with it what I please."

And so, she threw herself into cybernetic technology. Hate drove her. The kind of hate that only the abandoned can understand. It led her to accomplish more than her mother had, to show her father the magic he had discarded like trash. She knew she'd been a silly little girl back then, but that foundation was the seed of her accomplishment. Her hormones in puberty magnified her hate for her parents even more. That hate began to numb into competitive drive, with her mother as her phantom rival. The girl moved from one subject to the next as she mastered each field. After biology, quantum computing technology, and after that, neuroscience. Unlike the rest of the world, multitaskers who settled for knowing a little about everything, she trusted the value of doing only one thing at a time. And each time, she tapped into her hate to motivate herself.

Meanwhile, her real mother sat there, peering through space-time, searching for a celestial end in the infinite. The girl thought it a foolish thing to study, when one could simply glance into a mirror and see an endless number of things more fascinating, ready to peel off and put under a scope. She became a cybernetic surgeon. She converted an iE into an actual artificial eye and found that having nine tails was nothing compared to a cybernetic one that was linked to her brain. But the iE neurolink was her masterpiece. She engineered and programmed it to crack through firewalls and obtain root access to other systems. She was the first in the history of the world to accomplish these things, but she hoarded this knowledge, which was easy, since she still had no friends. These breakthroughs would have made her twin whole.

She was about to turn twenty-one and was ready to show her mother how she had surpassed her. Her mother, whom she hadn't seen since that day by the banyan tree. Her mother had been wrong. She didn't suffer from BIID or some other affliction. She was simply adding and enhancing. She would make the mother see it for herself if she had to. See that Ascalon Lee would have been able to fix her sister. Akira was back on the island by this time, which surprised the girl. But it was true the best telescopes on earth were there: atop a high mountain in the middle of the ocean, with the only nearby light pollution from island residents who slept soundly at night after catering to tourists. Her father must have been furious with her mother's return, drinking in an impotent rage. The girl made plans to travel to the island to show her mother. It wasn't her first trip back. She had offered Jerry Caldwell a skyscraper home security system she had invented herself and left something else there, just in case. But as the girl jetted across the Pacific on this trip, hoping to show her mother, it was her mother who showed her.

The discovery of Sessho-seki. The world trembled. The girl was onboard when she heard the news, and just as she had as a child, she wept to the point that she couldn't breathe. She spent the flight in the lavatory, ashamed. She could never surpass her mother. She no longer loved her father, a bitter alcoholic who spent his time taking tourists on deep dives, none deep enough to cleanse him of his dark secret. She only had Jerry, whom, if she was being honest, she didn't love either. Years ago, the girl had studied her own brain chemistry and noticed there were certain substances she lacked and others she had an abundance of. She could easily have cured herself then, if she'd thought there was something to cure.

She spent the next few months wallowing while the world wailed, grieving for itself before its death. She spent this time in alleys and basements, participating in the apocalyptic bacchanal and bathing in all the pleasures she'd forsaken her entire life, only to find that they did not give her lasting pleasure. She made money by media blasting the plague anxiety off the brains of the wealthy and frolicking on the Dark Web. She launched several backdoor hacks from there. The impending doom of Sessho-seki seemed to render cybersecurity updates moot.

Then came the news of Ascalon, the weapon that would save the world. *Ascalon!* Her name, even if no one else knew. Maybe her mother had loved her after all.

But she wouldn't approach Akira just yet. She wanted to learn what her mother had unraveled first, so she could hold an intelligible conversation with her on the mysteries of the universe. She worked under the tutelage of a pure oddity, a brilliant but happy man who, unlike most geniuses, had all the substances in his brain perfectly balanced. He loved to wear silly ties and would later be found hanging from one of them.

An impossible suicide. The girl, who had started calling herself Ascalon again, despite all the derisive comments that accompanied the name change, which only added to her drive, had learned something crucial from this man before his passing. He believed that Sessho-seki did not exist. At first, she couldn't believe it. But then, she began to run calculations. Calculations became algorithms, algorithms became simulations, and simulations became theories. Exhausted after her twenty-two-hour workdays, she crawled into an AMP chamber that her trust fund money procured for her, that she had modified herself. She wanted to sleep, but she wanted to dream imaginatively while sleeping. So the chamber not only showered her with the hibernation-inducing molecules that would shut her body down to the precipice of death, it flooded her with a compound extracted from a tropical tree known to send one on a fantastical mental voyage. She'd experimented with the substance in all those back alleys and basements and found that it was the only thing she missed from that period of her life. Even in sleep, she never stopped thinking about Sessho-seki and the Ascalon Project.

The first simulation was Sessho-seki. The second was the Ascalon Project. The third, a theoretical model of Akira's brain. For this, she needed to investigate the personal. To learn and document everything about Akira Kimura. While the world spent its last gasp looking up, Ascalon spent it looking in. She had always been better with a microscope than a telescope. And it was easy learning that started from the lips of the father and ended in books about Akira.

By this time, the purge was beginning. And she followed and watched with cloaked surveillance technology. She bore witness to the father, now a drunken, buffoonish terrorist, being tricked into the water and reduced to marine snow. The string of scientists, the first of which had been her former mentor—perhaps her first friend, she was never sure—toppled from their lofty towers of understanding by death or shame. She watched this angel of death splash the president's man and his scientist into the ocean. It was the only time Ascalon was afraid. She thought it foolish of him to risk Akira, but he knew what he was doing. The girl watched that event personally from the shore, the image of the SEAL plummeting as eternal in her mind as paint on a copper canvas. She began to weave a theoretical map of Akira's brain and used her own corticolimbic system as its base. After all, she inherited it from her mother, as most daughters do. Once she finished the model, she ran the three simulations together. She held Akira Kimura in even higher esteem. The woman was indeed becoming a god.

That's when she decided to approach the mother for the first time since childhood. The construction of Ascalon, the great cosmic ray, was fast approaching. It made sense that Ascalon, the girl, reunite with her mother quickly as well.

Akira Kimura, however, was difficult to get to, not just because of her guard and the endless walls of security, but because her mother did not communicate by iE. She could not be messaged or hacked. But the girl knew where the mother looked daily: through the God's Eye.

So the girl hacked that. And when Akira Kimura sat in front of the telescope, the girl remotely steered its gaze back to her birthplace. The scene of her mother's original sacrifice and sin. And the mother knew who was sending the message. She was a genius, after all. The mother contacted Jerry Caldwell, and a meeting was set.

Oh, the blissful excitement that danced inside the girl's head! She would meet her mother, not as a pathetic, self-harming child, but as a disciple, worth both herself and her twin. They were to meet at the mother's penthouse, 177 atmospheres under the sea. Akira, Jerry, and Ascalon. No bodyguards. No iEs. It pained the girl, who wanted to show her mother what she'd built. An iE that completely interfaced with the brain. One that could infiltrate other systems. She was very, very close to being able to construct one that could split mind and body. One that could store consciousness and live outside a human shell. The girl stupidly thought it was something her mother could never build. She knew the world wasn't ending. Perhaps she and her mother could become partners in the new world that rose from the ashes of the old.

She removed the iE and cut her hair so that it would drape over the crater and scar. It was the first time in her life that she cut to beautify instead of replace. She went to the seascraper, giddy, landed, and instructed her iE to wait for her here. Perhaps after she told her mother what she had accomplished, Akira would want to see her great work. It was late, and the lobby was empty. She stepped up to the facial recognition scan.

And when it read her as not Tamamo Nomae, but Ascalon Lee, she smiled. Her mother would finally recognize the daughter and introduce her to the world! She would no longer be seen as a monster, but as the off-spring of a god. Jupiter's Minerva, Brahma's Ganapati, Akira's Ascalon. And the world would worship the girl as they did her mother.

Akira and Jerry waited for the girl in the penthouse. Upon exiting the elevator, she first looked at Jerry Caldwell. So pretty. So polished. Born with everything. A natural candidate for friends in every sphere. She hated her in that moment for the privilege and care she had been granted her entire life. Then she turned to the mother, trembled, and involuntarily burst into tears. Before she knew what she was doing, she was clinging to the god-woman's ankles, sobbing "Mother! Thank you!" over and over again. "Thank you for saving me! For saving all of us!"

Oh, how she groveled. Jerry tried to pull her up, but she refused. Jerry didn't see what the girl did. Hadn't dreamed what she'd dreamed. The end of holy wars, cold wars, world wars, and trade wars. Clean waters, clean air, a clean Earth, a clean collective conscience, a place where children could once again play amongst themselves away from the gaze of paranoid parental supervision. Humans living beyond human years, beyond meager standards. The future, wearing down and crushing the pillars of soon forgotten times and places. All from a single thought. Not the binding of a microorganism to a host, but something more powerful, an intangible thought flooding through humanity's collective mind, passed down from generation to generation. A scar in the sky an eternal reminder of this thought: *we are all lucky to be alive.*

Even if it was all a scam.

Akira pulled the girl up and brushed her hair from her face. Ashamed, Ascalon looked down. The mother gently raised the girl's chin and inspected the crater, even pulled open the lid to gaze upon its total darkness. And the first words from the mother to the daughter after nearly twenty years were, "Self-mutilation has a long and practical history with young women. Women disfigured themselves to prevent rape. To protect themselves from even their fathers and brothers. The act may even be in our DNA by now."

The crying girl nodded, but she did not agree. She wanted to explain to her mother that this was autonomy. When she had done this to her eye, she'd felt her drowned half come back to life. She was that much closer to perfection, and with her mother's help, she could get there.

As if reading the girl's mind, the mother reached into her pocket and pulled out a small orb. An eye! Had she already improved upon what the girl had invented? No, she was far too busy with the Ascalon Project. And the girl had kept her scientific discoveries a secret. The mother stuck the artificial eye in the empty socket. The girl tried to look through it, but saw nothing—it was only glass. "Now let me look at you," the mother said. The girl feared looking directly at her mother but did what she was told. "You look much more like me than your father," Akira said flatly.

And the girl wept again, harder this time. She had finally recognized their kinship! Might there even be love, finally? "I . . . I know," the girl stuttered. "I know what you've done. What you've done for all of us."

"What do you mean?"

"The trick. It's the trick of a god."

The mother raised an eyebrow, looked at Jerry, and said, "Could you leave us for a few minutes?"

Jerry paused, then nodded. She went into another room and closed the door. The mother turned back to the girl. "The trick?"

"Mother, I know," the girl said. "There's no asteroid. No weapon. Just machines that will create a permanent light. A reminder of everything you've given."

The mother sighed and shook her head. The girl rubbed at her eye. The mother grabbed the girl's hand, and the girl began to calm. "I did all the calculations," the girl said. "Ran every possible simulation."

"Then you calculated incorrectly."

"I know what Idris Eshana did for you. I've spent years studying this, mother. Shadowing you. I've figured it out. Are you not proud?"

Her mother certainly didn't look proud.

"I see what you see," the girl said.

"And what is that?"

"A better world."

The girl was calm now. She began to feel sleepy. Had her body expended too much adrenaline trying to see through the eye earlier? "And you recorded these cal‑culations and simulations? All this supposed evidence?" the mother asked.

"I recorded everything," the girl said. "Even the fall into the ocean of the president's man and his witch. Even Father's death. You will still be worshipped forever."

The mother nodded. "Come with me," she said. She led the now tired girl to the bedroom, which was empty except for an open AMP chamber. The girl rubbed her eye again, this time out of weariness. She looked at the ocean‑facing walls of glass with real sea spiders climbing all over them. Then she understood.

"The eye," the girl gasped.

"Yes, the eye," said the mother.

The girl fought the sleepiness. "But I'm trying to help you."

The girl imagined the AMP from the eye coursing through her body and became even more tired. "There's one lesson that your father taught me," the mother said. "Only one. He grew up on the island and was raised to spear fish in these waters. He taught me how to spear fish. How to hold my breath long enough to kill."

The girl gasped, or tried to. She couldn't tell if she'd managed it. The mother gently lay the girl back into the open chamber. "Don't worry," the mother said. "I won't kill my last living child. But you will sleep."

"For how long?" she asked, barely able to formulate the words.

The mother popped out the girl's fake eye and inspected it. "Where did you leave your iE?" the mother asked.

So she didn't know. If she did, she would have demanded the girl bring it in with her. She just wanted it to cover her tracks.

"For how long?" she asked again. She activated emergency protocol. The iE received the silent neural transmission and zipped away. Now, Akira frowned at the fake eye. Then she turned to the girl and stared at her empty socket. Something was clicking inside her.

"Where is it?" the mother asked.

"I'm sorry, Mother, but you won't find it."

The mother pressed a button to shine a light on the girl's face; it pierced the empty socket. Her frown slowly transformed into a gasp. She said it before the girl could: "Love the likes scarcely imagined."

"Rage the likes of which you would not believe," her daughter said back.

"Shelley was too wordy."

The mother put the eye back in the girl's socket. She closed the chamber and pressed a button. It rose to vertical so the girl could see the sheets of glass infested with sea spiders, the ocean deep, dark, and endless behind them. How silly it was of her to think she could surprise a person who was incapable of being surprised. There was no doing something that Akira Kimura didn't see coming. Akira demanded that she sleep, so she would sleep.

With realization, there are only two versions. You're either in time or too late. The girl was too late. Jerry Caldwell stepped into the room and tried to save the girl with savage arguments and fluttering hands. Akira was patient at first, but finally had to invoke the name of her guard. If Jerry persisted, the mother would unleash him on everyone in this room. Including Akira herself.

And so, the world would end.

Jerry Caldwell had made her strongest closing argument and lost. She stepped in front of the AMP chamber, took one last teary-eyed look at the girl, and walked out. That was the last time Jerry Caldwell and Akira Kimura would ever be in the same room.

The mother looked through the glass at the barely conscious girl. She began to hum a pretty tune that made the girl even sleepier. The only thing keeping her awake were the vibrations of anxiety. Then the mother transitioned from a hum to words with the same melody.

Ascalon is not only the name of the savior
It's the name of the daughter
The one I gave up
Find her for me and tell her that I'm sorry

No longer able to move her arms and legs, the girl focused on her tail. It was a part of her, but it wasn't. There was no blood flowing through it. It wasn't connected to her metabolism and wouldn't go into deep sleep like the rest of her. But it was connected to her primary motor cortex through her corticospinal tract, and her primary motor cortex was shutting down. She tried to inch her tail toward the release button inside the chamber, but the tail moved slower than the 30 micrometers per minute that death moved. She didn't know what to do.

She had no desire to sleep, but it was hopeless. All she had was that final conscious thought. *Tail. Release.*

"The world cannot know what you know until I'm gone," the mother said. "You and I cannot exist at the same time."

And the girl, who had thought herself fearless her entire life, only now realized that was a lie. Her greatest fear was being alone. It was why she'd cried so hard when she'd been forced to leave her father. It was why she longed for both her twin and her mother. She had always thought of her solitude as temporary. Something that she had her whole life to fix. But now, she would be trapped in it forever. She had failed. Tail. Release. *Tail. Release.*

She slipped into sleep repeating this futile mantra.

All the girl can remember of the time of her sleep are flashes of light in the otherwise total darkness of the midnight zone. During her hibernation, there were rare instances of torpor, of sleep less deep, during which her tail would lightly twitch. This also allowed her to witness, in the briefest glimpses, the construction of an underwater cityscape. She noticed the fabrics of the different seasons, even in the deep. Sometimes, she believes, she saw her mother standing above her, surgical mask covering everything but her eyes. Scalpel in hand. But these moments were all so brief. Bits and pieces of incomplete thought, some of which floated from the unconscious up to the surface. Comet dust. Stock market crash, stock market rally. Everything in existence moves above absolute zero. A birthday party. A blindfolded girl being spun by her friends. Koku: the amount of rice it takes to feed a person for one year. Blue water, blue people. People of all colors. Those spiders in the glass: how many generations of them have passed? Genetically engineered plants that grab nitrogen from the air. *Tail. Release.* A tomb. Metal skies and rain like lava. Kinetic energy turned electric. Nuclear disarmament. The game is over. All you can do is decide how you will lose. Human action is predictable. Will is unbreakable because it is more than human. God, frozen and divided. *Tail. Release.* The zombie galaxy. Expanding Earth theory. Eternalism, not block universe. Wisdom only comes from personal pain, just like insanity. Sessho-seki smashing into Earth again and again and again.

The girl spent nearly thirty years alone in this waking dream.

But this didn't matter, she later forced herself to believe. She embraced her mother's notion of time, without its linear qualities. We had transformed, becoming the pinnacle of human civilization. Knowing what everything was while forgetting how any of it worked.

Then, after thirty years, the tail finally hit its mark. She freed herself. She could not walk or see. She was birthed from the chamber just as vulnerable and broken as her twin decades before. All she knew was, she couldn't stay here. Her mother would find her and put her back inside. Or maybe strangle and drown her, like she did the sister. There was no one to welcome her back. No one to delight in the news that she'd escaped.

There were only those who would regret it.

She struggled to remove the poisonous eye, the only

thing the mother had ever given her. A trick, like the one she'd unleashed upon the world. The girl placed the eye on the floor. It did not roll. The penthouse foundation was perfectly level. Then, with her tail, the girl impaled the eye on that foundation. It broke to pieces.

The girl crawled to the wall and guided herself to the lift. She would need *her* eye. And it wasn't far. It was at Jerry Caldwell's, hidden in the heart of her holo art. The girl's body was weak, except for the tail. She used it to force herself upright. The tail, which she had always seen as her sister's, had saved her. She stumbled into a heli-taxi and made it to Jerry's. Having built the security system, she easily bypassed it. She retrieved her eye and made it out undetected, finally able to see again.

For the first year, like a sufferer of Cotard's syndrome, she truly believed she was dead. She began to build her own tomb beneath the lava. The islanders, recent transplants who spent their iE-free days cleaning and composting and their nights on natural hallucinogens, finally found her digging in the deserted obsidian fields. In awe of her mechanical eye and her powerful tail that broke through rock, they began to help her. Even from the beginning of construction, it became apparent to her. She was building her mother's tomb, not her own. She wasn't the one approaching death; she hadn't earned it.

When the tomb was done, she headed toward the waterfall where she and her sister were born. The little grave was right where her father had drunkenly told her it had been. He'd buried the body at the beginning of the ancient trail, away from the water so the remains wouldn't be washed away. The girl dug up and collected the bones in a tiny coffin, then made one of her own, sleeping alongside her sister. She really did feel like she was already dead after decades in that chamber. But over time, she finally began to wake up. She felt less lonely lying next to the twin.

Making a child feel less alone. That was a mother's job.

So began Ascalon's mission.

She reached out to Jerry Caldwell and regained her trust. Then she began to work. To strengthen her body. She resumed her studies as well. On the birds who came to sit on the black rocks above. On dissection. Neuroscience. She dyed her skin blue and hair pink so no one would recognize her when she ventured out, although it had been thirty years and that was unlikely. She studied the mannerisms of teen boys and managed to pass as one. A temporary disguise. Then she began to watch her mother. At first nervously and at a distance, but Akira didn't appear to be searching for her. Didn't appear to worry in the slightest. This made the girl even angrier. Her mother didn't care. She didn't even change the security protocol of her penthouse. She just continued to stare out at the stars every night, as if everything else around her was too predictable and mundane to merit her gaze. Furious, the girl turned her attention to the guard. What a sad, silly existence. She may have been trapped in an AMP chamber for three decades, but she hadn't built her own prison. He had built his several times over. A parade of wives and children. A tedious, unprofitable occupation. Spiraling debt. Ha! She could see his eyes constantly wandering. Maybe to decades ago, when he'd been relevant. Maybe to greens and reds, which she knows from his medical records he cannot see. But slowly, over months of observation, she realized there was more to his colorblindness. She collected DNA samples, which was easy enough. Human beings shed DNA wherever they go. The DNA she acquired was from nose hair clippings left in a sink. She studied him on a genetic level and found something fascinating. A mutation. Mutations are common enough, but this one was extremely rare. An unusually high number of olfactory sensory neuron receptors. And a synesthete. He saw what he smelled. And that was murder, wasn't it? Was it an accidental enhancement? Possibly. He had grown up in the brief age of legal genetic enhancement, and such an enhancement could only occur pre-birth. Unfortunate that she could not recreate this enhancement for herself.

But he could be a potential ally. An easy one to acquire. Someone itching to become relevant again. Given his special sense, he would be easy to put on the trail. Like the girl, he is a slave, not only to his gifts, but to taste as well. The taste of fresh blood. It has been a long time, and right now, he is starving.

I will ask him when the time is right.

It has been said that matter tells space how to curve, and space tells matter how to move. *I am space. Black, encompassing, alone. And now I must carve my mother into a god.*

22

When anyone is out on the docks with Ascalon, Sabrina demands that they hold her hand the entire time. The next morning, Ascalon and I are out for a walk, and I'm holding her hand, which she does not like. I think about the differences between her and John and my first daughter, Brianne, though I don't remember much about her. Brianne was a constant fountain of head-banging temper tantrums, which probably made it easier for me to go off to war. As for John, he was a scared, clingy baby who only had to be told "careful" or "no" once, and I think about how, in the end, this obedience and fear didn't keep him alive. I look down at Ascalon, who is leaning over the edge trying to escape my grasp. If I let go, she will plunge straight into the water. I sigh. It's still a sore spot that that psycho laughed at my existence in her book. A sore spot that my parents may have tried to soup up my genetic code, mucked it up, and never even told me. Sabrina, she's still at home spinning from the idea that Sessho-seki, the cause of global calamity—of her parents' suicide—may not have existed. She was so young then, just a kid, but she remembers the panic. Her parents' obsession and the neglect that followed. I don't believe Ascalon Lee. I was there. It was real. When I told Sabrina this, she asked if I ever saw it. I admitted I didn't. Her frown in response was almost enough to make me doubt my judgment.

I glance at my new, drone-delivered iE then scoop up Ascalon, hug her, and kiss her cheek. She doesn't care for that much either. She says, "Crawl, crawl!" which means she wants to walk. John loved to be carried. These children are so different, or maybe I'm remembering John wrong. As for Brianne, I never even knew her as a toddler.

I wonder how Akira remembered her own daughters. I don't understand how she did what she did to both of them. I put Ascalon down, and she bolts. From behind, she looks like a tiny orangutan running. Teetering side to side while speeding forward, long arms dangling freely. I catch up to her and grab her hand. She accepts it this time. I have no idea what's changed.

The docks yawn with morning activity. The vac tube train breaches the surface. A few early birds in battered work attire step inside the tube, and the train is sucked down underwater and follows a path that resembles old indoor plumbing. A couple of heli-taxi pilots sip piping hot coffee out of dense foam-fit thermoses, waiting for their first fares. It always struck me as funny that we drink out of the same stuff we wear. I guess it makes sense. It keeps the coffee hot but can also ice it for the cold-brew folks. A couple, at least a hundred years old, sit on a bench, looking up at Ascalon's Scar. They are old enough to remember. A group of red teens on their way to school walk toward us, whispering and giggling in each other's ears. A couple off to the side, VR while walking. These games nowadays. You can turn a stroll to school into high adventure. Isn't reality strange enough? I wanna unplug them. I squint to block some of that red my new eyes are still adjusting to. I look at their wrists. All of them are wearing identical beaded bracelets. The beads are as clear as water, one on each bracelet etched with katakana characters in gold. They stop to admire Ascalon.

"So cute!" one of the red girls, squatting in front of Ascalon, says. She's a friendly kid.

Ascalon pulls at the girl's bracelet. The girl laughs. She takes it off her wrist and gives it to Ascalon. "She can keep it," the girl says.

"No, that's okay," I say. "You don't have to give it to her."

The girl shrugs. "I'll get another one. They're free."

"Oh yeah?" I ask. "From where?"

The girl frowns. "They're everywhere. In memory of Akira Kimura."

The teens head to the vac tube train stop to wait for the ride they already missed. I look back at the old couple sitting on the bench. They're wearing the bracelets, too. I squat in front of Ascalon to take a closer look. Surprisingly, the character isn't Akira's family name, but the same katakana for Ascalon I saw out there on that tombstone. So it begins. Gods don't make us into their images, we make gods into ours. I think about *The Book of Ascalon*. I understand the pain its author has been through, even though she's murdered those closest to her and has threatened my family. I've had run-ins with my share of criminals, and they tend to have things in common. Bruised fruit tends to mold more quickly than the rest. This is no exception. I'm no exception. Akira, too. Lost her father at a young age. Hid behind her education and was thrust into a new country not that long after. Made some bad decisions—really bad ones—and got scared of losing everything she'd built. Nothing leads to more mistakes than trembling empires. Fucking criminals, trying to preserve their own importance. And I'm one of them.

Two friendly looking women in suits walk toward me and Ascalon. They stop in front of us. I put a hand on the handle of the gun tucked in the small of my back. "What a cute baby," the one with curly hair says.

I pick Ascalon up with my free arm. She's busy trying to rip the bracelet on her wrist apart. "Thanks," I say.

"We're with the FBI," the other with straight black hair says. They send their IDs to my iE. Both named Ascalon. They send a Federal subpoena next. I take my hand off my gun. "Nothing here about Jerry Caldwell," I say. My daughter is really pulling at the bracelet now, stretching the rubber band that holds it together to its very limits.

"The grand jury is convening over the matter of Akira Kimura's death," curly haired Ascalon says. "The Caldwell murder is a state matter."

I read the subpoena on my new iE. Three days. They aren't wasting time. I know better than to ask questions or get into any kind of conversation. I need a lawyer. And the best one I know is dead, killed by a one-eyed psychopath trying to write the next holy book for the entire human race. I know what she would have told me. *Limit your exposure*, Jerry used to always say. I can't afford a lawyer. I can't afford to fight. I feel myself hugging my kid a little tighter than she likes, but she's rolling with it. Maybe she can sense my anxiety. My god, I think. These last few days. My dad's favorite old cliché comes to mind: *The hits just keep on coming.* "Thanks," I say, trying to keep my expression neutral. "I'll be there."

The two agents wave goodbye to Ascalon, then walk away. They're wearing the bracelets as well. I look at my baby. "I know what you're thinking," I say. "I should tell them everything."

Still working the bracelet, she ignores me, which she's wonderfully good at. I look over as the docks work themselves up from a yawn into a stretch. The early morning exercisers, the old who cannot sleep past six in the morning. Kids in front of the vac tube train stop off to underwater school.

We turn around and start heading back, and as we do, I ping Akeem and ask him for a favor. He agrees. And even though I've got twenty years on him, he ends the call by saying, in a fatherly tone, that no one goes it alone.

I'm in real trouble here. This grand jury thing. A special prosecutor. Probably the best. Special prosecutors have taken down presidents before. I'm not terrified, because I know I didn't do it and that they don't have the evidence to put me away, but they might be able to get me on tampering with a crime scene, or start digging into my past. It's funny . . . A day ago, I was ready to spend the rest of my life in jail for a crime I didn't commit. Now I'm scared shitless of someone who's just gonna ask questions. Maybe that's because when I was on Vomit Island, I knew my family was set. That gem was gonna put Sabrina and Ascalon up for life. But if I go down now, they'll be in danger. And I've seen the face of that danger, along with the capabilities of the dangerous mind behind it.

Ascalon stretches the bracelet and lets go. It slingshots into the water. "Exactly, kid," I say. "Exactly." She laughs. I fake a laugh with her, then put her down and grab her hand before heading home. I look up at the sky. *It was real*, I tell myself. *The evidence is right there.* But doubt begins to creep in. I picture Sabrina's frown again. I haven't been thinking about what I actually saw back then. I've been thinking about what I didn't see.

When we get inside, Sabrina is programming the walls a light shade of green and red. It's blinding to me, but she means well, probably figures that it'll help me get used to the colors, so I don't say that it looks like Christmas exploded in here. She's amazing, this wife of mine. I wonder if this is a common occurrence in marriage—turn drama into matrimonial parody when crisis hits. Ascalon's commentary on our lives hit Sabrina harder than it did me. "When did devotion to family become something to laugh at?" she said.

"When her mother snapped her sister's neck," I said. It worried me that Sabrina was so focused on the part about us and not all the other stuff. The other stuff was definitely more of a threat.

I put Ascalon down for a nap and tell Sabrina about the FBI and the subpoena. But Ascalon won't sleep. She's crying for her mother. Sabrina bites her lip to strategize, just like she used to back in her pulse racket days. "The Feds," she says. "First, they ruin you. Then they throw you in jail."

For Less Thans like us, we never feel so acutely poor as when we hit legal troubles. "True," I say. "But you need to be guilty for them to do all that."

"It was a long time ago. It was martial law. Executive order."

"Not all of them."

Sabrina sighs and shakes her head. Ascalon is still crying.

"I should go in and plead guilty to Jerry's murder," I say. And I wonder why I say it. Am I testing my wife? That's just plain stupid. I head to Ascalon's room. "You'll get the bail money back sooner," I can't help adding.

Sabrina follows. "No."

I step into the room and pick up Ascalon. She stops crying. I brush her little bald head with my lips. She smells brand-new. "I'm toast," I say. "I can face the Federal stuff on Vomit Island."

"What about Ascalon Lee?"

"I pinged Akeem. We talked about it, and I'd like you guys to stay with him for now. His place is isolated, and he's got top-notch security."

"Where are you going?"

"I need to talk to someone."

"Who?" Sabrina asks. She puts Ascalon down. Ascalon crawls into the living room like she senses the beginning of an argument and wants no part of it.

"Chief of Staff Chang," I say.

"Why? Is he still alive?"

"Hanging in there at 115, the last I heard."

"Where?" Sabrina asks.

"I don't know. Easy enough to find out, though."

"But you're not supposed to leave the state. And we have that other mess to deal with. Why is this so important?"

I grab Sabrina's hand and squeeze. "I need to know if Sessho-seki was real," I almost whisper. And it's true, even if I know it's selfish. "I need to know if all of this was for nothing."

"And Ascalon Lee?" Sabrina asks.

I touch my nose and think about Ascalon Lee and how she probed it. It's not sore anymore, and I'm worried I'll forget. Stop appreciating what I've got and unwittingly loosen my hold on it. But the fear of death is already fading from me. And I know that's stupid. I start having other stupid thoughts, like maybe we're designed to die the way our fathers did. Mine went by deep-diving too many times. I feel like I'm doing the same thing.

"She's no Ascalon. She's The Killing Rock, and she's coming for me. But I'll be ready."

Sabrina kisses me on my cheek, lets go of my hand, and heads to the living room. I think about the prospect of spending the rest of my life in jail without my wife, without my child, and it shakes me. For the past few years, even up until couple of days ago, that thought didn't bother me. What changed, and why so quickly? I'm questioning how well I know myself. The colorblind boy who watched his father die. The pianist, the art history major, the army sniper. The cop with synesthesia who thought he could see, smell, and hear murder. Husband of four, father of three—one lost. A friend to The Money, surrounding himself with them despite the fact that he never had any. The man whose self-worth hinged on a handful of clever murders. What kind of man prides himself on killing innocent people? The answer is easy. A bad one. Even if those were done in service of saving the world, which it turns out they may not have been. I pray that Akira didn't do all of this for her own deification.

I walk to the living room. Ascalon points to the wall and says, "Ish." For some reason, "ish" means "show." She wants her program projected. Sabrina turns it on. A fly chased by a frog. A frog chased by a cat. A cat chased by a dog. They run in circles around the room. A true classic. "I want to come with you," Sabrina says.

"I'd like nothing more. But I have a hunch."

"A hunch about what?"

"She knows where I am. She'll follow me, and maybe I can

end it," I say. "Far away from you and Ascalon. I'll call a heli-taxi for you two to head to Akeem's. You'll be safe there."

Sabrina hugs me and tells me she loves me. I say the same. I kiss Ascalon on the forehead and look at her. She ignores me, her toes clenched as usual as she watches her show. I put on a thin, hooded overcoat and put Ascalon Lee's book into one of its pockets. I take out the last remaining 1911 from a vacuum-sealed drawer in the kitchen and look at it. The mirror-polished stainless steel, the decorative detective badge on its handle. A relic, like me. But an effective relic, maybe also like me. I leave it on the kitchen counter before I walk out the door. This family is down to one gun now, and I want Sabrina to hold on to it. While I'm walking along the docks to the hover, I wonder if this kind of love can last. I wonder how much a person can put up with until it breaks. At least if I die, bail will go back to them, and Ascalon Lee has no reason to be interested in my family.

I climb into Sabrina's hover, work the pedals, and take off. I head to the shuttleport, where one of Akeem's private shuttles awaits. I notice that my own toes are clenched. That's a habit of mine too, isn't it? Before pulling a trigger, while I pilot, working a case. I think about Ascalon doing the same thing in the float burbs below. Children sometimes remind us who we are. It's sad that we need to be reminded.

23

Chief of Staff Chang lives in Muskogee, Oklahoma, which is about fifty miles south of Tulsa, the south end of The Great Leachate. I spend the trip calling up some Shelley on my iE. First, I get a bunch of confusing old-ass poetry by some guy. Then my iE notifies me that the Romantic poet had a wife, who wrote *Frankenstein*. I obviously know it but have never read it. I get about ten percent in before deciding that you've gotta be stark raving mad to get through this book, much less quote it from memory. Makes sense for that particular mother and daughter pairing.

I fly over the great towers of cubed trash covering the 200,000 square miles of contaminated puddle that stretches from Lake Michigan. The vast majority of Midwesterners migrated out when the groundwater started killing people, so the government decided to cover it with the nation's trash. Then it took foreign trash for profit. The money helped to pay for the Desert Storm wars, which weren't wars between countries, but wars between governments and corporations. It took those to get the world off fossil fuels, just like it took wars to get off monarchy, slavery, and genocide. I caught the tail end of Desert Storm, but the Leachate Migration was before my time. Word is that there are hidden tunnels amidst the trash where the poor live—The Zeroes, who the rest of us aren't sure really exist.

Muskogee was a river port town back in the day. Those are as extinct as silver mining and dude ranch towns. Penicillin still flows through its waters, since we gave up on fixing the landlocked and turned to the ocean before I was born. Muskogee is one of the few middle-American specs left from the twenty-first century, still run by cords and wires. A place, like many, that never bounced back from the Leachate Migration and the Great Sun Storm that dropped the planes out of the sky when Akira and I were kids. Like the other nearby municipalities, it's one broken hip away from becoming a ghost town. While I'm on Akeem's human waste-fueled, private shuttle hovering over this dust bowl, I think about something Akira told me once. A thought Ascalon Lee also had in forced hibernation. We live in a zombie galaxy that died seven billion years ago. We revolve around a postmortem star, built from the cosmic debris of the one before it. We, like Muskogee down below, don't matter to anyone but the planet's current inhabitants.

After I land at the deserted air strip, I ask my iE how to get transportation into town. It pings a taxi for me, and I sit and wait. I'm surprised when I see a ground-based automobile rumble to me. The driver, a woman smoking an actual cigarette, asks me where to. I ask her if she knows where Chief of Staff Chang lives. She asks me who the hell Chief of Staff Chang is, and says that as far as she knows, there ain't no Chinamen that live in these parts. So I ask her to take me to town. She nods and drops me off at the hardware store. Never having been in a hardware store before, I step inside.

I always figured do-it-yourself was as extinct as river port towns, but it appears to be on life support in Muskogee. The place is packed with plastic tubes, fixtures, and actual metal screws and bolts. The only person inside is the owner, a really tall old guy, maybe seven feet, with cataracts and a bent back. He asks if he can help me. I ask him about Chief of Staff Chang. He nods and says the old man lives out in old Park Tree Plaza building. He says I can't miss it. Like him, it's the tallest in town.

"Thanks," I say.

"What do you want with him, anyway?" the owner asks.

"I've gotta ask him something," I say. "Hear his take, which is maybe the truth."

"He lives on the sixth floor," the owner says. "Penthouse. I go out there once a month to make sure the place is running, replace the odd part here and there."

"How is he?" I ask.

"He and this town are competing to see who outlasts the other. My money's on him."

"I don't mean to sound like an asshole, but why would you stay in a town you know is dying?"

The tall man grins. "Keeping a thing alive gives me purpose. What's yours?"

I nod but don't answer. "Is the Plaza in walking distance?"

"About a mile up Thurston. Corner of Blackstone."

I thank him. It then occurs to me that I have no weapon, not that I need one to talk to a 115-year-old man. But I've got caveman blood in me and figure I should grab something just in case. She's out there somewhere. But for some reason,

I feel good about where I've landed, a place with streets and corners. No suction-cup security or tat-dyed kids. I'll see that blue woman coming from a mile away, especially during the day. I purchase a used utility heat blade that's probably older than me. I put it in the pocket opposite the one with Ascalon's book and head out.

It's a strange feeling walking up an actual street fronted by buildings made of concrete. Passing parked cars on rubber wheels. Old-school drones wash windows and sweep the streets. There's a green exterminator van that rolls by. I grip the knife's hilt, ready to tango if it stops and trouble jumps out. Exterminators seem redundant for this place, with all the poison flooding through the environment. I wonder where the van is heading.

A block up, the streets are empty. I think about the few people who live here and figure they're just like the rest of us. People who see this occasionally wonderful, occasionally horrible, monotonous existence as good enough. It's all a spinning grinder that sputters along until its bearings pop and clank on a perfectly level floor, rolling around chasing something that ain't there. I'd love to believe in one last surprise when my springs fracture and my life belt snaps instead of some inevitable malfunction, a frightening, regretful, final pain. There ain't no pill for that. No chamber. Ask Akira or Jerry or Kathy or John. My parents. The people I killed. I think back to Professor Brum and wonder if things might've been different had she lived.

I get to Park Tree Plaza, which sits in front of a massive tree and next to a broken-down Ferris wheel. It's an old condo, and I'm talking twentieth-century old, basically a tall box built of cinderblocks. I swing open the glass door and enter the lobby. Floor cobbled with ceramic tile. Grass growing through cracked grouting. I turn right and head to the elevator. I press the button. Red. I'm beginning to notice how many buttons in this world are red. It lights up, and I'm surprised how fast the elevator doors open. I step inside, and there's only one button, a plastic black one that reads six. All that's left of the other buttons are metal threads protruding from the elevator wall. I press six. The elevator sounds like it runs on belts made of old metal chains. If I were a machine, this is probably what my body would sound like.

The elevator stops, and I step into the penthouse. The floor is blanketed with cubes of linoleum that curl at the corners. To the left is a tiny kitchen with cracked marble counters. The white concrete walls lead up to a ceiling spackled with a strange, crumbling plaster. I step past the kitchen and enter the living room. There's a sofa that I think used to be white but is brown now. And a portrait. Even though it flickers, I recognized the face. Brum. It hangs from the wall across the sofa.

Dead ahead, an old man in a wheelchair is parked out on a lanai draped in blinding green artificial grass. I head to him, passing drapes choked with cat hair. I look around. No sign of a cat. Under Brum's portrait, there's a suspended bed that monitors body functions while its occupant sleeps. I imagine it's hard to sleep when you're hooked up to one, waiting for the buzz that alerts you that it might be all over. I walk by another box on wheels, a death predictor, a gadget that estimates your chances of making it through the day. The chief's reads seventy-five percent.

I pause at the sliding glass door. There's a plant growing through the cracks of concrete balcony. Specks of planter and wicker litter the artificial grass. Trumpet creeper, my iE tells me. I can't tell where the red-flowered vines root from, possibly in this floor or one of the dead stories beneath us. The sun is setting, and the old man is staring at a giant tree below, watching hundreds of green birds come home to roost. I can't see them too well, the birds. They flock into leaves just as green as they are. Wind blows, and the rustling leaves sound like rain. A primitive energy in me stirs at the sight of all this life. I slide the door open and step onto the balcony.

Chief of Staff Chang looks up at me and smiles. The bags under his eyes look like wilted abalones. I doubt he remembers who I am. Do *I* even have an accurate picture of who I was back then? I remember him as fat. He would've been a young adult when all the chickens died, when corn syrup still nourished the country, and before an ounce of beef or pork cost as much as the same weight in gold. Now I see him and think, maybe he wasn't fat. Maybe he was just a big guy. But he looks small now, hunched over in his wheelchair, which sits on actual rubber wheels. He points a crooked, arthritic finger down at the tree. "I sit here every morning. Every evening. And I can't for the life of me figure out what the spatters of white on the leaves are. Paint? Pollution blown over from The Leachate?"

I look down at his pleasantly demented grin and don't have the heart to tell him the white spatters are bird shit. I don't even know how I knew what they were so quickly. Maybe all I've ever really noticed in life is the shit. But I'm seeing other things now. Like how hubris can be contagious. The chief caught it from Brum, and I caught it from Akira. "I remember you," Chief of Staff Chang says. "She said you'd come for me."

I take off my hood. "I'm not gonna kill you. I just wanna know."

The chief sneers. "Know what?"

I kneel down beside him. He's got a thick plaid sleeping bag draped across his lap, a plush cascade of reds and blacks that skirt the bottom of his wheelchair. "Was Brum right? Was there no asteroid?"

"She was my wife."

The wind blows. The leaves rattle, and the Ferris wheel creaks. "I'm sorry," I say.

The chief looks at me. "We kept it a secret because it would've sent the wrong message."

I nod. "Political bias."

"I *was* biased," the chief says. "She was my wife."

I stand back up and feel my weight in my knees. I look over the balcony. "Was she right?"

"You know, as old as I am, I still have pretty good eyesight."

I stare out at the tree. "My eyes are shot."

"I believed her," the chief says.

Belief. This is a dead end. I squat down again, which is a mistake because my back and knees are killing me, and I question whether I'll be able to get back up. I stare at the old man and think, maybe in the end, there's just belief and nonbelief, and math has simply become our latest tool of rationalization, filled with trickery like any other language. A tool to win an argument. Otherwise, scientists would never disagree. Never argue. Never revise or downright flip their positions. I remember Akira once telling me about a book that came out right after Einstein figured out relativity. The book was called something like, *100 Scientists Explain Why*

Einstein Is Wrong. Maybe what even math can't overcome is the human condition, which is, in its essence, the fact that nobody ever wants to be proven wrong. Including me.

"All that time, we knew she was lying," the chief says. "Well, at least my wife did. But we went about it all wrong. For some reason, we felt like the clock was ticking. It wasn't. We could've been patient. We could've proven that Sessho-seki and the Ascalon Project were shams *after* the supposed asteroid was destroyed. But Karlin, she was so outraged that it was like she was racing that ray to destroy The Killing Rock. She kept badgering the president."

I look out at the giant tree again. The green birds circle and chirp, looking for their spot in the canopy. Ribbons of wood drip from the thick branches. The birds look like the dead one Ascalon was holding in the painting, but bigger. I imagine the chief sitting out here at every sunset thinking about what he's lost—what I took from him. I know the pain that stays with you from this loss, and I'm ashamed of knowingly inflicting it on others just to keep a lie breathing. "Evidence?" I ask.

The chief lifts his arm, grabs my shirt, and pulls me close, surprisingly strong for his age. His hand is shaking. "The full-body scans," he whispers. "Don't you remember?"

I do. The pedestal and rings of blue light. "What about them?"

"Karlin. She gave up on trying to disprove Akira with math. She knew she'd lost that battle. So she contacted the engineers that were contracted to build the damn machine in the first place. They gave her access, and she obsessed over Akira's scans. Specifically, her brain. She took them to her neuroscience pals in DC."

"What she did was illegal," I say. "That data was my jurisdiction, not hers."

Chang scoffs. "Like you even knew what you were looking at. That's exactly why it was your jurisdiction."

I grit my teeth. "So what about these scans?"

"The parts of Akira's prefrontal cortex where lies are created were lit up like midnight on New Year's. Every single day."

I shake my head. "That's not conclusive. We don't even use that tech in interrogation."

"You don't use it because of civil liberties. Otherwise, you would."

I swallow. "So what happened?"

"I told Karlin to sit on the scans. Like you said, she was working outside her jurisdiction. But she couldn't help herself. She went to the president. He looked at the scans and told her, 'What am I looking at? Blurry snapshots of Bigfoot? A UFO?' Karlin told him brain imaging of Akira Kimura. And he snapped. He'd had enough. He told her he expected her resignation by week's end. And that was when we headed to Water City. We were going to confront Akira with those scans and give her one last chance to admit that she was wrong before we went whistleblowing to Congress."

I sigh. "That was a bad move."

The chief nods. "Imagine the frustration of being the only one to know the truth."

I think about Akira. "Or the pleasure of it."

Chang grimly nods. "You ever been married to someone obsessed and on a mission?"

I think of Kathy. "I have."

"Could you have stopped her?"

No, I couldn't. Just like Chang couldn't stop Brum. Like Sabrina can't stop me. The best of us support, even while we watch the wagon wheels crumble beneath us. "You still have the data? It's not rock-hard evidence. In fact, it's pretty slim, but do you still have it?"

"Don't you think I would've released it all those years back if I did? The data was stripped from us. Classified. And when Karlin was killed, the White House confiscated her iE and buried it under another layer of top-secret. So the only arguments I had were my word and a vague recollection of science I didn't even understand. I knew I had zero credibility, but I had to say something, even if it sounded like mad ranting."

"So the White House covered it up? They didn't believe Akira?"

"Don't you see? At that point, politically, they had to believe her. The president went all in for her. Most people believed her. He couldn't walk back the Ascalon Project, even if he wanted to. Akira Kimura became the most powerful person on the planet."

"Why are you telling me this now?" I ask.

"Because you're here asking. I'm guessing this is the end for me, and I want someone to know the truth. It gives a me sick satisfaction that it's you. That self-loathing kick in yet?"

He's persuasive. I don't wanna be convinced, but I can't help it. Murders built on a lie. I look down at the artificial grass, which is littered with tiny fragments of chipped planter from when the plant outgrew its potted life. I wonder how long it took its roots to rip through the planter. Seeing roots so deeply embedded in the now cracked concrete, I wonder if one could remove the plant without bringing the whole balcony down. Nope. just like Akira's lie, the plant has grown too big to amputate safely. This trip was a mistake. Ultimately, the only thing I've gotten out of it is a guilt that could pull me down like quicksand if I'm not careful.

"I don't know if I can go further with this," I say. "You don't have any evidence, and I've got even less. I've got a wife and kid to think about."

The chief sneers. "A coward in a line of many."

"Maybe," I say. "But in the end, history will judge her. And it doesn't need my help."

"It's been nearly forty years," the chief says. "History has already failed us."

"Your wife wanted to be right so badly, it ruined her," I say. "And you. And me. Maybe all of us."

"Truth will ruin a man," says the chief.

I look out at the birds. They're settling in now, perched deep in the tree where they cannot be seen. They're Australian, these green birds, and it makes me almost want to laugh, the sight of the beautiful, tropical pestilence here in the middle of Oklahoma, probably returning from picking at rubbish at The Great Leachate. Even the huge tree, a banyan, looks Asian or tropical, and here it is in Muskogee, population two, so far as I can tell. Back on the islands, we would have these things eradicated. Indigenous species only. But here in forgotten middle America, nature is just taking its violent course. This is how the world is made. I remove *The Book of Ascalon* from my coat and drop it in the chief's lap. "As someone who hates Akira, you'll find this an interesting read," I say.

The chief lifts it and squints. "What is this?"

"She had twin girls. She murdered one. The other . . . Well, she's become something else."

The chief looks up at me. "She's a terrible human being."
I shrug. "We're all terrible."

"You have a chance to be better," he says. "Make this right."

"That book is handwritten," I say. "Probably the only copy. Take care of it. I'll have the Feds come and pick it up. But you might want to read it first."

I open the sliding glass door and enter. I head to the exit. The chief wheels after me. "You're not going to do anything?" he asks.

"You were the chief of staff, and you couldn't do anything. It's been forty years, and I'm a newly retired cop. What the hell do you think I can do for you?"

Chang's only response is a long stare with forty years' worth of frustration.

I think about the state of the world. Our tech, our ecology, our low crime rate, our lack of war. Anyone with enough crypto can go anywhere in the ocean. Those without can lose themselves in simulated worlds that speak to their tastes. Ancient Rome, feudal Japan, the American West—even post-apocalyptic settings have finally become sellable again this long after our close call. This ain't a utopia, but it's a better place than it would've been if Akira hadn't painted the sky. We are bound by that scar, a constant reminder that we're lucky to be alive. The world now is a better place than the one John briefly lived in. It's the kind of world Kathy would have loved to have seen. My first wife and kid, Vanessa and Brianne, are probably living it up in the EU. No more terrorists, global warming, nukes. The water mafia in Pakistan, the sea cucumber mafia in South Africa, gone. The pandemic in Sudan contained and eradicated. High methane-producing livestock like cows and pigs stopped being mass farmed. Then the global chicken plague got us, unwillingly, on a better diet. No more feasting on bowls with near-extinct creatures. Now it's all plant-based, sea-based. The ocean's no longer choking on plastic, which Kathy would have celebrated. Gigantic cubes of trash rotate in an endless recycling queue. For a century, we were all melting glaciers at incredible velocity while kite-high on painkillers, shopping, gaming, scrolling through social media, and chasing celebrity that the earth began to slosh and wobble. And that's stopped now. It's a better world for Ascalon than it was for me.

Sure, it's not perfect. We Less Thans still live paycheck to paycheck. Like those seascrapers, the ceiling separating The Have Nots from The Money is constructed with shatterproof glass. Soon, it'll be as hard as the crust of a small neutron star. Parents still fight about who's contributing more by way of paying bills, housecleaning, and childrearing. Poor countries have still been abandoned in the global economy. There are pockets of abject poverty on every continent. On ours, The Great Leachate. Nobody's sure what the numbers are, because no one reports on The Zeroes. Journalism became PRM— Public Relations Media—before I was born. The feed reports on plot-driven, angry affairs, personal and global, and new diseases on the rise, at least one per species. It never really asks how or why. It just asks, *What's next?*, then speculates.

And sure, we stopped global warming. In fact, Ascalon's Scar struck us like Cupid's arrow, charming us into our still-current love affair with the planet. But like the end of all wars, the carnage remains. The groundwater and penicillin rivers were deemed unfixable when they realized how much it would cost. On a personal level, medical bills are still flabbergastingly high for basic procedures. There are childcare costs. Mortgage costs. And other costs we don't realize we're paying until Death, the ultimate repo man, comes to reclaim our liquidated souls. We use our raised life expectancies just to work for longer. Extend our credit even further. We hide, show off, and protect everything behind sheets of gorilla glass. Plus, there are no more cigarettes or fried chicken.

I wonder how much all the bullshit matters. Is thinking like a parent the same as thinking like a coward? The truth is, I'm scared. The last few days have shaken me. I turn and look the chief in the eye, to give him some respect with my final refusal. "She's dead," I say. "Why aren't you satisfied with that?"

He looks at me, puzzled. "She's not dead."

I feel my face work itself into a frown. "What are you talking about?"

"She was just here two days ago."

I start to walk away. I want nothing to do with this craziness. "She was down there, tinkering with the Ferris wheel. I figured she was either spying on me or here to kill me. I've been waiting for the day she'd come for decades. I tried to go down there. Even in this state, my rage took over. But by the time I got there, she was gone. I figured that's why you showed up here today. She finally decided to punch my ticket."

"Impossible, buddy. I saw her cut to pieces myself."

"Look." He projects a holo from his iE. It's a glitchy, older model, but from a distance, the figure climbing the wheel and calling the green birds to her does look like a young Akira.

Ascalon.

After the name sounds in my head, I see a cloud of green smoke above the chief's head. And I cannot move. Of course, my uninformed attempt to blot this ability out has utterly failed. The ophthalmologist has allowed me to see red and green with only my eyes. I figured, take away one gear, and the machine is supposed to break. I don't register a smell, but I clearly see the green gyre widen above his sparsely haired crown. "No," I say.

"What are you looking at?" the chief asks. "Did you hear me?"

I try to snap out of it. Both of our iEs drop to the floor, spark then sizzle. I step to the wheelchair to pull the chief inside. Then I hear music. I stop. The Ferris wheel groans to life. "Entry of the Gladiators" blares from it, and the hundreds of green birds, quiet during sunset, are roused by the music.

The entire colony takes wing into a longitudinal lift high up and pitches back down to about thirty feet above us. They bank and begin to circle, flapping in unison and gliding around as if all thousand of them are tied to us by the same string. They are beautiful. Orange beaks, heads slightly yellow, bodies green, tails spears of blue. All from the same ancestors.

Then, the string is snipped. They pitch up so high, their green feathers become shadow. They reach their ceiling and seem to stall. They hang up there for a moment, wings spread, completely still, like beautiful origami. Then the colony crumples, and the birds sink together, speeding straight at us.

The squawking is awful as they pick apart the chief. His screams are even worse. He tries to swat them away with the book but drops it. I take out my blade and swing wildly at them, but there are too many. When he stops screaming, it occurs to me that they might come for me next. I grab *The Book of Ascalon* off the artificial turf, dive inside, and shut the sliding door. There's not much left of the chief by the time the door is shut. The birds turn to me now and fly into the glass. So many of them that I can no longer see outside. The carnival music gets louder and louder. The tempered glass door begins to crack. I heat my blade, although I wouldn't be able to fend that many of them off even with a flamethrower.

What is it that Ascalon told me? That there's nothing I can do that she hasn't seen yet. Feathers burst and the glass door spiders from seam to seam. Then the carnival music shuts off. The birds peel away and head back to the tree. The Ferris wheel creaks to a standstill. I take a couple steps back. And I feel her there. I turn around.

There she is, flesh-colored now. Beautiful and terrible, like the birds outside. For a split second, looking even more like Akira than Akira did. But then the differences crystalize. They aren't as numerous as they were the last time I saw her. Taller, more muscular. The scar. The tail. The gleaming yellow eye. I step back toward the sliding door and I knock out the glass with the hilt of my knife. I step through the shattered doorway, walking backward on clenched toes until I can feel my back hit the balcony railing.

"Give me the book," she says.

Before she can say anything, I touch the heated blade to it. A flame sparks at the edge of the first page, her life's work about to be incinerated. Ascalon sprints toward me. I wait until she's at arm's length, then lean back against the rail and let myself topple over, book still in hand. Ascalon grabs me by my ankle. But I'm way heavier than she is. She's been dragged over the edge of the rail too—it looks like her tail wrapped around the rail just in time.

And here we are, dangling upside down over a railing. Me holding a heat blade and a burning book, her holding onto my ankle with both hands. "You're certifiable," she says, smiling.

"You didn't think you were the only one," I say.

She begins to pull us up. I start swinging. "Stop," she says. "I'm trying to help you."

I swing up and plunge the heat blade into her shoulder. She doesn't even wince. In fact, I swear she's smiling. But her tail spasms around the rail. I hear it begin to crack. I drop the burning book and scramble up Ascalon's body. It'd be nice to have a pair of Akeem's grip gloves right now. I grab onto the railing and pull myself over. I drop onto the artificial grass and look up. The rail snaps, but the barbed end of Ascalon's tail plunges into the remaining concrete. I stand and look over the edge. Ascalon pulls the heat blade from her shoulder. I grab her tail and pull with everything I've got.

"I see why my mother loved you," she says.

And I ask myself why I'm trying to save her, and the answer is immediate. Because it's the hard thing to do.

I get her back over the balcony. We both fall hard into the chief's puddle. I feel his blood sticking to my back. Ascalon's struggling to get the end of her tail out of the concrete. I snatch the heat blade from her and get on top, kneeling over her, and the ease of it makes me feel like she's letting me. She's still smiling. I put the heat blade an inch from her eye. The fake one, not the one that's the spitting image of her mother's. The smile doesn't fade. She wraps her hands around mine and pulls the blade closer to her. Now it's me straining to pull away.

When I try to talk, I realize I'm out of breath. "I'm trying to help you," I struggle to say.

"You don't want to know what I found when I probed you?" she asks.

"You told me," I say.

Still smiling, she sighs. "Then do you wonder what I left?"

I do. I imagine being back in Jerry's penthouse, Ascalon's tail reaching so far up, it felt like it was piercing my brain. Not searching for something, but planting something. It's worried me since I woke up. But whatever's buried up there, I don't got it in me to try and dig it out.

"I knew you'd come here to Chang after reading what I wrote," she says.

"Why'd you kill him? No one believed him then. They sure as hell weren't about to now."

"I will preserve my mother's legacy. I'm more thorough than she was. Even a tiny, seemingly insignificant wound can fester. Can you see the extent of my abilities now?"

I look down at her serene face and know killing her is the smart thing to do. But when I see the plowed skin running from her forehead to her cheek in a straight line, I imagine the girl in the red sweater, back to her mother to hide her self-inflicted scar. The same kid, years later, put to sleep by Akira. No prince's kiss to wake her, only her own will. Always alone. But she's delusional and dangerous, which is probably one of the reasons why her mother put her to sleep in the first place.

"Tell me where you've hidden my mother's iE," she says.

Her insistence on this enrages me. "Even if she had one, should I know where the fuck it is?"

"You'll find it. She had no one else to leave it to."

"I'm not even gonna look for it."

"You can't help yourself. You're drawn to murdered things."

For once in my life, I've gotta be better than Akira. Not smarter, because that's not possible. Just better. And something in me deep down truly believes she got what she deserved. "I don't care what you're planning," I say. "Just leave me out of it."

"You don't understand," she says calmly. "You cannot separate yourself from this. You are part of the fabric of it. And I will pull on your thread as necessary." She grins at me. "You saw again, didn't you?"

I nod.

"Why would you want to give up such a gift?"

I think about that. "Personal peace."

"You were stupid to try to blind yourself. Now you can only half-see."

I feel something sharp rip through my back. The tip of her tail protrudes from my shoulder. I grasp the heat blade and shuck Ascalon's yellow eye. "Now you can only half-see, too," I gasp.

She finally screams and throws me to the side with her tail. I form a fist and punch her in the temple. We both get up. I'm standing there, heat blade in one hand and her artificial eye in the other, vibrating, feeling like my second heart is gonna explode. Just like her, I won't stop. She's gonna have to fucking kill me.

"Now is not your time," she says, standing there as if I

haven't just taken her eye out. "But soon, we will both be dead."

After all the yammering she did at Jerry's, I'm surprised this is the first time I notice she has Akira's voice. Maybe it's because Akira never said crazy stuff like this. Or because I worshipped her. But recognizing the similarity makes me hate Ascalon Lee. "I want zero to do with this. You keep coming for me, and I'll end you."

She smirks and climbs on the balcony. "Keep the eye. But you won't want to see what I see."

The end of her tail splits into a robotic hand, and she springs down to the giant tree, catching herself on a branch with it. The leaves rattle, and sleeping birds squawk and fly. I can't see her in all that green, and I don't know what I'd do if I could.

It's the birds that worry me now. I back up and trip over the doorway frame, then hurry to scramble back to my feet. I stagger inside and rip off my shirt, bundle it, and press it against my wound. I'm losing blood. Fast. I step past the chief's death predictor. It reads zero percent. I wonder if it's reading him or me. I feel awful about what she did to him. What I did to him.

I step inside the chief's bathroom to find a towel, maybe some gauze or a first aid kit. There's gotta be something in this place, considering his age. A couple of white hand towels hang on rings to the left of the sink. I grab them and turn on the water. I rinse off the heat blade first. A puff of steam explodes from the sink, almost burning my face. The mirror clouds. I wipe it with the other towel and look in the mirror.

All I see is guilty man covered in red. Maybe Ascalon is right. It was a flawed experiment to give up the colorblindness,

but it only seemed right after learning how it could be manipulated. I just wish I wasn't still seeing what I used to. The
blade, still hot, is clean now. I press it against my exit wound
and scream. I'm barely able to stay conscious. I turn my back
to the mirror and press the hot blade against my skin again,
this time to close the entry wound. I drop the blade and fall
to the floor.

For some reason, I see my daughter Ascalon playing with
her colored blocks. Carefully stacking them eight high. Then,
like she always does, she knocks them down. We never stop
doing that. It's time to go home now.

I wake up. I was out for a few seconds there. I pull myself
to my feet and think. I've got her iE. I'm guessing it's all
there—the numbers, the sleep, the grand conspiracy. Murder.
A child ruined by her mother. I'll turn it over to the Feds.
It's a better witness to a grand jury than I am. It should also
contain evidence of Jerry's murder. Of Akira's. Of the murders
I committed. It's time I stopped trying to save my own ass.

As for Akira having an iE, impossible. I would have
known. I would have seen it. Poor chief. Why did Ascalon
come for him now? I suppose if I were her, I'd be paranoid,
too. He was the last living dissenter, but he had no proof of
anything, only wild accusations. But why kill him at this age,
and in such an elaborate spectacle? Then I understand. This
wasn't for Chang. It was for me. If I didn't get in line, this was
my future.

I head to the elevator with no idea how I'm gonna get back
to Akeem's shuttle. I can't call a cab, not covered in blood like
this. And I'm still worried about those damn birds. I press
the down button. It doesn't light up. I head for the stairs and
find that I can't stop shaking. I stop and breathe. *Think, old*

man. You can't just walk back in this condition. Maybe the chief kept some kind of transport on the roof. I'm crawling up the stairs and barely manage to make it all the way.

I stumble out onto the roof. There's nothing up here except for gravel and a pink-clouded sunset. I'm out of ideas. Except one. *Quit your hang-ups,* I tell myself. I ping Sabrina my location and ask for help. I keep an eye out for the birds. They've vanished. Sabrina tells me she and Akeem are coming. I tell her not to bring Ascalon. She says Akeem's kids adore her and will keep an eye on her.

Sabrina's trip to Oklahoma will be at least a couple hours, so I slouch against what looks like an air vent and look for anything that will distract me from the pain. And I see it. Outside of town, miles beyond the tree and broken-down Ferris wheel, fields and fields of stacked and scrapped nuclear warheads fronting The Great Leachate like toppled pillars. Within a year after Sessho-seki, global nuclear disarmament. It might've taken a grand lie to do it, but she did it. Fucking Akira. How I sometimes forget everything she did for us. How we all do. I wonder how long it takes man to ruin a good world. To rebuild another one. Just like my daughter and me, stacking up blocks, knocking them down, and stacking them right back up. I think about Akira's daughter and the painting and the perfect scar running from the top of her forehead to her cheek, traversing across the crater that once held her human eye. Then I look up and spot Ascalon's Scar, twinkling in the now-dark sky. I laugh to myself. It's all fake, isn't it? An illusion, although it doesn't matter if it is one. All that matters is we believe it. I stare at the Scar in wonder as things fade from green to red to black.

24

I'm dreaming and I know it. It's a simple dream. I wake up. My iE tells me it's 1:54 A.M., so I go back to sleep. After what feels like a few hours, I wake up again. It's still 1:54. I stand, the usual creaky morning pain absent. I immediately wonder if I'm dead. I step forward. It works, so space, it seems, still exists. But I'm unsure about time. It's still 1:54. I lie back down, tell myself *Fuck it*, and go back to sleep.

This time, when I come to, I'm onboard Akeem's private intercontinental shuttle, or PIS, in the sleep quarters in the rear of the ship. First, I ask for the time. I quickly remember that my iE is back at Chang's, fried just like his. Then I check my pockets and am relieved to feel Ascalon's eye there. On the bed beside me is the remains of the chief, covered in plastic. I focus and try to spot green rising from him, leading me somewhere. Nothing. I look out the window. We're in dive mode, coming down from the stratosphere. Sitting up, I look around the sleeping quarters, which are decorated with ancient Roman artifacts encased in glass. It's one of the things me and Akeem have in common, a hobbyist's interest in the Roman Empire, but mine culminates in some downloaded history holo casts on my iE. His, The Money version, culminates in priceless six-sided dice carved from animal bone. A bronze arrowhead. Various coins. The biggest case contains what appear to be surgical instruments, which makes me squirm.

The door to the SQ slides open, and Akeem walks in with a military-grade med drone behind him. It's only when I see the hovering drone that I become conscious of the pain. "Where's Sabrina?" I ask.

"In the copilot's seat," he says. "She's not very happy with you right now."

"I figured."

"Plus," Akeem nods at the chief's body, "she had to lug what was left of him onboard. I thought she was crazy for picking up all the bones, but she said it was evidence to get you off the hook. Do you ever wonder if you're worth it, man?"

I nod. "Every day."

"She told me about the grand jury thing. What the hell's going on?" Akeem asks.

"You don't wanna know," I say. "Listen, my friend. Don't get too close to this. I'm toxic right now."

Akeem sighs and nods. "The med drone stitched you up. Put some healing gel on that wound. You're pumped full of pain meds right now, so take it easy."

"Thanks." I point at the glass case with surgical instruments. "I gotta tell you," I say. "That's the last thing I wanna see right now."

"Dug up from Vesuvius." He opens the case and pulls them out one by one. It's the first time I notice he's wearing one of those beaded bracelets in honor of Akira. "Forceps," he says. "Catheter. Scalpel. Vaginal speculum. I'm not sure we've come very far since then."

I force myself to stand. My body is creaking, especially my hip and shoulder. I step to the glass case, look at the ancient surgical instruments, and shiver. I remember sitting in class sixty-plus years ago learning about the Romans. I remember the fifth emperor, Nero, and the story that he played his fiddle while Rome burned, which was impossible because the fiddle hadn't been invented yet. All of this is over 2,200 years old. I wonder what will pass as fact and fiction in another 2,200 years. Will Akira still be a god? Will her "accomplishments" eclipse the crimes committed for her to be great? Now her transgressions have found their consequences in her daughter, who has perpetuated the killing.

I glance once more at what's left of the chief. No green. I feel like I'm experiencing withdrawals. I attempted to kick this, but now I'm desperate for its directional pull. That ambergris scent. Especially when it showed up above the chief—why only then? Because of the sheer magnitude of her intent?

"I don't suppose you heard," Akeem says.

I turn to Akeem. "Heard what?"

"The islanders are turning Akira's crypt into a little town for tourists. They're lobbying for her remains to be buried there once her body's finished going around the world."

Ascalon made that, not Akira. I wonder if the islanders know who they're rebuilding for. I eye Akeem's bracelet. His beads are pure platinum. The Money even spends more in tribute. "Where is she now?"

"They postponed the funeral procession indefinitely."

"Why?"

"Too many spectators demanding to see the body."

I shake my head. "Believe me. They don't want to." I

wanna relay what Chief Chang said before he died. But then he chimes in.

"I'm tired of the whole thing at this point," he says. "It's all anyone talks about. I've got Akira fatigue."

"Thanks, Akeem. I owe you one."

"Then do this for me."

"What?"

"When we land, apologize to your wife. And . . ."

"And what?"

"Stop acting so goddamn crazy."

Akeem exits the SQ. I think about what he's said. Crazy might be underplaying it. In the past five days, I've broken procedure at a murder scene, withheld crucial information, quit my job, nearly abandoned my wife and child, pulled a heat blade on one of my best friends, burned down a mausoleum, almost voluntarily went to prison for life, had life-altering eye surgery, and flew to Muskogee, Oklahoma, just to watch parakeets tear a person apart. What the fuck am I doing with my life? I'm eighty years old and feel two hundred. But I'm not tired of this. Despite everything, I feel even more alive than the day Akira came to me at the skeleton of Volcano Vista and asked for my help. Ascalon has the same power over me as her mother. I hope that's not because she drugged me or planted some explosive in my brain.

I take her eye out of my pocket and I look at it. It's beautiful. Smaller than an iE, a brilliant bird's-eye yellow with a black pupil. We all have specific mini-singularities built into our eyes. Her eye lacks the facets of a normal iE. It's smooth. Perfect. Except for the bio tissue that dangles from it that was connected to Ascalon's brain. This tech is impossible. Maybe she really is as brilliant as the mother was. If Akira had an eye like this, I would have noticed.

As for Ascalon, I don't want to fight her. I don't want to kill her. And I definitely don't want to know what it is she ultimately wants. Because I'm afraid I'll discover that I want the same thing. I look back at the eye and picture it being cracked, like one of Akeem's chicken eggs, the yolk mixed with a shaman's stick to glimpse into the past. But not by me.

Then the tissue begins to shrivel, like death in fast-forward. The roots fall from the eye. Then the green begins to pulse. Maybe I've been pumped with too many meds. I don't want to watch, but I do anyway. The greens grow thin and long, orbiting the sphere, streamers of color twirling around it. I squeeze my eyes shut and open them again. The wisps are still there. I blow on them, but they don't disperse. Instead, they spin faster like a pinwheel when my breath hits them. The yellow eye turns to gaze directly at me. I should just put it back in my pocket and chalk all this up to drug-induced hallucination, but I blow on it again.

The eye begins to spin. It rises from my palm. I take a couple of steps back.

The wisps of green and red gyre further and further outward, bouncing off the walls of the SQ. I'm leaning against a window now, watching the spirals fill the room like a miniature galaxy. Then the scent hits. Pure ambergris, stronger than I've ever smelled before. Music starts, too—softly at first, but quickly becoming deafening. The tune of Ascalon's song pounds at my eardrums.

I cover my ears, and the music blares louder in turn. I close my eyes again. I can feel the tears trickling from my eyes. I open them. More green and red than I've ever seen. Thick. Choking. I wonder if this is real.

How did Akira fail to find this device all those years ago? I think about the toy ball that took out the chief and corporal. Then it hits me. She didn't need to find the device. She had Idris Eshana, the inventor of the iE, in her pocket. She just needed to observe the severed connections in her daughter's head and figure out how to attach them to a more advanced iE. Ascalon Lee's sleep-state vision of her mother with a scalpel. She didn't just keep her daughter in AMP to protect herself. She kept her daughter in suspended animation to study her. *Akira had an iE.*

I grab the eye and barge out of the SQ. Akeem is sitting, changing his boots. I stagger by him. He stands. "What's going on?"

The eye is trying to spin in my clenched fist. I turn around. "Do you have grip gloves?"

"I always keep grip gloves on me." He pulls them from his back pocket. I snatch them from him and slip one on with my teeth. After it's on, I put the eye in the palm of the gloved hand. "Drop the landing gear," I say.

"Are you crazy? We're going too fast for that."

I manage to get the other glove and head to the elevator to the mech bay. Akeem follows. "Have you lost your mind?"

Sabrina enters the main cabin from the cockpit. She's startled by the sight of me. "What are you doing?"

I wanna tell her, but I've got no time. I step into the elevator and close the door. She calls for me. I look down at my hand. The greens and reds slip through the cracks between my gloved fingers. If there was ever a time I wish I didn't see them, it's now. The elevator stops at the mech bay. I exit and charge down the narrow path to the landing gear. I hope the shuttle holds up, and that I make it in time.

I find the lever to put down the landing gear and pull it. A loud beeping. Red lights flashing. Airstream floods the bay, almost yanking me out. I grab onto the lever. The landing gear is ripped from the fuselage. The shuttle drops. Fast. I'm thinking that this may have been a mistake until I look down at my closed fist. I know I've been wrong before, but no way, not this time. The greens and reds leak out in endless streams. I let go of the eye. It's swept out of the shuttle just as it explodes.

The shock waves hit the vehicle, which rumbles and beeps even louder. It begins to dive down, nose first. We're a dead stick. I hang on and hope Sabrina and Akeem can level us out. The airstream is so strong, it feels like it's peeling off my skin. The shuttle begins to level, then slow, but the shrill beeping doesn't stop. Through the hole on the floor where the landing gear once was, I see we've broken through the scud. Now, there's just ocean. The pleats and crests look frozen from this high up. I figure I should be in panicked prayer right about now, but I'm not. I'm calm and reflective. Maybe it's the drugs. Maybe not. I catch a glimpse of the edge of an island. A beach, maybe. I imagine children playing there, building sandcastles. Then everything is just clouds. The shuttle bumps up and down. This is the death rattle. There's nothing left to do but hang on and let my mind race. I tell myself that consciousness is just our brains using memory to predict reality. We predict ourselves into existence. Once we stop doing it, we fear we don't exist anymore. I tell myself not to fear this, but to embrace it. I'm so tired of predicting. I figured fixing my colorblindness would water down the unique psychedelic cocktail in my brain. I was wrong. I misdiagnosed myself. Maybe I'm just flat-out crazy. I tell myself we're all just castles of sand, destined to be washed away by rising tides.

Then the shuttle jinks, trying to avoid everything below it. We finally hit the ocean surface. Hard. And now I'm not thinking. I'm just holding on. It floats up and hits again. The beeping stops. The fuselage cracks in half, and the half I'm in skids sideways, then tumbles. It comes to a stop before starting to fill with water. I let go and try to splash my way out, but it's sinking fast. I'm underwater now, the husk descending cracked end first. I dive down with everything I've got. I barely manage to pull myself down through the crack and head for the surface. I'm running out of air.

I break through and take a giant gasp, then get my bearings and start swimming through the shuttle wreckage, looking for Sabrina and Akeem. I don't know how I just survived. But when the odds are stacked against us, we never really know how we pull it off. So we credit something intangible, like god or an ideal version of ourselves. Then we lose our fear and attempt riskier and riskier things until the gamble doesn't pay off. I hope my wife is alive.

Off to the left, I see Sabrina treading water. Relief washes over me. I swim to her, fighting off the pain between my shoulder blades. We reach each other.

"What happened?" she asks.

"Ascalon's eye," I say. "Self-destructed. Akeem?"

"I don't know. When we started going down, he went to the cockpit and took the controls."

"Shit. He probably strapped in."

I dive down into the water but can't see much. Too deep. I

pop back up. No sign of the cockpit. I go back down until my ears feel like they're gonna burst. Surprisingly, I feel a hand tugging at me. Sabrina's. I shake it off and dive deeper, but the deeper I go, the less I see. I return to the surface, panting. "Stop!" Sabrina screams.

"What?"

Sabrina points. I follow her finger and see an inflatable raft. It's Akeem and the med bot heading to us. When he gets closer, I see that the med bot is rowing while Akeem is reclined against the bow, hands laced behind the back of his head. He's grinning and smoking a cigar. I shake my head. This motherfucker.

He pulls Sabrina in first then me. The med bot starts prodding me. "How the hell did you get out of the cockpit?" I ask.

Akeem shrugs. "I've spent most of my life in this ocean. It'll never kill me. I'm blessed."

Sabrina shakes her head. I look out to the horizon, trying to guess where the hell we are. I have no clue. Ascalon warned me not to hold onto the eye for too long. But if she'd wanted, she easily could've killed me several times over by now. She's keeping me alive because she wants something.

I look east and imagine the eye rising from the ocean, green and red flesh sprouting from it. First, the brain. A lightning storm of firing neurons. Then a spinal cord emerging from the brain, growing down toward the water's surface. Lightning strikes, a pink flash and boom. Organs pulsing as they appear, each one lighting up. Nerves reaching out from the spinal cord like tentacles to the organs. Then bones and muscle. Skin, marbled green and red. A mythical sea monster, built step by step, just as a savior was taken apart. It wasn't Akira toying with me. Ascalon put the piano in The

Savior's Eye and led me to that mausoleum. She was the one who drew me to Jerry's and the painting, then set me up for Jerry's murder. It may even have been her who sent me the gem that got me out on bail. She had known I would visit Chief Chang. She predicted my every step, playing me like a chess piece. But why me?

I stare at this hallucination and notice something funny. It resembles Akira more than it does Ascalon. It sings a song I know well. I see the lyrics in red. I shut my eyes, not wanting to see it anymore, but that doesn't help, because I can still hear the song. Certain letters in the lyrics grow bolder.

Ascalon is not just the name of the savior
It's the name of the daughter
The one I gave up
Find her for me and tell her that I'm sorry

The bold letters become even larger while the others fade away. Soon I see:

I am the savior. I am the daughter. I am dio.

Whatever she's put in me is making me see this. I want to get rid of it but don't know how.

Sabrina shakes me. I look at her then look back. The monster and the letters are gone. Now there are only Coast Guard hovers coming to the rescue. "What were you looking at?" Sabrina asks.

"I don't wanna know," says Akeem. He begins to cough. "It's been a while since I smoked a cigar." He coughs again, more violently this time. A speck of blood spurts from his mouth. He tosses the lit cigar overboard. Sabrina eyes the hovers, willing them to get here quicker. The med bot moves from me to Akeem.

"Dio," I whisper.

Akeem slaps the med bot away. "What did you say?" he asks.

"Dio," I say. "What does it mean?"

"And you call yourself a student of Roman history." Akeem laughs, then coughs again.

"Stop talking," Sabrina says. "You've got internal bleeding. The hovers are almost here."

"I'll pray to dio then," Akeem says. I look at him. "Dio," he says. "Means 'god.' Derived from the Latin 'deus.'"

Akeem coughs uncontrollably, and my imagination goes running again. A little girl, born perfect. All her deformities thrust upon her sister in the womb. Then an aching loneliness, the longing to have part of her sister in her. So, she carves in some of the deformities, both of the twins existing within her. Rejected by her father. Rejected by her mother. Neither wants to be around a reminder of what they left behind under the waterfall that day. So, she makes herself into something more. Still rejected. And this time put into a deep sleep, no Prince Charming coming to save her. She can no longer be Ascalon. No one will accept her.

I think of the creature I just imagined rising from the ocean. *It's not real*, I pray. But it was as clear and powerful a sight as the first time I saw green or red. And I know it's there.

25

The second case I primarily worked on wasn't exactly *Murder on the Orient Express*. A sixty-five-year-old male pinged 911 and reported that his senile mother had disappeared. Uniforms responded, and at first, the man wouldn't let them into his apartment. When he finally agreed to let them in, on the condition that they wouldn't touch a thing, they saw why. The place was so messy, it was tough to walk through. Enough packaged food to last a nuclear winter. So much crap in the delivery chute that it was clogged. One officer stepped on a sea urchin shell and crushed it. The man threw a fit and attacked the officer. The uniforms cuffed him and brought him in. When I questioned him at the station, he told me he hadn't left his apartment in years. He didn't feel comfortable around anyone besides his mother. And when she went missing, his condition prevented him from going outside to look for her. In Japan, they called guys like this hikikomori. The man had basically dropped out of society.

After interrogating him for about ten minutes, it was pretty obvious to me that he'd offed his mother. He clenched his jaw every time she was mentioned. He said he spent every single day trying to get the apartment organized, but she always misplaced things and tore the place up looking for them. He said he'd felt trapped in hell. He couldn't leave, but he couldn't stay, either. I asked him why his place was in such disarray now that his mother was gone. He leaned across the table and whispered the answer. Every day, he would organize, but when he woke up in the morning, the place would be in shambles again. "It's her ghost," he said. She was punishing him. I asked him what she was punishing him for. He said for being a bad son.

When I entered the crime scene, the greens were already there to greet me. Rising like steam from a rice cooker. Seeping from the seal of the freezer. The entire floor was smoky with green like dry ice at senior prom. It took some time, but I found the mother scattered throughout the apartment piece by piece. Hands sealed in the rice cooker. Feet in the freezer. Head wrapped up and crammed under the floorboards. After I found all the pieces, I went back to the son and asked why he'd cut her up like that. He said that even after death, his mother rose every night to rummage through the apartment looking for her stuff. So, one day, he dug her up and cut off her hands, thinking she couldn't possibly move things without her hands. But it didn't work, so he dug her up again and cut off her feet, thinking that she couldn't move from room to room without her feet. But that didn't work either. By the end, he was just cutting out of rage. Rage at her for being responsible for his existence, which he didn't care for anymore. I didn't have the heart to tell him that he'd been the one waking up in the middle of the night and messing his place up. I left that to the shrinks at the max security psych ward, where he would spend the rest of his life. I wonder if he's still alive. If he ever believed them.

I'm thinking all this while laid up in Akeem's personal med ward, nanotech healing my broken ribs and shredded shoulder and looking unsuccessfully for whatever Ascalon Lee left inside me. Akeem is one room over getting a massive organ overhaul—newly farmed stomach and small intestine—and Sabrina is out playing with baby Ascalon somewhere, hardly a scratch on her, which makes me glad. It makes sense, really. Not many fall better than a former collegiate all-star athlete. It's been six days since Akira's death, but it feels like it's been six years. The Feds, still the most powerful entity on earth, are flying here this afternoon to question me. They've already run a full autopsy on what's left of Chief Chang and investigated the crime scene in Muskogee. They know it wasn't me who killed him. But me, I'm not so sure. So when they asked me if I knew who was responsible for his death, I told them that. And that won't satisfy them for long.

They're bringing the special prosecutor with them on this next go-round. Probably smart and experienced. A real patriot with all the time and resources in the world. My iE is gone, but its data still exists. Maybe I'll sign over access. I'll let them rewind through decades of mistakes and let my history be the judge of who I am. But for the first time in a long time, I'm not thinking about the past. I'm actually thinking about the future, like Akira did. Both knew this wasn't a habit of mine, which blinded me when dealing with them.

I'm eighty, and only now do I see where my synesthesia ends. I didn't see death coming when it came to Kathy and John. Or Akira. My sight is limited, as all sight is. But just because others can't see something, doesn't mean it doesn't exist. Akira knew this, as well as its implications—that you could convince people of the existence of something they couldn't see. She always was a prolific inventor. But her fabrications—like her inability to play the piano, her role as Ascalon's aunt, her need for security instead of a hit man—they've played us all like chess pieces. In the end, I'm finding it hard to believe that The Killing Rock was coming for us at all. So maybe Chang was right. She had years to plan Sessho-seki and engineer whatever she shot into space. Maybe her daughter was the real Ascalon Project. But Ascalon has killed her and wants something badly. I think I know how she plans to get it.

So, when I see Sabrina on security vid running toward my room, Ascalon in her arms, I already know what she's here to tell me. She passes Akeem's armed guards standing in front of his door and politely waves without breaking stride before stepping inside. "Did you hear? It's all over the feed."

I nod. "People are starting to say that Akira's still alive."

"You saw?"

I strain to stand. The ribs and shoulder still ache. I stretch until the pain is unbearable. "Yeah, out on the water."

"What are you talking about?"

I begin to dress. I wince in pain. "That's why the Feds and special prosecutor want to talk to me."

"I thought they wanted to talk to you about Akira's murder?"

"Kind of. Akira's body is gone. I get it now. That's why the funeral procession was canceled. It was stolen on the third day. Probably incinerated on a timer, actually."

Ascalon pushes away from Sabrina and says, "Crawl, crawl." Sabrina puts her down. Crawling is what I imagine all the microscopic mech critters in my shoulder and ribs are doing. Searching for tissue to fix, foreign objects to destroy. For a second, I think I can feel them squirming around in there, then remind myself that's impossible. "Incinerated by whom?" she asks.

"I need to figure out a way to get my rail gun back," I say, slipping on my pants. Ascalon wobbles to the bed and tries to climb up. I pick her up and wince, then put her down on it. "Listen," I say. I know that's the wrong way to start a sentence. It's always followed by shit someone doesn't wanna hear.

"I was so stupid. I didn't see it."

"See what?" Sabrina asks.

"Ascalon. She's spent thirty-odd years involuntarily asleep planning this, and the last three awake executing it. Why did she cut up her mother like that? Not just for revenge. For tissue. From every organ. And to plant the devices that would burn her mother up after she was done. And she was looking for something. Something she couldn't find."

Ascalon starts jumping on the bed. Sabrina, looking disappointed, heads to her and tries to gently sit her down. The baby cries.

"Looking for what?" Sabrina asks.

"Her mother's iE."

Sabrina frowns. "You said so yourself. Akira never had one."

"She wouldn't have had one like ours," I say. "She's Akira. She would've had something special. And she wouldn't want anyone to know she had it." I tap the side of my temple. "She would've put it in here. And it wouldn't be the first time she kept something from me."

"So the book isn't some made-up story," Sabrina says. "But why is her daughter doing this? What's her endgame?"

"I'm betting she's got her mother's blood type. The same mitochondria. And now she has enough tissue samples and the funds to grow all the genetically compatible organs she needs. I didn't catch it at first, but she's undergone some surgery. Changing her voice. She wants to look and sound exactly like her mother."

Sabrina tries to calm Ascalon down. "What do you have to do with all this?"

"I knew Akira better than anyone. And everyone else who knew her well is dead. Ishana. The president. Jerry. Chief of Staff Chang. That tour guide. I'm the only one left."

"What does she want from you?" Sabrina asks.

"She wants me to find Akira's iE."

"Why?"

I squint and look for green above Sabrina's and Ascalon's heads. Nothing. I need to finish this, or there will be. "The hell with it. I'll take the 1911."

Sabrina pulls it from her back and hands it to me. I check if it's loaded. "But why?" Ascalon is cackling, bouncing up and down on the bed again.

"To *become* Akira Kimura."

Sabrina sighs and closes her eyes. Ascalon takes a bad step and falls off the bed headfirst. I'm there to catch her. She laughs and laughs and laughs. I kiss her on the cheek. I blow at the wisps of her thin hair. I take in the fresh baby smell from her head. I love this kid.

"Do you know where she is?" Sabrina asks.

I nod. "Pretty sure. One hundred and seventy-seven atmospheres deep."

"Volcano Vista," Sabrina says.

I nod. "Her new place."

I put Ascalon down on the floor, and she runs to her mother, who scoops her up. I've gotta try. For my wife and my kid. I move in for a hug. Sabrina sighs in my arms. Ascalon pushes my face away. A chip off the old block. "I love you," I struggle to say. Not because I don't mean it, but because it's something I've always struggled to say.

"I love you, too," Sabrina says.

I shake my head. "When the Feds and the prosecutor come, tell them where to find me. And when he wakes up, tell Akeem thanks for everything."

"He left a message for you."

"What?" I say.

Sabrina takes something out of her pocket and tosses it to me. It's the gem. "He said for you to take this and shove it up your ass."

I smile and set it on the counter. "I—"

Sabrina nods. "I'll give him the bail money once you're cleared."

I look at her. "I'm sorry about all of this."

"I know," she says. "Come back in one piece."

I laugh when I imagine coming back in several pieces. Ascalon points behind me. "Gre," she says in a wispy voice.

It's how she says green. I turn around to look at what she's pointing at.

"Gre," Ascalon says again.

Puzzled, Sabrina and I look at each other. Ascalon points again. "Re," she says.

Red. We both look around the room. There isn't a single red or green thing in here. Ascalon points behind me again. "Gre. Re," she says.

I turn around, almost expecting to see a ghost hovering

above me. But I see nothing. Then they start forming. The wisps. Faint. I follow them with my eyes.

They're coming from the gem.

I touch my nose. She wasn't trying to put something inside me. She was *looking* for something. I pick up the gem and run it under X-ray. The blue projection pops up. There it is, encased in the middle of the gem. A tiny data chip. A sliver of gallium nitride that stores a lifetime. Everything Akira has ever seen or done since the inception of her first and only iE.

Or maybe nothing. Maybe pure data.

I look at Ascalon. She smiles like she knows that I finally see what she's seeing, and that brings us closer together. She has my synesthesia. So much for imaginary. It's real, genetic— and hereditary. "I'm sorry, kid," I say.

Ascalon looks at the gem and claps her hands.

Sabrina grabs me by the arm. I look at her. I don't think she caught on to what me and Ascalon are seeing. "What is it?"

I point at holo projection. "There's a data chip in the gem."

Sabrina squints. "Why?"

"It's her iE."

I pick up the gem, hold it up to the light, and inspect its hundreds of green facets. I'm in awe of its value. Not the gem, but what's inside. The mind of a god.

"That's why Ascalon Lee probed you," Sabrina says. "She was looking for it."

I nod. "Akira left this to me. Why?" I'm asking myself as much as I'm asking Sabrina. Akira could've destroyed this herself or never even made one in the first place.

Sabrina peers at the slight chip. "She wanted you to do something with it."

I turn to my wife. "What? Why choose me for that?"

She shrugs. "Who else is there?"

I reexamine the sliver. So small that it could pass for a crack or a chip. I wouldn't even have noticed if it weren't very faintly smoldering in green and red—the smell, or the particles, cloaked by the dense crystal around it. She's right. Shit, I'm the only one left. Me. I'm fighting back those old feelings of love and admiration. I look at Sabrina, hoping that just the sight of her will help me in that fight.

"That's why Ascalon Lee cut up her mother," Sabrina says. "To find this."

"It's why she left me alive."

"She knew Akira would leave it to you without even telling you."

I put the gem in my pocket. "She knew Akira would leave clues that only I could see. That it would take me some time to find it."

"You're not going to give it to her, are you?" Sabrina asks.

"I don't know what I'm going to do, but there's no room for either of them in our lives." I sigh. This demented, genius pair, larger than life. What if they were given the chance to start over? Most people use their iEs to communicate. To share their favorite frivolous things. To vid themselves eating. Fucking. Doing the basest things animals do, but in high-class environments, as if to say this is what makes us a higher species. They use iEs to consume entertainment. To gossip. To game. Walk in simulation. Bathe themselves in it. Drown themselves it. To gain fifteen minutes' worth of knowledge, then call themselves experts. Some people decide to have their iEs' data destroyed upon death. Others hire an editor to digitally clean the narrative into something falsely coherent and relevant, then release it to the public or pass it down to their kids. But these two used it to store knowledge that they created. World-shaking knowledge. One embedded it somewhere inside herself, probably near her brain. The other's is her eye. They directly linked this tech to their consciousness. My mind whirls at the potential of this. Programming ourselves to perform mundane tasks in the subconscious, much like our brains command our lungs to breathe and our hearts to beat. Sure, most people would still just use this to pull up vids to jerk off to, but in the hands of certain people, this technology could have terrifying consequences. Should I destroy this?

"Be careful," Sabrina says.

"I don't want to kill her," I say.

"I worry more about her killing you."

I run my hand over Ascalon's head. Her hair is so fine, so soft. "If I don't come back—"

"I'll kill her," she says.

I believe her. I step to the nearest shelf to rummage through the medical supplies and find what I'm looking for. I pocket it. I kiss Sabrina and walk out. It's time to compartmentalize. To stop thinking about my family for my family. It's time to work myself into a nice, violent lather thinking about all the things I hate. Those of us who bitch about our first-world problems. The ones who say privileged shit like, *Imagined problems can be worse than real ones*. They never are, except to those who don't have real ones.

While I'm climbing into the hover, I think about the idiotic grand jury process the Feds want to put me through. Threatening me with perjury charges and prison time if I slip up. Most crimes are illegal across the board—theft, assault, murder—but the act of lying is prosecuted in a million different forms and gradients. Fraud, slander, false advertising, perjury. You can lie to your spouse and kids all you want. Just don't lie to the Feds.

I lift off, and the wind howls. The incoming tropical storm has been downgraded to a depression. I look down at Akeem's ridiculously opulent estate floating in the middle of the ocean. I force myself to hate it. Fuck The Money. And The Less Thans? Fuck them, too. We're all the same. We just want to matter. To learn just enough to seem important. Once our lives didn't depend on learning anymore, we stopped studying. We bob around in schools, relishing in our superiority to the fish and animals around us, but the only thing that differentiates us is that we realize our own mortality.

By the time I fly through the wet, choppy air and land at the lot a half mile from the entrance of Volcano Vista, mostly I'm just sad. If I'm going out soon, I don't wanna go out like Chief Chang. An angry old man. Or a paranoid recluse like Akira. At the hand of her own daughter. I don't wanna be taken by surprise, either, like Jerry Caldwell or the innocents I put in the ground myself. It's dark now, and I'm walking along the garden path to the seascraper between trees that seep silently in the humidity. Under the dim polyp lights that brighten when I near, a moth sips the tears of a sleeping bird.

Up ahead, more light. Hundreds, maybe thousands of firefly specks in front of the grand arch of Volcano Vista. Sound. Commotion. People. Did someone pull a fire alarm? Hard to imagine at this time of night. Nobody likes to be pulled out of bed in the middle of the night, and The Money, who populates the bottom half of the seascraper, has the power to make sure it doesn't happen. I step into the clearing and see what appears to be a candlelight vigil. The crowd seems to be leaning toward the arch, like plants tilted toward sunlight for nourishment. I squeeze past them. They're all wearing their beaded bracelets in tribute. I hear whispers. "Someone saw her," an old man says. "She's down there. Alive," says a young woman.

I break through to the front. Cops have the entrance barricaded. A few media crews are on the scene. I spot the superintendent chatting with security under the arch.

Then a strong gust of storm wind and a collective gasp.

The thousands of specs of candle lights lift and float into the dark sky like jellyfish bells. The entire crowd watches, astonished. Even the superintendent and the guards are looking up, pointing. "See, she's alive!" someone screams.

For some reason, I expect the superintendent's eyes to turn toward mine, but they don't. Instead, he's watching the floating lights scatter in the night sky, and his eyes begin to tear. Incredible. He's sobbing. Every person I pass is holding a bulb of light in front of them, like an offering, hoping theirs will glide from their hands like the others. I hear more shouts. "She has risen," they say. "She's come back for us!"

I step through the barricade and head to the entrance. I turn to look, and the superintendent and the guards are still bewitched. A little girl exits the lobby while I turn, and we bump into each other. Her lighted bulb falls from her hands and hits the ground. It flickers, then dims. She begins to cry. I slip through the door, and the clamor of the crowd softens.

I cross the solar-paneled flooring and walk under the crystal, water-filled chandeliers lit blue by bioluminescent algae that only glow at night. I step to the elevator and scan. The doors slide open. I step in and begin my descent.

This time, I'm not looking at my reflection in the glass. I've spent my whole goddamn life doing that. If I'm going to get out of this in one piece, it's time to learn how to look across the past, present, *and* future at once.

A spook fish passes by in the twilight zone. Its bright-green barrel eyes are embedded inside its transparent head, which lights up like a SEAL cockpit at night. I remember the spook fish can see out through its own head. I need to do the same.

What did Sabrina want me to remember? That our survival instinct, which makes it easy for us to forget trauma, also makes us unappreciative of close calls and second chances. As usual, she's right. I think about her words as I set out across the catwalk flanked by trauma and final chances. I need to make sure I remember my way back.

26

As I'm heading down, I use the time to make sure I'm ready. 1911, fifteen in the mag. Unlike my rail gun, the 1911 isn't powerful enough to punch through the glass, so my aim doesn't have to be perfect. I brought the old heat blade from Muskogee as well, just in case. I try to anticipate what might be down there. Ascalon, perhaps a different color, maybe armed. No, she probably assumes her tail and mind are enough. And they damn well might be. Something tells me I haven't seen either in their full capacity yet.

Passing atmosphere forty, I recall the last time I was here. Watching Akira slide into pieces. I wonder which parts Ascalon took and made her own. Not just tissue from organs—she's got the chops to graft entire appendages. Maybe the hands? The feet? Definitely the hands—they would give her fingerprint ID. I never even thought to confirm it was really her when they first slid off in the chamber. Procedure. It would've served me that day after all. I check the 1911 again. I hope this old thing doesn't jam. I reach into my pocket and take out the two small nose-filler orbs that I swiped from Akeem's med bay before leaving. Normally, they're used to stop a broken nose from bleeding. But me, I've got other uses for them. Protective. I need to see clearly. I can't let Ascalon use my sight against me. I hope it'll work, but hell if I know. A full-on mask would probably be better, but I don't want to tip her off. And when I think back on her sticking her damn tail up my nostrils, these things also irrationally give me a bit of peace of mind. The gel fillers disappear up my nostrils and expand. My lips part slightly so that I can breathe out of my mouth.

Finally, the penthouse. 177. I step inside.

The lights, tracks of orange latticed on the ceiling, are muted. They make the room feel like it's daybreak. I look down at the floor. I hope she hasn't implemented the same suction-tech security that was at Jerry's. I take my first steps gingerly, eyes on the floor. Nothing happens. I walk through the near empty penthouse and pass the artifact telescope. The ocean floor lights up, and the entire room brightens. I glance though the window. The cannonball and the fuselage are still there, but the whale bones, which I last saw being devoured by zombie worms, are gone.

I step into the next room. It's dim and chilly. Ascalon is sitting cross-legged in front of the low tea table. Steam rises from the kettle. I look at her. Actually look. She really is a replica of her mother now. The scar on her face is gone, and the white lab coat she's wearing make that undeniable. There are, however, patches of blue left on her bare forearms. Just remnants from her last tat pill.

"Please, sit." She's even got Akira's voice now, cold and condescending. It's almost like being back in the classroom of your least favorite teacher.

I sit across from her, my gun pointed at her under the table.

I look at her hands. Faint scars at the wrists. She smirks as she scoops green powder into the kettle that sits atop a tiny heater. She mixes it in the pot water with a bamboo whisk. The steam rises in the cold air. "Her heart is beating in my chest now."

I nod. "You gonna pour that tea, or should I do it myself?"

She stops whisking. "I will pour," she says.

She fills my cup, and I look down at the smoking tea. I take a chance and sip from it. She does the same. I look up at her face. A new yellow iE. It's really the only thing that differentiates her from her mother now. The other eye is definitely Akira's. A dark disk of a pupil that I always associated with knowledge.

"I can't believe she let you run wild for three years," I say.

Ascalon shrugs in agreement. "I thought there was a good chance that once she discovered I broke free, she would come after me as well." She smiles. "Every day in the first year, I expected to see you, her right hand, coming for me. But I believed myself to be dead anyway, so what did it matter?"

"She never told me."

"I know."

"Why?"

Ascalon takes another sip. "Guilt. Embarrassment. Those are the things my mother feared. Not death. The piano story from her childhood is true."

This surprises me. How would she know? "And the song?" I ask.

"She sang it the day she put me into that . . . that thing." She eyes the AMP chamber. "I just took it and improved on it. Something I'm used to doing."

"Did the islanders really just let you dig that hole?"

"They dug it for me," she says. "They built the entire place by my specifications. They believed it was what my mother wanted. And again, she didn't interfere."

"She wasn't even the one who pinged me to meet."

"No. That was me. You understand now, don't you?"

"Understand what?" I ask.

"She let all of this happen," Ascalon says. She blows on her tea. Wisps of steam float off the top. "Which means she wanted it."

I finish my cup. Ascalon pours me some more. The scars on her wrists are already fainter. She's steady with the kettle, even with her mother's hands freshly sewn on.

"Are you ready to help me?"

"You've threatened my family and almost killed me more than once, and you want me to help you?" I ask.

"Let's not go by the scoreboard. You murdered my father. You cut my eye out of my face and set fire to the book I spent months writing. I'm sorry about your shoulder. I lost my temper. And as for the explosion, I warned you. If you'd let the eye blow you to pieces, you weren't the warrior I thought you were anyway. The one who can see murder."

She pauses. "Seeing yourself as superior can be helpful, you know."

"How's that?"

"Once you do, you have to live up to it," she says.

"Why not just be you?" I ask, already knowing the answer.

"People worship her. No one worships me." She pauses. "But perhaps this way, they will."

I stand up and sigh. I step to the AMP chamber and knock on it lightly with my knuckles, which don't have any punch left. "They'll never believe you," I say.

Ascalon calmly takes a sip of tea. "No, but they'll believe *you*. And once you hand over her iE to me and I transfer her data to my own," she says, tapping at the side of her eye, "it will be impossible to distinguish between us."

"Maybe," I say.

A holo shoots from her eye onto the table. It's a live feed of the crowd outside. "Don't you see it? They want so badly to believe." It begins to rain, and a gust scoops up the lights of those not hanging on tightly enough.

Ascalon refills her cup. "I will expunge all the data concerning your past transgressions. I'll pay you handsomely. The kind of wealth that will provide amply for multiple generations. You've turned down my offer to make you like you were forty years ago. I extend that offer again."

I think about that. "I was less forty years ago."

Ascalon shrugs. "My mother's wealth was vast, much greater than people knew. She inherited the bulk of the Idris Eshana estate. Your wealth would surpass your friend Akeem Buhari's. And Jerry Caldwell's. Which, by the way, I inherited as well."

The thought keeps me quiet. I run my hand along the chamber. It's a tough hunk of metal. Even more bulletproof than the glass that surrounds us. "Maybe we're better off now that she's dead."

"We?" she says. "Who do you mean by that? Humanity?" She laughs, and her tail moves, which makes me reflexively point the gun at her. She ignores it. "You know, you have the tendency to imagine kinship with people you don't even know when under duress. It's remarkable, really. Stress typically leads people to do the opposite."

She's looking down at her tea, calculating our next moves.

It's one of those conversations that could change everything. A single word can save or destroy us.

"You should've been paid properly the first time," Ascalon says. "It was disrespectful of them not to, considering the extent of your service. But I'll make amends. And I promise you that I'll never ask you to kill."

To become one of The Money. My wife, my daughter, future generations, all taken care of. What the Caldwells have, what the Eshanas have, what Akeem has—maybe it's what I've always wanted, deep down. Maybe that's why all my friends are rich. Why I've always spent money like I have. I was always trying to be one of them. Maybe I always did see it as the reward for the "extent of my service," the one I was really hoping for. I was a goddamn unpaid assassin. And I never got a piece of that fame and fortune. I wanted them to give me something without me having to ask for it, which is exactly what Ascalon is doing right now. But I was blind to the color of blood and the color of money for most of my life. I couldn't see the cost of either. I run my fingers over the AMP chamber's control panel. *See through your own head*, I tell myself. *See through your head*.

She points to her eye. "What was your self-diagnosis?"

"Psychodynamic merging. Charles Bonnet syndrome delirium. Astronomer's gambit."

"Which?" she asks.

"All of the above."

She smiles. "Not even close," she says. She eyes the 1911. "Some sniper you are. By the way, you never thanked me for ridding you of that ridiculous police captain."

"You want me to be grateful for that? Every time you do something, people wanna pin it on me."

"That's not my fault."

I don't say anything. I just stare at her. Impatient, Ascalon slams her hand down on the table. "My fingers are hers. My teeth. The very fiber of my organs. I'm one of world's greatest surgeons. One of its greatest scholars. She owed me a life, so I took it."

I nod. "Hers."

Ascalon frowns. "It was the only one worth having."

I nod, mesmerized by the steam still rising from the kettle. I focus back on her. *See through your head, old man.*

"One last thing I'll do for you," she says. "To satisfy your deluded notion that you're pursuing the truth. I'll finance a probe mission to travel to Ascalon's Scar, where we'll analyze the supposed point of impact. I'll show you what's there." Ascalon shrugs. "Whether she did what she claimed she did, and your crimes were justified. We will, of course, keep the results to ourselves."

I sit back down, gun still pointed at her. In my heart of hearts, I believe the chief, but a part of me wonders what Akira shot up into space. What Ascalon's Scar really is. Why Akira left me her iE, what she wanted me to do with it. I take the gem out of my pocket and put it on the table. It's just about the greenest thing I've ever seen. "Maybe a probe mission isn't necessary."

She stands from behind the table, and it's tough not to be in awe. I can't really imagine her as a once-helpless baby being carried out of the woods by her father. It feels like the woman standing in front of me is incapable of any weakness, past, present, or future.

I wonder if Akira had any expectations when she was pregnant. If she wanted her baby to coo, laugh, be affectionate, and to be the same with that child. Probably not. And I'm so much like her. I don't coo or laugh. I'm not affectionate. I just complain. And when I think about all the things I love, that makes me ache.

She leans over me. "You have no idea the kind of pain she's caused me," she says.

I nod. "I know."

"It's beautiful," Ascalon says. She reaches down for the gem with Akira's hand, but I pick it back up off the table. I see cold fury light up in her eyes, but she pauses.

"Wait," I say. "What if there's nothing in it?"

"It's the final piece," she says.

"If her thoughts are on it, you will *become* her."

"You know, I see why my mother loved you," Ascalon says. "Your brain chemistry is perfect—it makes you curious but deferential to expertise. Violent but obedient. Chemically analyzed psychological profiles are as reliable as oracles."

"Why did she leave this to me?" I say.

"Do you even care at this point? I'm about to make you a very rich man."

"And the improvements." I say.

"I'll make them myself. And if you really do want me to balance those chemicals out and fix your nose. I'll do that, too. A pity, but I'll accommodate."

"And I want the truth," I say. "About everything."

"We'll discover it together. We'll work closely, just like all those years ago."

If I'm being honest, I want all of those things she just offered. Every single one of them, more than I've ever wanted anything. For some weird reason, a childhood memory pops up at this moment. My great-grandmother. She's speaking a foreign language, telling me to eat slowly. But I don't listen. I just keep shoveling the food in my mouth. I don't eat slowly. I devour.

I grab the gem and pocket it. Her eyes, open so wide I can see all their whites, are focused on my face. Without even looking at it, she cranks up the heat on the little burner sitting between us. Blue light beneath the kettle flares. It begins to whistle, and steam jets out. "I *am* Akira Kimura," she says. She smiles, eyes still locked on mine. And what she does next, I don't see coming.

She blows the steam coming from the kettle into my face. I blink. Then I begin to choke. Something whips through the air and lashes my hand. I feel the skin on my knuckles peel. The gun goes spinning across the floor.

Ascalon stands. She walks to me. I'm in a ball, clutching my face. She reaches into my pocket and pulls out the gem. "My apologies," she says, gazing at the gem. "It's quite a clever poison. It only activates when it hits three degrees beyond boiling point. It enters through the nose and throat, much like the anesthetics of old, but far more powerful. Non-lethal, of course. It's the same one I used on my mother."

I cough until my throat is hoarse. Then I suck in air. "You don't need it to become her," I manage to sputter. "You're close enough, and the world is hungry for her return."

"Perhaps."

I have to keep distracting her while I catch my breath. "You need it for peace of mind. To make sure she never *actually* comes back. After you analyze it, you're going to destroy it."

"My mother was right. We cannot exist at the same time."

"The tomb wasn't for Akira. It was for you. The old Ascalon Lee."

"Yes."

"And once I give this to you, you'll kill me."

I don't wait for an answer, scrambling for the gun.

A morning star with heat-blade spikes slams the glass floor in front of me. It cracks. My eyes follow the handle. It's the end of Ascalon's tail. I roll to the side and go for the gun again. I grab it milliseconds before the morning star strikes the spot where it lay. Coughing, I roll on my back and point the 1911 at Ascalon.

She hits the gun out of my hand with her tail before I can fire. My hand sizzles in pain. I scramble for the pistol again and manage to get hold of it with my other hand, but her tail comes swinging at my head before I can point it at her. I roll away, and the lit spikes of the tail hits the glass wall, which spiders. *It's a gun. Get some distance*, I tell myself. I head for the door.

"You should be paralyzed by now," she says. "What is this nonsense?"

The door slides shut on me before I can get out. She slams her tail against another panel. It hits so hard, my ears hurt. I turn and fire recklessly, not hitting a thing. Next thing I know, she's tackled me. We tumble to the floor, and she pins me. "This is pointless," she says.

I don't know how many more strikes the glass floor and walls can take before shattering. I can almost hear them groaning against the pressure of the midnight zone. If the water bursts in, neither of us will survive. For all I know, the entire scraper could crumble. "Okay," I say. I blow both nostrils as hard as I can. The two small orbs shoot out of my nose. I had a feeling they'd be useful. I just didn't know how.

"Clever man," she says. I slowly pull my blade from its sheath with my unbattered hand.

Now the reds and greens are flowing out of her, snaking into every crack and crevice in the glass walls. She swipes the tea table and smashes it to pieces. "It took her three and a half years to fool the world," she says. "I'll do it in less. How much does your wife know?"

"Fuck you," I snarl, almost afraid raising my voice will start a death flood. The walls groan even louder around us, but she doesn't so much as glance at them.

"It doesn't matter. I'll find out," she says. "She won't make it through anyway."

I slip the blade through her ribs. She spins off me and screams.

I throw the knife at the AMP chamber's outer control panel. The capsule pops open, and the blade clangs on the floor. Her scream sounds like the pain of her entire life is coming out of her.

I sprint to the chamber and dive in, gun still with me. I catch a glimpse of her storming toward me, tail raging. I press the "on" button inside the chamber and roll on my back. The hatch slowly begins to close. I aim and pop off a round. She spins, and I hit her in the shoulder. Fuck, she's quick. She drops the gem, and it slides across the floor.

She chases it.

My mother, a glass engineer, taught me about its structure and its limits. I fire. Again and again. I empty the clip. Not at Ascalon, but thirteen rounds at a single spot on the glass before the chamber shuts. I turn to the control panel and pump up the AMP.

The penthouse glass walls explode. Ascalon leaps onto

the capsule, gem in hand. She ignores the water bursting in and hammers away at the window. Her screams are muffled.

The AMP chamber is sucked out and tumbles across the seafloor. Ascalon, imbued with superhuman strength, still manages to hold on. We're on the seafloor. The end of her tail strikes the glass again and again. Cracks form. I'm waiting for her lungs to collapse. For her sinuses and ears to rupture. Maybe they have, but the tail won't stop. Ascalon's face, pressed against the now cracked window and surprisingly intact, bears a look of pure hatred. The same look she had on her face in the painting. She screams again. But down here, nobody's listening. Just like nobody was listening up there her whole life.

Ascalon headbutts the glass while her tail goes to work on the capsule. I hear the crunch of twisting hoses and metal being torn off the chamber—they're mere echoes this deep. The AMP kicks in hard, overriding my fear. My consciousness flickers, transitioning to a lullaby.

Ascalon is not just the name of the savior
It's the name of the daughter
The one I gave up
Find her for me and tell her that I'm sorry

"I'm sorry," I whisper. The last thing I see is her banging on the glass with the gem. She looks terrified. And I know it's not just of dying, but of being alone. She wants me to enter the endless darkness with her. *Love me.* I see her mouth the words. I hate myself for being the final disappointment of her life.

The song and the muffled hammering fade in this echo

chamber, which is the only thing keeping me isolated from the deadly cold and pressure outside. Here I am, in my midnight zone coffin of regrets and terrible mistakes. I hear something shatter. Has she succeeded? I fall asleep in the deep-water blackout. Maybe all of us are destined to rest at the bottom of the ocean.

27

It's been a year since the death of Akira, and no one's at work because it's a global holiday. Everybody on the island is crowded around The Savior's Eye, waiting for the president to flip the switch and turn on the water statue that will commemorate the life and death of the greatest scientist who has ever walked the earth, Akira Kimura, the Savior. The massive crowd is breathless in anticipation, whispering words to each other like "hero," "genius," "martyr," words that remind us what we aspire to but often think we are. I'm there, too, with Sabrina and Ascalon, still on the mend from being presumed dead and sitting there at the bottom of the ocean. It took a week for Akeem's geothermal mining company to find me. It took another week to figure out how to bring me up safely alongside Volcano Vista, which miraculously survived its bottom floor being swept out from under it. It took another month to safely wake me. And finally, a few more months on top of that to gradually shrink the nitrogen bubbles that had ballooned throughout my body during that time. I've still got joint pain. One doc tells me it's just age. Another tells me I've got bone necrosis from the "accident." Me, I'm tired of being in the middle of an argument, so I just take my meds and live my life. Sabrina says she needs me around to watch Ascalon grow up. I like to think that she also wants me to stick around because I'm decent company.

The president gives his speech, and I'm thinking about all the things he doesn't say. After I came to, I talked to the FBI, then testified in front of a senate oversight committee. Half of them believed me before I testified, half didn't, which was coincidentally how the results turned out. There was no hard evidence for me to present to the committee, anyway. Ascalon's book and old iE data were burned up, along with my own iE. And her body, along with the gem, were never recovered. Akira's body had indeed incinerated itself spontaneously before her funeral tour. Maybe Ascalon knew what she was doing all along. The completion of Akira's deification needed one last component to be cemented. Heresy. Something that contradicted her work, a foil to her perfection. Only when a swell of opposition is crushed does deification become permanent. Most people didn't believe Ascalon Lee existed—even when I said her name over and over, I knew how false it rang. The most generic name in the world. And when it was calculated that the cost of sending a probe to investigate Ascalon's Scar was almost as much as the Ascalon Project forty years before, the opposition was firmly silenced—certainly none of the skeptics would be willing to put up that kind of money on the word of a burned-out cop. I think about what Akira once said to me, long ago. *Science isn't genius. It's budget.* There would be no probe, not in my lifetime.

I look down at my kid, who has her face buried in her mother's shoulder. She hates crowds. I wonder if her generation will discover the truth.

Akira always said everything was binary. But what she didn't acknowledge is that the binary becomes one. Those zeroes and ones, they're a single message. Light and dark, sides of the same coin. This is what Ascalon tried and failed to achieve. In the end, Akira became the singularity, leaving no room for the real Ascalon who so desperately sought love—who killed for it, just not quite in the way I did. The only Ascalon that will be remembered is the one whose scar cuts across the sky.

The president turns the spigot. The crowd cheers. This president is pretty much the same as most of the ones who came before her. My dad used to say a presidential election was a way to reassure us how stupid America is every four years. And every single time, America has passed the test.

At first, the fountain just gurgles up a stream of water a couple stories high. The president looks embarrassed, then visibly sighs in relief when the water shoots up hundreds of feet and begins to take form. I'm still thinking about what I'm going to do for a living. The one thing the senate oversight committee did believe, as well as the Feds and locals, is that I didn't kill Jerry Caldwell, so Sabrina, Ascalon, and I are living comfortably on the returned bail money that Akeem refused to take back. He offered me a job at one of his geothermal plants, but I owe him too damn much at this point, and I'm hesitant to go down deep again. The department says they'll take me back, but looking for greens and reds is something I'm worried I'll get addicted to if I spend too much time on the job. So now I start most of my days by taking my meds, then going out before sunrise to watch the seabirds glide over the float burbs.

The statue takes shape, and it's as grand as promised.

Thousands of feet tall. Big enough to stomp the hell out of the Statue of Liberty, Christ the Redeemer, and Spring Temple Buddha. Made up of enough water to quench the thirst of the billions watching this manmade geyser. Of course, the thing is, it doesn't really look like her. It looks more like the love child of Amaterasu and the Colossus of Rhodes, her finger pointing up at Ascalon's Scar. I never saw Akira point at anything except in that one dream, where two of her pointed at the girl in the red sweater in the painting. But the water continues to stream, dug deep from the core of the tallest mountain in the world. A forgotten goddess breathing life into an imperfectly remembered one. The crowd breaks down in tears.

"Let's go," Sabrina says. "We can beat the air traffic out of here."

I nod and stare at her for a minute. Sabrina and I have been getting along well this last year. Maybe we finally figured out the difference between trying to make someone happy and trying to make someone be happy.

Before we go, the inscription at its base flashes in huge letters in the sky:

> *Science is the process of transforming imagination into truth.*
>
> —*Akira Kimura*

Ain't that the truth. Just like religion before it. And after it.

We slip through the crammed crowd and head for the SEAL. Space junks whiz by overhead in celebratory formation.

I spent most of my life believing that history was where

you found truth. That you could just revisit a past thing again and again until you discovered it. Akira and Ascalon thought they could see more—the present and future. But the present is just a flash we remember later. And sometimes it's best to spend the present walking forward, because even if we stay completely still to look, the moment is over, and we're already behind.

Do I still wonder on occasion why Akira left me her iE? Sure, but I keep moving forward, like we all do every day. Wake and slip into clean foam fits. Check our iEs. Drone in food delivery. Step into vac tubes or fly up in hovers. Message. Game. Scroll through the feed. Spend time in an AMP chamber. How many of us really know the science behind all this? Almost none. We were never riper to succumb to a global magic trick.

But I choose to leave all that wondering behind. I've got a new mantra. *Procedure.* Walk forward and thrive without judgment, without mirrors. And most importantly, be thankful for every fleeting thing you've got in this near-apocalypse garbed in a riot of color.